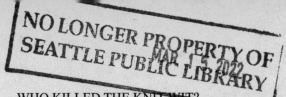

WHO KILLED THE KNIT WIT?

When Wilfred announced from the grill that the shrimp was nearly done, Pamela and Bettina had set aside the question of why Flo might have wanted to kill Critter. Now Bettina revisited the issue, first summarizing for Wilfred what Pamela had told her about bloodroot, Flo's access to it, and her role in serving the coffee at the knitting bee's afternoon break.

"So," she concluded, "Flo had means and opportunity. But as far as we're aware, no connection with Critter that would make her want him dead."

"On the other hand," Pamela chimed in, "we know of two other women who had definite motives."

"The ex-wife and the ex-girlfriend," Wilfred supplied.

"No definite access to bloodroot," Pamela noted, "though we don't know that that was the poison the killer used. But we think we've figured out the identity of the ex-girlfriend—"

"Not really girlfriend," Bettina corrected her. "More like seduced and abandoned. From what you overheard, it didn't sound like Critter ever really cared for her at all."

"I'm looking forward to talking to Bitsy tomorrow," Pamela said. "Once I hear her voice, I'll know for sure if she's the 'seduced and abandoned' we're looking for."

"And if she isn't?" Bettina inquired.

Pamela shrugged. "We'll keep looking. But we've got Yvonne to follow up with too, and now we've got Dermott . . ."

Books by Peggy Ehrhart

MURDER, SHE KNIT

DIED IN THE WOOL

KNIT ONE, DIE TWO

SILENT KNIT, DEADLY KNIT

A FATAL YARN

KNIT OF THE LIVING DEAD

KNITTY GRITTY MURDER

DEATH OF A KNIT WIT

CHRISTMAS CARD MURDER
(with Leslie Meier and Lee Hollis)

Published by Kensington Publishing Corp.

A Knit & Nibble Mystery

DEATH OF A KNIT WIT

PEGGY EHRHART

Kensington Publishing Corp.
www.kensingtonbooks.com

KENSINGTON BOOKS are published by

Kensington Publishing Corp.
119 West 40th Street
New York, NY 10018

All Kensington titles, imprints, and distributed lines are available at special quantity discounts for bulk purchases for sales promotion, premiums, fund-raising, educational, or institutional use.

Special book excerpts or customized printings can also be created to fit specific needs. For details, write or phone the office of the Kensington Sales Manager: Attn.: Sales Department. Kensington Publishing Corp., 119 West 40th Street, New York, NY 10018. Phone: 1-800-221-2647.

The K and Teapot logo is a trademark of Kensington Publishing Corp.

First Printing: March 2022
ISBN: 978-1-4967-3390-0

ISBN: 978-1-4967-3392-4 (ebook)

10 9 8 7 6 5 4 3 2 1

Printed in the United States of America

For my sister Penny, with thanks.

ACKNOWLEDGMENTS

Abundant thanks to my agent, Evan Marshall, and to my editor at Kensington Books, John Scognamiglio.

CHAPTER 1

Pamela Paterson smiled to herself. The conference had gone so smoothly, unfolding just as she and the other organizers had planned. The participants—artists, teachers, collectors, hobbyists—had flown in from all over the country to spend a week in workshops, lectures, and discussions focused on anything and everything to do with fiber arts and crafts. The Wendelstaff College campus had been the perfect venue, with dorms and classrooms empty in the last week before students returned for the fall semester.

Now the conference was wrapping up. The keynote speaker's luncheon talk was nearing its end, then would come a few more workshops and the afternoon session of the knitting bee that had been Pamela's idea. That evening a gala banquet would climax a satisfying week devoted to fiber.

At the moment, all eyes were focused on a podium at one end of the Wendelstaff dining hall. There Dr. Robert Greer-Gordon Critter stood behind a lectern, every inch the professor with his well-trimmed hair graying at the temples, his horn-rimmed glasses, and the bow tie that lent a jaunty note to his expertly tailored tweeds.

"And so to conclude," he intoned, lifting what was presumably the last page of his talk, "not nearly enough credit has heretofore been given to the role of spun fiber in the advance of civilization and the success of the human enterprise."

He removed his glasses, smiled, and nodded in acknowledgment of the applause that followed.

"Questions?" He glanced around the large room.

A woman sitting at a table near the podium hopped to her feet and began speaking. "I read your book," she said in an accusing tone. "And you jump to conclusions no one with a solid grounding in the archeological evidence for spindle development would have jumped to. In fact I would even say—"

Critter waved a dismissive hand and smiled a dismissive smile. "I leave the minutia to those who can't see the forest for the trees. I am a theorist." He looked out over the room. "Next question?"

"You can't just brush me off like that." The woman remained on her feet. She was fiftyish, and attractive, wearing a dress sewn from rustic, gaily dyed fabric. "Anyone can make up theories if they don't have to pay attention to facts. For example, spindles have been unearthed in regions that actually never made the technological advances you point to as a result of spun fibers, and—"

Critter smiled again, but less confidently. "Other questions?" He pointedly looked toward the room's farthest corner. Pamela swiveled her head to follow his gaze. A hand waved in the air and he nodded gratefully. But before the new questioner could even rise, the persistent woman near the podium went on.

"What about the Westvelt hoard? Spindles galore, and yet until the Romans—"

"You, in the back." Critter nodded, raising his voice.

But the woman was not to be silenced. "And the Mesopotamian burial chambers?" Her voice rose in pitch. "You don't even—"

"I don't even what?" Critter leaned over the lectern, a frown disfiguring his bland features.

"Have any ideas of your own, except the bad ones!"

Critter swept up the bundle of papers containing his talk and stepped back from the lectern. "Thank you very much!" he growled, nodding at the dean of humanities, Louise Tate, who had introduced him. "*Very much.*" He retreated toward the exit behind the podium as the woman called after him, "You stole all my good ideas and polluted them with your bad ideas."

A college maintenance man, gray-haired but fit, who had been helping with the conference lingered near the door. Critter paused for a moment before pushing the door open. The maintenance man nodded, fished a pack of cigarettes from his pocket, and extended it toward the professor.

As the door closed behind him, Dean Tate closed her eyes and let her shoulders sag. She was a petite blonde woman with a pixie-cut hairstyle. "Oh . . . my . . . goodness," she sighed as Pamela approached. She looked up and smiled weakly, as if sensing that Pamela's intent was to commiserate. "I knew the split wasn't amicable," she moaned, "but I thought Yvonne would just be happy to go her own way with him out of her life."

"I guess you know her." Pamela pulled up the chair on which Critter had perched while Dean Tate detailed his many accomplishments for the audience that had assembled to hear him.

Dean Tate nodded. "Yvonne Critter—now it's Yvonne Graves—was a regular at School of Humanities social events until a few years ago, when their marriage started to disintegrate."

"At least she waited till his talk was over," Pamela said. "So the conference-goers didn't miss out. I'm sure a lot of them came to the conference because they had read *Spinning Civilization* and were eager to see and hear R. G.-G. Critter in person."

"You're so kind!" Dean Tate reached for Pamela's hand. "I do sometimes need a reminder to look on the bright side." She shook her head. "But honestly, sometimes I feel that I'm the principal of a middle school and not a dean at all. The childish intrigues! The gossip! The feuds! You'd think professors' minds would be on higher things." She leaned forward confidingly. "You're lucky you work at home."

Pamela did feel lucky. As associate editor of *Fiber Craft* magazine, she spent most workdays at the computer in her pleasant home office, where she evaluated articles submitted to the magazine and copyedited ones that had been selected for publication. Rarely did her job require an in-person appearance anywhere—only the occasional meeting at the magazine's offices in the city or events like this one: the conference on fiber arts and crafts co-sponsored by *Fiber Craft* and Wendelstaff College.

Pamela looked at her watch. "I should get back over to Sufficiency House," she said. "The knitters will be wondering where I've disappeared to."

"You'll be seeing R. G.-G. again." Dean Tate raised her brows and twisted her lips into a humorless smile. "He's planning to drop in at Sufficiency House for coffee this afternoon. I hope he's recovered by then."

The exit behind the podium was closest to the parking lot where Pamela's car waited. As she walked past the attractive cluster of tall shrubs that softened the utilitarian lines of the dining hall, she heard a familiar male voice. The voice was as assertive as it had been when explaining to a rapt audience how important spun fiber had been to the advance of civilization. But now it seemed to be responding to a lament.

"You jumped right into it," the male voice said. "Nobody forced you."

"But you acted like you . . . cared for me," a woman whimpered. "And I trusted you. And now I feel so . . . let down. Like I was a fool."

"We're both grown-ups."

Pamela halted. How could anyone be so cruel in the face of such misery? Even someone who'd just endured public criticism of his new book?

"I admired you," the woman went on. "You're brilliant. And when you kissed me and . . . the rest . . . and it seemed that we were going to be . . . a couple, I was so amazed, I had to pinch myself."

If the conversation hadn't already revealed that this woman was not Yvonne, her voice—with its nasal twang and unexpected diphthongs—hinted at a stratum of society far removed from the educated circles that were home to Dr. Critter.

* * *

Sufficiency House was at the northern edge of Arborville, just across the border from the town where Wendelstaff College was located. It had been the home of a Depression-era crusader, Micah Dorset, who taught classes and wrote pamphlets encouraging people to grow their own food and make their own clothes. It had been given to Wendelstaff several decades previously by Dorset's heirs and now existed as a museum and information center.

Ten minutes later Pamela nosed her car to the curb in front of the house, a Craftsman bungalow painted a soothing shade of green. A wide porch spanned the entire width of the house, shaded by a low roof supported by massive angular pillars. Sufficiency House occupied a lot on a residential street, but it differed from its neighbors in that instead of a lawn, its front yard had been given over to food production.

Rows of waist-high tomato plants bearing heavy fruit in every shade from green to deep red gave way to luxuriant vines from which dangled pods bulging with beans and peas. Feathery dark-green carrot tops and darker green beet leaves announced that root vegetables lay beneath the ground. A tidy brick walk led from the sidewalk to the porch steps.

Pamela paused to admire the tomatoes, wishing that her yard was sunny enough to grow more than a few tomato plants. She stroked a hairy leaf and inhaled the tomato aroma that rose even from the plant's foliage.

As she climbed the steps, the front door opened and Flower Ransom—or Flo, as she preferred to be called—sang out a greeting. Flo was Sufficiency House's live-in caretaker and docent. As she had once told Pamela, she had shortened the name given her at birth by her hippie parents into a single syllable with a more old-timey feel. Totally caught up in her position, she wore her gray-streaked hair in an austere roll at the back of her head and limited her wardrobe to clothing that would have been worn in Micah Dorset's era. Today's ensemble was a much-washed cotton housedress faded to an indeterminate shade of pale blue, accessorized with lace-up shoes in brown leather.

"We're keeping up the momentum," she chirped, stepping aside to let Pamela enter.

Seated around the room, some on the nubbly tan sofa, one in a roomy upholstered chair with broad wooden arms, one on a matching hassock, and others on wooden chairs imported from other parts of the house, were knitters. Their ages varied, but all were women.

The knitting bee had been Pamela's contribution to the conference program, open to all with an interest in knitting. Participants were invited to bring their projects, or—if they were not yet knitters—to bring yarn and knitting needles. After morning coffee, experienced knitters had paired with beginners. Soon needles had begun clicking, and the room had resounded with the pleasant chatter of women whose hands were busy but whose minds were free to roam. Such bees were common during the Depression, she knew, when frugality was essential to survival and purchased clothing was a luxury out of reach for so many.

Pamela returned to the chair she had vacated earlier and drew her own in-progress work from her knitting bag. She had recently finished a sweater for her best friend, Bettina Fraser, a fellow member of Arborville's Knit and Nibble knitting club, but with skills less advanced.

The sweater for Bettina had used a complicated seer-sucker stitch that required careful counting of knits and purls, but Pamela's current work in progress was considerably simpler, if no less altruistic. Nell Bascomb, another member of Knit and Nibble, put her knitting talents to charitable use and Pamela had joined Nell in one of her do-good projects: winter scarves for the Guatemalan day laborers.

Happy that the garter stitch the scarf was worked in allowed her mind to wander at will, Pamela launched a new row and fell happily to work. The projects taking shape in the laps of the other knitting bee participants ranged from a very ambitious Fair Isle cardigan to the beginnings of a humble scarf not unlike the one that hung from Pamela's own needles.

Quiet conversations had sprung up around the room, gray heads bending toward brighter tresses—one young participant even had green hair. Experienced knitters were fielding questions from the beginners as other people chatted about their children or their husbands or their classes or their other hobbies.

Pamela's chair was right next to Flo's, and the seating arrangement was such that a large gap, allowing access to the dining room, yawned between Flo and the knitter on her other side. Pamela enjoyed hearing chatter around her as her mind wandered freely, unconstrained by the need to keep up her end of a conversation. But Flo had been so helpful in arranging the details of the bee, and if she was to have anyone to chat with, it would have to be Pamela. So Pamela mustered her social smile and dipped her head toward the sock nearing completion on Flo's busy needles.

The sock's color, a muted red, was quite unusual, and that provided Pamela with her opening gambit.

"I love that color," she said. "Is your yarn from the Timberley yarn shop?"

Timberley was the next town north of Arborville. It boasted a wider—and fancier—array of shops than those found in Arborville's commercial district, as befitting the higher per capita income of Timberley's residents. Among those shops was one that sold yarn from every fiber-producing region one could imagine. A knitter wanting to move beyond hobby-shop acrylic could easily spend as much on yarn there as one would pay for a sweater from the fanciest store at the mall.

"Oh, no!" Flo sounded horrified, though in a gentle way. "I try to live by Micah Dorset's tenets. 'Use it up, wear it out, make it do, or do without.' I unraveled a wool sweater that had already given me years of wear and I redyed the yarn with natural dye sourced from the Sufficiency House garden."

"The red is beautiful," Pamela said. "What color was the sweater you unraveled?"

"Beige, basically. It was that oatmeal kind of yarn. So the dye came up really nice." Flo had a pleasant, undemanding face, with guileless pale blue eyes. She looked no younger than her fifty or so years, but those years had been kind.

"What plant makes that shade?" Pamela asked, reaching over to finger the strand of yarn that led from the ball in Flo's lap to the work on her needles.

"Bloodroot," was the response. "Not the leaves or the petals though. You have to dig up the rhizomes. But it spreads willingly, so more always grows as long as you leave a few rhizomes behind."

At that moment, the door that led to the kitchen swung open and a young woman, a Wendelstaff student who Pamela recognized as one of the conference aides, popped out.

"Coffee and cookies are here," she announced. With the door open, a rich and tantalizing aroma advertised the coffee's presence.

Flo lowered her knitting into the basket at her chair's side and rose to her feet. Pointing around the room and murmuring the numbers to herself, she counted the knitters: ten, in addition to her and Pamela.

She darted through the dining room door and Pamela followed her through that room and into the kitchen. The Sufficiency House kitchen had been preserved in its 1930s state—or perhaps restored to that condition. Large black and white tiles in a checkerboard pattern covered the floor. The stove and refrigerator, both gleaming white enamel, were elevated on legs that seemed too spindly to bear their weight. A gray soapstone counter was interrupted by a deep metal sink.

A wooden table stood against the wall that wasn't occupied by counter or appliances. It now held coffee in a tall stainless steel dispenser with a spigot and hot water in a similar but smaller dispenser, as well as cream and sugar, a bowl containing tea bags, and a tray of large chocolate chip cookies.

Flo was busily filling mismatched but attractive china cups with coffee and nestling them into the saucers that awaited them on another, larger, tray.

"The cups and saucers are my own collection," Flo said, "from thrift stores and tag sales. When Sufficiency House hosts events, it seems appropriate to serve refreshments as they might have been served in Micah Dorset's time. People still had nice things from before the Depression, and I'm sure they enjoyed bringing them out."

She left to carry the first six cups of coffee to the dining room and take orders for tea, and Pamela followed with the tray of cookies. Additional trips supplied tea for the tea drinkers, more coffee, cream and sugar, small plates, napkins, and spoons. Some knitters perched on chairs at the dining room table, while others took their refreshments back to the living room, where they clustered around the coffee table.

Chatter, punctuated by laughter, grew louder under the influence of caffeine, and the atmosphere became quite partylike. Flo had remained in the dining room, but Pamela had pulled her chair up to the coffee table and was enjoying a conversation with the woman working on the Fair Isle sweater. The woman was describing her trip to the Shetland Islands for Wool Week in such glowing terms that Pamela had begun to mentally examine her budget for the next year with an eye to experiencing Wool Week for herself.

Her calculations were interrupted, however, when the door of Sufficiency House opened. A familiar voice boomed, "Good afternoon, ladies!" and R. G.-G. Critter strode into the room, elegantly professorial in his tweeds and horn-rimmed glasses. A faint drift of cigarette smoke followed in his wake, and from the porch a man called, "I'll be back for you in an hour."

CHAPTER 2

Critter paused in the middle of the room for a moment, as if to allow time for admiration. He had clearly recovered from the experience of having his work challenged by his ex-wife. Even if he hadn't, Flo's solicitous approach would have soothed his pride.

"Dr. Critter!" she exclaimed as a smile warmed her gentle face. "I'm so glad you were able to make it! Was that Bob Lombard on the porch?"

Critter nodded.

Pamela stood up to greet the guest as well. In an aside, Flo explained that Bob was one of Wendelstaff's maintenance people and he'd been invaluable in helping the conference run smoothly.

Some women had drifted in from the dining room and others had risen from their seats in the living room. Soon Critter was surrounded, accepting compliments on his talk and answering questions about his research. His aura seemed not to have been dimmed by his ex-wife's claim that all his good ideas were actually hers.

"And what are you all working on?" he inquired as compliments and questions trailed off, addressing himself particularly to the youngest participant in the bee, whose green hair detracted not one bit from her attractiveness.

She stepped away to seize up her knitting project, a simple scarf in an orange mohair, perhaps chosen for the eye-catching statement the finished product would make with her interesting hair color.

Flo had been observing at a distance, obviously pleased with the success of the refreshments and the warm welcome Critter was receiving. Suddenly, though, she raised a hand to her cheek and exclaimed, "I'm forgetting my manners! Dr. Critter, let me get you some coffee! And there are chocolate chip cookies."

She took a few steps toward the door that led to the dining room and the kitchen beyond. But Critter stopped her, saying, "I can serve myself." He directed a smile at the green-haired woman. "I'm very liberated."

As he stepped through the door to the dining room, Flo called, "Coffee's all the way back in the kitchen and there's one more cup and saucer."

Soon he was back, pulling one of the wooden chairs closer to the coffee table, sipping his coffee, and chatting with the women around him. A few on the sofa had taken up their knitting again, but others were still nibbling on cookies or finishing up their coffee. Pamela had returned to her chair. From her vantage point, she could see Flo tidying up the dining room table, stacking abandoned cups and saucers on the tray that had held the cookies.

A sound like a stifled hiccup drew her attention to the group around the coffee table. She could see only Critter's profile, but his face seemed flushed. Everyone around him was looking at him, but no one was laughing, or even smiling. She heard the sound again, like a dry cough, and it was coming from Critter, who had raised both hands to his chest. He began to snort.

At this point, Flo hurried in from the dining room, and a few women set their knitting down and rose to their feet. A plump middle-aged woman spoke up. "I'm a nurse," she said, and with a few long strides she reached Critter's chair and bent over him.

He flung his head back and began to gasp, and his face grew more flushed.

"An allergic reaction," the nurse said. She looked up. "Were there nuts in the cookies?" Bending back down, she addressed Critter. "Do you carry an EpiPen?"

"Not allergic," Critter managed to moan.

"He didn't have any cookies," the green-haired woman contributed.

Flo, meanwhile, had produced a cell phone from somewhere. Her fingers busied themselves on it as she murmured, "Nine-one-one." Then she raised it to her ear and recited the address of Sufficiency House.

Critter had begun to twitch, so frightfully that the wooden chair he was sitting on threatened to topple. The woman who had been sitting in the roomy upholstered chair jumped up and said, "Have him sit here." She pushed the chair sideways until it was lined up right next to Critter. The nurse and the green-haired woman each seized one of his arms, raised him slightly, and hefted him into it. He rested his head against its cushioned back, eyes closed, and began to pant. His hands, which had remained resting on his chest, clawed at his dapper bow tie.

"Loosen it! Loosen it!" someone urged. "He's choking."

Critter's mouth dropped open. A sound like a low-pitched whistle emerged from his throat, repeating again and again.

Pamela watched, feeling short of breath herself and wondering if whatever was afflicting Critter was spreading, soon to afflict everyone who had taken part in the knitting bee. She scanned the faces that were focused so intently on the distressed man in their midst. She saw concern, certainly, alarm—even curiosity. No one else, however, appeared to be ill.

She inhaled deeply. Surely her body was reacting to the stress of this very unexpected event. Should she be doing more? The bee had been her idea. But Flo had summoned an ambulance, and a nurse was standing by—though not knowing what had brought on his distress, there was apparently not much else she could do.

Fortunately, at that moment a faint, high-pitched wail signaled the ambulance's approach. The wail grew louder and louder, deafening almost, until it ceased abruptly, like a blasting radio that has suddenly lost its power supply. In the startling silence, Flo reached for Pamela's hand and Pamela returned her comforting squeeze. Then feet sounded on the porch and Flo darted toward the door to admit the EMTs.

Pamela nodded when the banquet server, a Wendel-staff student, asked if she had finished. The salmon she had requested when the conference registration form asked her to choose a banquet entrée sat almost untouched on her plate. The vision of Dr. Critter gasping in the living room of Sufficiency House had taken away her appetite.

The knitting bee had seemed such a good idea, and Sufficiency House had seemed the ideal venue—linking the craft's present-day popularity with its historical importance in eras of frugality. Her boss at *Fiber Craft* had been delighted when she proposed the bee, and since she lived so near Wendelstaff College and was already familiar with Sufficiency House, plans for the bee had coalesced nicely. But now the bee would forever be linked in people's minds with the recollection of Dr. Critter's distress. And at the point when knitters would have been putting away their knitting for the day and looking forward to the bee's continuation on Sunday, instead they watched EMTs strap Dr. Critter to a gurney and wheel him out to the waiting ambulance.

The banquet was taking place in the Wendelstaff College dining hall. The tables and chairs were arranged as they had been at lunch, but white linen tablecloths, candles in silvery candleholders, and floral centerpieces had been added. The overhead lights had been dimmed, softening the large room's modern angularity. Pamela had taken the first empty seat she saw, and was relieved that most of the people at her table seemed to know each other and didn't feel it necessary to draw her into their conversation.

The buzz of conversation echoed and blended into a low hum from which no words emerged distinctly. But some people—maybe even most people—were talking about the dramatic event that had occurred that afternoon at Sufficiency House, she was sure. The ten participants in the bee could each have told ten other people and they in turn . . . viral was the term for that kind of spread, she believed, and by now all two hundred conference participants surely knew that R. G.-G. Critter was spending the evening in the hospital rather than claiming his rightful place on the banquet podium, next to Dean Tate and Pamela's boss, the editor of *Fiber Craft*, who looked as chic as ever. Thankfully, the people at her own table seemed not even to know who she was—thus she was spared endless questions about what had transpired at Sufficiency House.

Though Pamela was at a table about as far from the podium as one could be, her boss seemed to be staring right at her. She had acknowledged Pamela with a wordless stare when they found themselves filing into the dining room elbow to elbow, as if there had been nothing more to say, since Pamela had been debriefed in a lengthy phone call an hour earlier.

Servers were coming around with dessert now, a choice between cheesecake or chocolate mousse, and other servers were following with coffee and tea. Pamela opted for cheesecake, thinking that at least it looked nourishing and at some point she was bound to feel hungry. Bob Lombard, who seemed to be the do-it-all maintenance man, was tinkering with the microphone. A gruff "check . . . check" established that the sound system was functioning, and he stood aside, beckoning to Dean Tate.

She started to rise but paused to fumble in the handbag that sat beside her on the floor, pulling up her phone and glancing at its screen. The glance turned into a stare. She poked at the screen with a finger, lifted the phone to her ear, and sat back down. As Pamela watched, the dean closed her eyes and her pleasant expression became grim.

She rose again and stepped to the microphone. At her first words—"I've just had some very tragic news"—the room was instantly quiet, as if a gust of wind had swept through, leaving only a still silence behind. "Tragic news," she went on, "from the hospital where Dr. Critter was taken this afternoon."

The tragic news could only be one thing, Pamela realized, and the cheesecake no longer looked the least bit appealing. In fact, her throat felt as tight as if she was doomed never to eat again, and her heart was making its agitation known with a steady ticking near her collarbone.

"Dr. Critter has died," Dean Tate announced, and sound returned to the dining hall as exclamations erupted at every table.

Pamela closed her eyes with relief as her car engine's purr trailed off into silence. She hadn't thought to turn her porch light on when she set out hours ago for the conference, but the September moon was bright and she'd left a few lamps on that morning for the three cats that were her housemates. The vision of her house, with lighted windows that beckoned, offered welcome comfort after her trying day.

More comfort was at hand.

"Pamela!" The voice reached Pamela as she stepped out onto her driveway. She turned to see Bettina waving from the driveway of the house directly opposite hers. At Bettina's side was a shaggy four-legged creature nearly half as tall as his mistress.

"How was it?" Bettina called. She tugged gently at the leash that tethered Woofus the shelter dog and began to advance across the street. Soon she was standing at Pamela's side. Woofus, however, lingered several feet behind with the leash stretched tight.

"He's been nervous today," Bettina explained. "The grandchildren were here." She focused on the dog for a moment, to murmur, "It's okay, boy. We'll go home in a minute."

She turned back to Pamela. "So—the knitting bee? How did the first day go?"

"Oh, Bettina!" Pamela wailed, and reached out both arms to anticipate the hug that she knew was coming. "It was just awful."

"Awful?" Bettina held out her free arm and Pamela collapsed against her friend. She was so much taller than Bettina that her chin ended up resting atop Bettina's head, cushioned by Bettina's well-tended scarlet curls. "What on earth . . . ?" Bettina inquired, her voice softened by concern.

"Dr. Critter is dead," Pamela moaned. "He stopped by Sufficiency House for coffee in the middle of the afternoon and he drank a cup of coffee and then he had some kind of a spell, choking and gasping for air. And Flo called an ambulance and then during the banquet Dean Tate announced that he had died."

"That's awful!" Bettina's muffled voice emerged from somewhere around Pamela's collarbone. Pamela stepped back to let her friend speak more clearly. "Truly awful," Bettina said. "But I'm sure people don't think that you"—she paused and raised her chin to meet Pamela's gaze—"that there was anything you could have done differently. People get ill."

As if commiserating, Woofus began to whimper. But then he began to strain at his leash, as if urging Bettina to escort him back to the safety of his own home. Bettina consoled him with a murmured "There, there, boy." She grasped Pamela's hand. "I am not leaving you alone though. I'll hand Woofus over to Wilfred and then I'll be right back."

Bettina returned quickly enough that only one cat, Catrina, had come out so far to welcome her mistress home. And Pamela had not advanced beyond the chair in her entry into which, overwhelmed by exhaustion, she had sunk the moment she stepped across the threshold.

"Now, now, now," Bettina exclaimed, bending down and seizing her friend's hand. "Let me make a soothing pot of tea—coffee will just agitate you more—and you can tell me all about it. As Wilfred would say, 'A sorrow shared is a sorrow halved.' "

Pamela started to stand up but felt herself sway and sat back down with a thump.

"Whoa!" Bettina bent down again, peering into Pamela's face with her brow furrowed and her mouth grim. "Did you drink the coffee at the bee too?"

"I did," Pamela said, waving a hand as if to shoo away the idea that she suspected was forming in Bettina's mind. "Everyone did, and nothing happened to anyone else. It's not the coffee. It's just . . . I didn't eat very much today."

Bettina rocked back and placed her hands on her hips. "You just came from a banquet," she said, barely suppressing a laugh.

Pamela shrugged. "I was so upset I couldn't eat, not even the cheesecake."

Now Bettina did laugh. "That's why you're thin and I'm not. When I'm upset, the first thing I do is open the refrigerator."

Not that Bettina had very much to be upset about. She had a husband who adored her, two happily married sons, grandchildren close at hand, and a job reporting for Arborville's weekly newspaper, the *Advocate*.

She pulled Pamela to her feet and said, "Lean on me if you have to. We're marching right out to the kitchen and I'm going to make you some scrambled eggs and toast. And we'll have a pot of tea besides."

Seated at the table in her cozy kitchen, with Catrina on her lap, Pamela watched Bettina crack eggs into a favorite blue speckled mixing bowl and slip two slices of whole-grain bread into the toaster. The squat brown teapot waited on the counter, already supplied with loose tea, and the kettle had been filled with water and set to boil on the stove. As Bettina worked, Catrina's daughter Ginger, who had inherited her color from her dashing father rather than her jet-black mother, ventured in from the dining room. She was followed by the newest member of the household, an elegant Siamese named Precious.

Both looked expectantly at Pamela, and then realizing that Bettina seemed to be in charge of food, transferred their gaze to her.

"I made sure they had a day's worth of food when I left this morning." Pamela returned their gaze. "But a little treat wouldn't hurt them." She started to rise, but Bettina waved her back into her chair.

"I don't want you fainting on me," she said, "and I know where you keep your cat food."

As the scrambled eggs finished cooking, Bettina stooped to a cupboard beneath the counter and plucked out a packet of chicken liver treats. She shook a goodly number of the plump nuggets into a shallow dish large enough for all three cats to gather around and set it in the corner occupied by the now-empty cat food bowls.

The kettle began to hoot then, and for a few moments Bettina was a blur of motion as she bustled here and there around the small kitchen. Soon scrambled eggs, golden and gleaming with butter, appeared before Pamela, accompanied by a slice of toast. Bettina added a pair of rose-garlanded cups and saucers from Pamela's wedding china, sugar in a cut-glass sugar bowl, and the squat brown teapot.

"I know you just like butter on your toast," Bettina said, "but the other piece is for me, and you must have some jam around here somewhere."

"There's strawberry in the refrigerator." Pamela nodded in that direction. "From when Penny was home. And I'll have a little too."

They were both settled comfortably then, opposite each other at the little table. Bettina waited until Pamela had nearly finished her eggs and toast before she said, "Now tell me exactly what happened."

Pamela began to elaborate on the events she had sketched out earlier, but she had gotten no further than Critter's arrival and Flo's greeting when she was interrupted by the telephone.

She half rose to lift the handset from its cradle and uttered a hesitant "Hello."

"Hey, Pamela!" said a pleasant, and familiar, voice. "It's Brian." When she hesitated in responding, the voice went on. "I heard what happened . . . with Critter. It's all over the campus listserv already."

Distracted from her toast and tea, Bettina watched and listened.

Pamela could think of nothing else to say but "Oh."

"Are you all right?" Brian's voice projected the same warm concern that made Bettina's Wilfred such a welcome presence in a crisis. "You worked so hard organizing the knitting bee . . . then this happened. And what a way to launch the fall semester! But Critter was never a very considerate guy."

"It wasn't his fault," Pamela murmured. "Not anybody's fault really."

"It looks like they're carrying on with the conference. Dean Tate's note to the campus community didn't say anything about cancelling."

"That's good, I guess," Pamela said. It *was* good, actually. She herself had always believed carrying on was the best recourse when troubling things happened.

"So how about getting together for coffee when things wind down tomorrow?" Participants had flights to catch or long drives back home, so the last conference events were set to finish by mid-afternoon. "Or dinner if you're free."

"Dinner," Pamela said. "Yes, I'd like that." And after confirming details of when and where to meet, she said goodbye and replaced the handset in its cradle.

CHAPTER 3

"Was that who I think it was?" Bettina inquired the moment a click indicated that the connection had been broken. She beamed at Pamela, her bright gaze enhanced by the whisper of lavender shadow on her eyelids.

"That depends on who you think it was." The opportunity for a bit of gentle teasing provoked Pamela's first smile in several hours.

"Your handsome professor friend from Wendelstaff?" Bettina responded, then she quickly added, "Just say yes or no. I learned my lesson with Richard Larkin. If I hadn't pushed you so hard maybe things would have turned out differently and he and Jocelyn wouldn't . . ."

Her voice trailed off as Pamela's smile was replaced by a frown.

"Okay, okay," Bettina said. "I'm ready for more tea.

How about you?" She reached for the teapot and topped up both cups. "And more toast?" She jumped to her feet.

The scrambled eggs quieted Pamela's complaining stomach, and the tea and toast with strawberry jam soothed her spirit. Bettina steered the conversation into realms less disquieting than Dr. Critter's sudden demise and less controversial than Pamela's romantic prospects, and soon Pamela felt quite herself again.

"I can sleep here tonight if you like," Bettina announced from the counter, where she was slipping plates and cups and saucers into the dishwasher.

"I'll be okay," Pamela said. "I really do feel better now."

After she saw Bettina to the door and sent her off with a hug, Pamela settled into her accustomed spot at the end of her sofa and, as a program involving zebras unfolded on the Nature Channel, picked up her knitting.

She nearly tucked it right back into her knitting bag when she remembered that she'd last handled the in-progress scarf that afternoon at the ill-fated bee. But good yarn wasn't for wasting and the scarf would soon be finished. Then it would go to Nell as part of her project distributing winter clothes to the day laborers. The best solution—to everything—was to carry on. Pamela thrust her right-hand needle through the first loop of yarn on her left-hand needle. Soon the rhythm of her needles synchronized with the rhythm of her breathing, and knitting began to work its soothing magic.

With Ginger perched on the sofa arm and a purring Catrina snuggled along her thigh as Precious lounged on the top platform of the cat climber, the world seemed a bit less topsy-turvy.

* * *

The alarm jarred Pamela out of a better sleep than she had expected, and she opened her eyes to a room brightened by the morning sun glowing behind the white eyelet curtains at her windows. For a moment she wondered why she had set her alarm clock when she normally slept until awakened by one or more cats demanding breakfast.

Then she remembered. Today was the second day of the knitting bee and she had wanted to make sure she was up early enough to get to Sufficiency House by nine a.m. With that recollection came others, less pleasant. But it was important to carry on, and coffee would help.

As she pushed the bedclothes aside and began to stir, two furry presences near her knees began to stir also. They glided upward and emerged from beneath blanket and sheet to greet her with fond stares from unblinking eyes, amber in Catrina's case and jade green in Ginger's.

Precious leapt from the sofa to join the little procession as it wended its way from the bottom of the staircase toward the kitchen doorway. The first order of business was generous scoops of chicken-fish medley in a fresh bowl for Catrina and her daughter to share and a scoop of liver and tuna for Precious, who had her own preferences.

Pamela measured water into the kettle, set it to boiling on the stove, and hurried outside to collect the *Register*. She got no farther than her front porch, however, before it became clear that the Sunday morning *Register* had something very dramatic to reveal—and that it had already been revealed to Bettina.

Bettina was halfway across the street, her filmy robe billowing out behind her and her bright scarlet hair still tousled from sleep. She had freed her copy of the *Register* from its plastic sleeve and was waving the unfolded newspaper as she ran. Pamela hopped down the steps and sped toward the curb.

"He was poisoned," Bettina called when Pamela drew closer. "He didn't just die. Someone poisoned him."

Pamela felt herself teeter and willed her body to remain upright.

"Here!" Bettina pointed at the bold headline on the front page: POLICE SUSPECT MURDER IN WENDELSTAFF PROF'S DEATH. "It's all right here!"

After stooping for her own copy of the *Register*, Pamela let Bettina tug her back the way she had come, up the porch steps, and into her own house. The fearsome hooting of the kettle provided an appropriate soundtrack as Pamela, perched on the edge of the chair in the entry, skimmed the article beneath the dramatic headline.

"I'll do something about that kettle," Bettina announced after a minute. Pamela continued to study the article. An autopsy was yet to be scheduled, but doctors who treated Dr. Critter when he arrived at the emergency room recognized that his symptoms weren't consistent with any known natural causes.

She closed her eyes and sighed a deep sigh. It must have been the coffee, though all the knitters had drunk it too. She hadn't made the coffee—it had been brought over from the Wendelstaff dining hall. But the bee had been her idea. It was hard not to feel that Dr. Critter's death had somehow come about because of her actions. And how on earth was her boss at *Fiber Craft* going to react?

The hooting had ceased, and the aroma of coffee emanating from the kitchen suggested Bettina had put the boiling water to good use. She pulled herself to her feet and made her way to the kitchen. Bettina had set out the rose-garlanded cups and saucers, along with the cut-glass sugar bowl and cream pitcher—though only Bettina liked sugar and cream in her coffee.

As Pamela took her seat, a *ka-chunk!* from the direction of the counter announced that toast had popped up.

"You have to eat," Bettina urged as she scurried about. Soon she had provided her friend with a cup of steaming coffee and a piece of toast, and had taken her own seat across the little table.

Pamela ate her toast, gratefully, and drank her coffee, but the lively conversation that usually flowed between her and Bettina over coffee was absent. Instead, her dialogue was with herself, and internal.

What did this new and shocking development portend for the conference? A morning's worth of sessions had been scheduled on the campus, followed by lunch in the dining hall, and then a farewell convocation in Wendelstaff's auditorium. And the knitters expected the bee to reconvene at nine a.m. for three solid hours of knitting, to conclude when they joined the other conference attendees for lunch.

"My cell phone," Pamela exclaimed suddenly, springing up from her chair as Bettina blinked in a startled way over the rim of her coffee cup.

Pamela seldom turned her cell phone on unless she was using it, and she now anticipated a torrent of messages lurking in her voice mail box. Surely decisions had been made, by Dean Tate and Pamela's *Fiber Craft* boss and the other conference organizers, about whether and how to carry on.

Her phone lay on the kitchen counter near her calendar and appointment book. Explaining her errand to Bettina, she snatched it up and stepped into the entry, holding her breath and willing her overactive heart to calm down. She pushed the button that would bring the phone to life, and touched the icons that would make it yield whatever messages it had stored. But there was no word at all from anyone, conference-related or not. A quick trip upstairs to check messages on her computer similarly brought no enlightenment about what the day might hold.

It was, however, barely eight a.m. Surely the rest of the conference would be canceled, but many of the participants, including the knitters, might not yet have heard that Dr. Critter's death was being investigated as murder. They might at this very moment be making their way to Sufficiency House, knitting bags in hand.

Once Bettina had been thanked and seen to the door, Pamela hurried upstairs to dress. Unlike Bettina, whose extensive wardrobe reflected an imagination and flair that made her stand out from her suburban cohort, Pamela paid barely any attention to clothes. For the conference she had substituted a pair of black slacks for her usual jeans. Now she stepped into the same slacks, pairing them with a blouse in the casual style that she preferred.

As soon as she turned onto the residential street that Sufficiency House shared with neighbors of similar vintage and design, it was clear—and would have been clear to any of the knitters—that something very untoward was afoot. Two police cars, sleek black and white and emblazoned with the Arborville town logo, were parked at the curb, looking out of place with the garden bounty of Sufficiency House's front yard as a backdrop. A stern-looking officer who Pamela didn't recognize was standing on the sidewalk at the end of the brick walk that bisected the garden and led to the house's front steps.

A few knitters were arriving on foot, their steps slowing as they noticed the police cars. Pamela nosed her serviceable compact into a spot a few car lengths behind the nearest police car. She climbed out to be greeted by cries more curious than distressed.

"What's going on?" the older of the knitters, a plump gray-haired woman, inquired, and the younger knitter echoed the question.

Pamela sighed and stepped across the street to meet them. "I guess you haven't seen any news this morning," she said, "or talked to anyone who has."

"This was a getaway weekend for me," the younger knitter said. "A chance to get away from the news."

The older knitter nodded and added, "I slept better last night than I have in months."

"Dr. Critter's death wasn't natural," Pamela explained.

The younger knitter, a freckly strawberry blonde, opened her pale eyes wide. "Murder?" she whispered.

"That's what the police told the local newspaper." Pamela nodded. "It was in the *County Register* this morning and I expect it's on the radio and TV and all over the internet too.

At this point, the stern officer, who had left his post at the end of the brick walk, approached. He glanced at the knitting bags that Pamela and the other two women carried and said, "Are you here for the knitting?"

"Yes," Pamela volunteered and the other two women nodded.

"And the three of you were here yesterday?"

When they all nodded again, he held out his arm in an "after you" gesture and motioned them toward the brick walk with his other hand. Pamela led the way, past the tomato plants and bean vines and up the steps onto the bungalow's broad porch. There Officer Sanchez, one of Arborville's female officers, opened the front door and invited them inside.

The scene in the living room of Sufficiency House was not that different from what it had been the previous day, except for the presence of Officer Sanchez—and the fact that the door between the living room and the dining room was closed. Two knitters shared the nubbly tan sofa, and an untended knitting bag between them suggested that a third knitter would be returning soon. Another knitter sat in the roomy upholstered chair and another on the matching hassock. The remainder perched on wooden chairs. Flo was there, of course, looking surprisingly serene in her faded housedress. All the women were knitting.

Why not? Pamela said to herself. Her own knitting bag was a comforting weight in her hand. Loathe to waste a moment that could be devoted to useful labor, women had always devoted spare moments to handiwork. And knitting had undoubtedly soothed knitters through many a stressful time.

Flo, who had reclaimed the wooden chair near the dining room door, looked up from the red sock in progress on her needles. She said nothing but her pale lips twisted in a sad grimace.

"They're interviewing us one by one," volunteered the young green-haired woman from her perch on the hassock. She tipped her head toward the closed door. "In there."

Pamela and the two women she had entered with claimed the remaining wooden chairs, and Pamela drew her knitting project from her knitting bag. The scarf had been nearly finished yesterday, and she had worked on it a bit while watching the program on zebras last night. But the convenient thing about a scarf—when one needed a knitting project to calm one's nerves—was that it could be just as long as the knitter wanted it to be. She tugged a length of yarn from the skein she drew from her knitting bag, picked up her right-hand needle, and launched a new row.

As she worked, she realized that besides the closed door and the presence of Officer Sanchez, there was another way in which the Sunday morning bee—for indeed it had become a bee again—differed from Saturday's bee. The room was perfectly silent. Whether the knitters were hesitant to say anything at all in the presence of a police officer—even one as unthreatening as Officer Sanchez, with her sweet heart-shaped face and her tidy knot of dark hair—or simply had nothing to say, Pamela wasn't sure. But silent the room was.

Thus, when a sharp click and a squeak signaled the opening of the dining room door, knitters looked up as startled as if a shotgun had been fired. The first person to step through the doorway was the woman who had captivated Pamela the previous day with her description of Wool Week in the Shetland Islands. She made her way to the sofa, where she claimed her knitting bag and sat down.

The next person to step through the doorway was Detective Lucas Clayborn, Arborville's sole police detective, wearing a sports jacket and tie as nondescript as his middle-aged face. He surveyed the room, his survey pausing when his gaze reached Pamela.

"Ms. Paterson," he said by way of greeting. "Would you mind joining me in here?"

He edged back a few feet and held the door open wider as Pamela hastily set scarf and needles aside. Once her hands were empty she discovered that her fingers were trembling.

The dining room looked as it had the previous day, except that the door leading from it into the kitchen was closed, and it was crisscrossed with bands of yellow crime-scene tape. Detective Clayborn gestured for Pamela to take a seat near the head of the table, where a pen and a small notepad marked his own place. He lowered himself into his seat and regarded her for a moment. Were it not for a certain probing quality to his gaze, he might have been taken for an insurance salesman about to make a pitch for additional coverage.

"I understand it was you who organized this . . . knitting bee." The pause and his slight frown suggested the term was new to his vocabulary.

"Yes," Pamela said. "It was me."

"Why?"

"I'm . . . interested in knitting." Detective Clayborn actually knew this already. Curiously, charming as Arborville, New Jersey, was, more than one murder had taken place within its borders. And even more curiously, Pamela's interest and expertise in knitting had often led her to recognize clues overlooked by the police.

He made no answer. As the silence grew oppressive, Pamela added, "The conference was partly sponsored by my employer, *Fiber Craft* magazine, so I wanted to do my part to make it a success. And the knitting bee idea, frugality and all, tied in well with Sufficiency House's mission and allowed Wendelstaff College to highlight the house and its programs."

Detective Clayborn nodded, then—thankfully—spoke. "How far in advance was Dr. Critter's visit to the knitting bee planned?"

"Not very." Pamela shrugged. "I think he just decided Saturday morning that it would be interesting to drop in and see what the knitters were doing." She was relieved to note that her fingers were no longer trembling, though Detective Clayborn's stare could be quite unnerving. The pad of paper on the table before him had been open to a fresh page when she entered the room, but he had yet to make any mark on that page.

"Did you know he was going to be there during the coffee service?" he inquired suddenly.

Pamela nodded. "Dean Tate told me at lunch time." She was about to add that Flo might have had more warning but realized that Detective Clayborn would doubtless ask Flo the same questions that he was asking her. And why volunteer something that might suggest Flo was responsible for Dr. Critter's poisoning? Especially when Flo could have no possible reason for wishing him dead.

There were people who had possible reasons for wishing him dead, however, and Pamela suddenly heard herself blurting, "Did anyone tell you about what happened with his ex-wife at lunch? She hates him . . . uh, hated him."

Detective Clayborn's expression didn't change. "We'll be interviewing everyone relevant to the case." His voice was so lacking expression as to seem computer-generated.

She had been about to describe the conversation she had heard coming from the shrubbery as she left the dining hall. The participants hadn't been visible, but one was clearly Dr. Critter and the other was an unhappy woman cast aside after a brief affair. But she didn't describe it, because she already knew what his response would be.

Now he picked up the pen. "Pamela Paterson, I believe," he said. She nodded, and supplied her address, landline number, and cell phone number. "Don't leave town," he added.

Was there a hint of a twinkle in his eye as he uttered that stock phrase? She wasn't sure.

He started to rise, signaling that she was dismissed. As she stood, he said, "The rest of the conference is canceled, by the way. And you're free to go home."

CHAPTER 4

But Pamela didn't go home. Faced with a roomful of knitters—who had shown up for the bee at her invitation—bravely applying themselves to their projects while they waited to be summoned one by one into the presence of a police detective, she could not in good conscience retreat to the comfort of her own home. So she reclaimed her chair, took up the in-progress scarf, which had already grown longer than a normal scarf, and set to work once again, soothed in spite of herself by the rhythm of her needles.

Another knitter from the sofa had been ushered into the dining room as Pamela was ushered out. Soon that knitter was back and preparing to resume her knitting where she had left off.

"You don't have to stay." Pamela spoke up from across the room. "Unless he asked you to." The woman whose interview had preceded Pamela's had apparently packed up the beginnings of her Fair Isle cardigan and gone on her way.

Officer Sanchez nodded in agreement from her post by the door.

"I'll wait for her." The knitter tipped her head toward her companion on the sofa.

Gradually the room emptied. Pamela spoke a few words to each departing knitter, assuring them that, in case they were returning to homes beyond the reach of the *County Register*, she would use the group email list that had updated participants on details for the bee to keep them updated on the Dr. Critter poisoning case. And she apologized for the unfortunate event that had so overshadowed the communal satisfactions the knitters had anticipated. Responses were gracious and included more than a few hand-squeezes and hugs.

At last Flo was summoned into the dining room and Pamela was left alone, except for Officer Sanchez. She finished the row she was working on and held the scarf up, suspended from one needle. It had gotten extremely long and, even with her hand raised as high as possible, reached nearly to the floor. Perhaps Nell could give it to a very tall day laborer. As she finished casting off, the dining room door opened and Flo emerged, looking shaken.

"Oh, Pamela," she moaned, taking a few steps to the chair she had vacated and sinking into it. "I've never done anything before that made the police want to question me."

Pamela folded the scarf into as compact a bundle as she could manage and reached for Flo's hand. "It's just a routine thing," she said. "We were all here when Dr. Critter drank the coffee, so somebody could have noticed something that will be useful as they try to figure out who poisoned him and how they managed it."

She glanced at the door that Flo had closed behind her. "Where is Detective Clayborn now?"

"He went into the kitchen." Flo withdrew her hand and transferred it to her lap, where it joined her other hand in a nervous fidget that involved plucking at the faded cotton of her housedress. "I guess I can go upstairs." She looked toward Officer Sanchez for confirmation. "I live here, after all, and I want to lie down. This has all just been so . . ." Her voice thinned, faltered, and faded out.

Pamela gave her a hug and watched her make her way toward the stairs.

As Pamela climbed the steps to her front porch, her attention was pulled in two directions. From inside the house came the sound of a ringing telephone and from the street came the sound of someone calling her name. She turned to see Bettina just reaching the curb, but heeding the phone she sped up, dashed across the porch, and fumbled her key into the lock. She hurried toward the kitchen but left the front door ajar as an invitation to Bettina to enter.

"Mom!" exclaimed the voice on the other end of the line. "I've been calling and calling all morning! I know you don't leave your cell phone on but don't you ever even look at your messages?"

"It's been kind of a strange morning," Pamela replied, lowering herself into the nearest chair.

"I know, Mom." Penny's tone was resigned. "I know all about it. Lorie texted me and then I looked at the *Register* online." Lorie was one of Penny's old friends from Arborville High. "I could come home," Penny added.

"No!" Pamela said quickly. "I'm fine. Really fine, and"—footsteps drew her attention to the doorway—"Bettina is here now and everything will be just . . . fine."

"You'll let the police handle it? Not like those other times when someone was killed and it had something to do with knitting?" Penny's voice sounded so mournful that Pamela suddenly wished her daughter *was* closer, not at college four hours away in Boston.

"Of course I'll let the police handle it," Pamela said. "Why wouldn't I?"

"*Mo-o-om!*" Penny groaned. "You know why and I know why—but I'll take your word for it and I hope I'm not disappointed."

"You won't be."

They chatted for a few more minutes, about less fraught topics, and then Penny signed off with "Love you, Mom." Pamela turned her attention to Bettina, who had settled into the chair on the other side of the kitchen table. In the hours since her last trip across the street Bettina had exchanged robe and slippers for a shirtwaist dress in an autumnal plaid, paired with burgundy suede booties and accessorized with a necklace of large gold beads and matching earrings.

She regarded Pamela for a long minute and then said, "You're really fine?" Pamela nodded. "I suppose you've talked to Clayborn." Pamela nodded again.

Seemingly convinced that Pamela really *was* fine, Bettina changed the subject. "The high-school drama class is doing *Hansel and Gretel* at the library this afternoon," she said. "I'm reporting on it for the *Advocate*, and Wilfred and the Arborville grandchildren are coming along. But have dinner with us. We'll cook something out on the patio—take advantage of the weather while we still have a chance."

Pamela saw Bettina to the door then, nodding in response to her urgent "Be sure to eat some lunch though" and sending her on her way. She returned to the kitchen, but before opening the refrigerator, she sat back down and pushed the button and tapped the icon that would make her cell phone yield up its voice mail messages.

Yes, there were several from Penny, each sounding more concerned than the last. But there was also one from Brian Delano. She hesitated a moment, then played it.

"Hey, Pamela!" came the voice, deep and warm. "I heard the news . . . about Critter, and the rest of the conference being canceled. So I don't know where you are now, but I hope you're okay and . . . please give me a call if you can."

She would, but not just yet.

Bettina was probably right. She should eat something. Pamela set her phone aside, stood up, and opened the refrigerator. The contents seemed unfamiliar, as if eons had passed since she last peered inside, though she'd cooked a meal as recently as Friday night. So much had happened since then! But the remains of a meatloaf jogged her memory of that meal and a few slices of meatloaf on whole-grain bread made a welcome lunch.

Feeling somewhat better, she took up her phone again and returned Brian's call. Pamela's social calendar was not such that she frequently had to choose between two competing dinner invitations, but she realized that she was now faced with that dilemma.

When she'd spoken to Brian the previous day, she'd

agreed to meet him for dinner after the conference wound down. And she'd nodded in agreement when Bettina urged her to cross the street that evening for a barbecue.

She knew that, given Bettina's enthusiasm about the romantic possibilities offered by Brian Delano, she would be more than happy to excuse her from the barbecue. But Pamela had agreed to the *date* (Bettina would insist on calling it that) before the revelation that Dr. Critter had been poisoned and all the complications and stress that revelation had introduced.

Brian Delano was a relatively new acquaintance, an attractive and appealing man whose company she enjoyed. But she'd only met him in mid-May, and then he'd been away for all of July and August. The relationship at the point when he left hadn't progressed to the stage that daily FaceTime calls were needed to ease the ache of separation. They had emailed back and forth, and she'd enjoyed seeing samples of the photos that had been the point of his journey. But she wasn't in love with him, and their *dates* still involved a certain formality.

Bettina and Wilfred, on the other hand, were like family. Time spent with them was a comfort in itself, with the knowledge that her words would be attended to if she spoke but her silence would be understood if she didn't.

"Hey, Pamela!" Brian's voice intruded on her thoughts. "How are you doing? I heard Sufficiency House was swarming with police this morning."

"They had the kitchen marked off with crime-scene tape," Pamela said. "And the Arborville police detective was interviewing the knitters from the bee. We all had coffee yesterday afternoon but nobody else had any kind of reaction and certainly nobody else died, so . . ."

"Sounds like the police have their work cut out for them."

Pamela nodded, but then realized that a nod wasn't audible and murmured agreement.

"So are you at Sufficiency House now?"

"I came home," Pamela said, and explained that she had wanted to stay with the knitters until the police finished with all of them but that that had happened by noon.

"I'll pick you up," Brian said. "It's a nice day. How about a drive along the Hudson and dinner at a country inn in one of those little towns?"

"Oh, Brian . . ." Pamela hesitated. "I just . . . I wouldn't be very good company."

"You don't have to be." He laughed, a kind of surprised laugh—as if she had misjudged him somehow. "We could just . . . be quiet together." When she didn't say anything, he added. "I would like that."

"I . . ." Pamela sighed. "My neighbors—old friends—across the street are worried about me and they invited me over and . . ." She sighed again. "So for tonight, I think I'll just stick here in Arborville. But I'd like to see you soon. I'll call you."

When he responded, his manner once more reminded her of Wilfred—secure and sympathetic enough to understand the need, at the moment, to spend the evening with old friends instead of him. As she said goodbye and broke the connection, she wondered if maybe she should have postponed the dinner with Bettina and Wilfred instead.

Pamela suspected that messages lurked in her email too, and preferring to read them on the larger screen of her office computer, she climbed the stairs. Precious looked up from Pamela's desk chair, where she had been dozing, her opalescent blue eyes startling against the sable of her dark face.

Pamela picked her up gently, slid into the chair, and placed the cat on her lap. She absentmindedly scratched Precious's head as she listened to the beeps and chirps with which her computer came to life.

Two messages waited in her inbox already and two more arrived as she watched. The old ones were both offerings of coupons, one from the hobby shop and the other from the office-supplies store. The new ones were more consequential: one from Dean Tate and the other from her boss at *Fiber Craft*.

Dean Tate thanked Pamela for her help with the conference and expressed regret that it had to end early and for such a lamentable reason. The message from her boss at *Fiber Craft* was more pointed.

"The knitting bee at Sufficiency House seemed a good idea," she wrote.

My idea, Pamela whispered to herself. *You might just as well say it.*

"The Wendelstaff dining service provided the coffee," she went on, "so I suppose this could have happened wherever on campus Dr. Critter joined the conference participants for the afternoon break, though the intimate setup at Sufficiency House and the house's layout with a back door entrance to the kitchen might have emboldened the killer."

I thought of that too, Pamela murmured.

"I'm aware that Sufficiency House is not in the same town as the college but rather just over the border in Arborville, where you live."

Pamela nodded, though there was no one to see the nod.

"I hope the Arborville police will soon figure out what happened and who's responsible. Living there you are perhaps more familiar with their abilities than I," her boss wound up.

More than you know, Pamela sighed, and closed the message.

Pamela had been grateful for the weekend chores that allowed her to distract herself until it was time to join Bettina and Wilfred for dinner. She had even taken a break from cleaning and laundry to bake a batch of oatmeal cookies. Now she set out across the street with a sizeable number of those cookies heaped on a wedding-china plate and covered with plastic wrap.

It had been clear from the moment she stepped onto her porch that a barbecue was in the offing. The aroma of charcoal well on its way to peak grilling condition reached her from the Frasers' yard, and as she made her way up their driveway, Bettina greeted her from the side of the garage.

"Come around this way," she said with a beckoning gesture. "We're out on the patio."

The Frasers' house was the oldest on Orchard Street, a Dutch Colonial once inhabited by the long-ago Dutch colonists who planted the apple orchard that had given the street its name. Bettina and Wilfred had enlarged and modernized the kitchen, which now communicated with the large patio though sliding glass doors. The kitchen and patio suited the Frasers' love of summer entertaining to a T.

Wilfred waved at Pamela from the barbecue grill, positioned several yards away from the patio on the grass, lest the wafting smoke become intense. He had tied an apron over the bib overalls he adopted as his uniform in retirement. Nothing had yet been set to grilling, but he was carefully monitoring the state of the coals.

"Hamburgers," Bettina said, "on some of those brioche buns from the Co-Op bakery counter. "Simple, but burgers are always a treat when they're cooked outdoors, and Wilfred so enjoys showing off his grilling technique."

In fact, Wilfred had been the primary cook both indoors and out since he retired, with the effect of considerably widening the Frasers' culinary horizons. Bettina had been a dutiful if uninspired cook, repeating the same seven menus week in and week out.

"And," Bettina went on, "it's still sweet corn season, so we're having corn on the cob."

Her attention turned to the cookies Pamela was carrying. "You didn't have to!" she exclaimed as Pamela offered her the plate. "But I'm glad you did!" She bent forward to examine the cookies more closely, then she raised her eyes to examine Pamela's face. "How are you?" she inquired, concern erasing the smile the cookies had summoned.

"I'm fine," Pamela said. "Really. Don't worry." She commanded her brain to muster proof and settled on "How was the play?" in hopes that interest in the quotidian would demonstrate that she was ready to leave the shocking events of the past few days behind.

"It was just wonderful!" Bettina smiled once again, a smile enhanced by the bright pink lipstick she'd chosen to coordinate with her stylish ensemble: a wide-legged jumpsuit in a print that evoked exotic blooms. "The actors signed autographs afterwards and my little grandsons were so thrilled." She hefted the plate of cookies. "Let's take these inside."

Pamela stepped ahead of her to slide the glass door open and followed her into the Frasers' spacious kitchen. Bettina set the plate of cookies on the scrubbed pine table that dominated the eating area of the kitchen and proceeded to the refrigerator.

"Beer?" she inquired, and without waiting for an answer, she lined up three frosty bottles on the tall counter that separated the eating area of the kitchen from the cooking area. "Glasses are already outside," she added, and they returned to the patio with the beer.

Bettina's skill and interest lay not in the cooking of food but in the serving. This evening she had covered the patio table with an aqua linen cloth and added placemats for good measure, in a rustic weave that alternated shades of blue and green in broad stripes. Atop the placemats sat her favorite sage-green pottery plates, accented with dark green linen napkins. The glasses that awaited the beer were tall and graceful, with simple lines that hinted at Scandinavian influence.

"And the little boys are happy to be back at school?" Pamela inquired, in a further effort to convince Bettina that darker thoughts had yielded to interest in the seasonal rituals of suburban life.

"Happy as they can be," Bettina chirped. "Little Freddy is in first grade now, so he goes all day. So proud of himself!"

She popped the cap off one of the beer bottles and tilted it over a glass, angling the glass too as a head of foam began to form, and offering the full glass to Pamela.

Wilfred joined them then, his ruddy face all the ruddier for his recent charcoal-monitoring duties. He filled a glass for Bettina and then one for himself.

"Quite the surprise in this morning's newspaper," he observed with a head shake after his first sip. "That professor's unexpected death was shocking enough, then to discover he was poisoned. It never rains but it pours."

CHAPTER 5

When Bettina seemed about to speak, after giving Wilfred a meaningful glance and nodding toward Pamela, Pamela seized her hand. Then she seized Wilfred's for good measure. "It's okay," she said. "There's no use pretending it didn't happen."

"But we don't have to talk about it now," Bettina said firmly.

"Dear wife, my lips are sealed! Besides, the coals are just about ready and there are hamburgers to grill."

"Corn!" Bettina exclaimed. Beer glass in hand, she headed for the sliding doors and Pamela followed, murmuring, "What can I do?"

A painted wooden tray on the scrubbed pine table held mustard, mayonnaise, catsup, sliced pickles in a little dish, salt and pepper, and a small basket containing three puffy golden buns.

A deep two-handled pot sat on the stove with a burner alight under it. Three ears of sweet corn lay on the counter, freed from their husks but with a few fine strands of corn silk clinging to the rows of pale yellow pearls that were their kernels.

"Coleslaw is in the refrigerator," Bettina said. "It needs a nice bowl. And the burger patties are in there too, on a plate."

Meanwhile, she lifted the lid on the two-handled pot. When a wisp of steam rose, she replaced the lid and turned the burner up.

As Pamela stood by the scrubbed pine table spooning the coleslaw into an oval bowl from Bettina's sage-green pottery set, Bettina carried the burger patties out to Wilfred. No sooner had Bettina left the kitchen than Woofus came nosing in from the dining room. He raised his shaggy head to study Pamela for a moment, then continued through the open doorway onto the patio.

"He knows Wilfred always cooks a little treat for him when there's a barbecue," Bettina explained when she returned. She glanced toward the stove where the lid on the two-handled pot had begun to jiggle.

In a few minutes, the aroma of grilling beef began to drift in from the yard. Bettina lowered the ears of corn into the pot, replaced the cover, and raised her wrist to consult her pretty watch.

Pamela carried the tray, to which she had added the bowl of slaw, through the door and set it on the table.

The timing was perfect. Just as Bettina stepped onto the patio and deposited a dish containing the steaming ears of corn on the table, along with a smaller dish containing a large pat of butter, Wilfred announced that the burgers were done.

"We're eating family style tonight," he added with a genial smile. "Bring your plates."

The buns in the basket had already been sliced open. Pamela put a bun on a plate, folded the top back, and advanced across the lawn to receive a burger. Bettina followed with her plate and Wilfred's.

One burger remained, however, after he had wielded his spatula to skillfully maneuver three of them from the grill onto the waiting buns. The extra burger wasn't as large as the others and in a moment its destiny became clear. Woofus had watched with great interest as the humans were provided with their dinner. Now Wilfred scooped the extra burger onto the plate that had held the burgers in their raw state. He used the spatula to break it up into smaller pieces, pushing them here and there and blowing on them to cool them.

"Every dog has his day," he explained, as he tossed a tidbit to Woofus, who caught it in midair and gulped it down with a grateful glance at Wilfred. Turning to Pamela and Bettina, he said, "Dear ladies, I will be with you in a minute. Please take your seats."

Back at the table, Pamela and Bettina set to work garnishing their burgers with the condiments presented on the tray. Soon Wilfred joined them and for a time there was silence—punctuated by sounds of pleasure, as well as by the crunching of sweet corn being eaten from the cob.

The Co-Op's brioche buns suited the burgers perfectly. They were the shape and size of a traditional hamburger bun, though almost golden in hue and with a more substantial texture when chewed, like good yeasty bread. The meat patty's tantalizing hint of char gave way to pink juiciness with each bite. The condiments Pamela had added augmented the juiciness and her fingers were soon slick with mayonnaise, catsup, and pickle juice, not to mention the butter dripping from the ear of corn as she nibbled at the tender kernels.

Bettina was the first to speak, surveying her plate with its half-eaten burger and corn cob with only a few rows of corn remaining. "This is a perfect late-summer meal," she sighed. "And we haven't even tasted the coleslaw yet."

"Let me do the honors," Wilfred said, and he leaned forward to scoop a generous portion of coleslaw onto each plate.

"Oh, Bettina!" Pamela moaned. "Your beautiful napkin!" She had begun wiping her fingers in preparation for taking up her fork to sample the coleslaw and realized the effect that process was having on the linen napkin.

"Do not give it another thought, dear lady!" Wilfred beamed at her. "The laundry guy has a cupboard full of cleaning potions."

"He's the laundry guy," Bettina explained, with a tilt of her head in Wilfred's direction. "As well as the coleslaw guy."

The Co-Op deli's coleslaw was a summer staple at Arborville's barbecues, but Wilfred's version took coleslaw to a new level. It was colorful, with shreds of carrot and red bell pepper intermingled with the cabbage, and upon tasting it Pamela noted that his dressing added a sharper tang of vinegar than usual to the conventional mayonnaise.

The pace of eating slowed down then and the conversation picked up, touching on the play again. Bettina explained that the production had been a summer project for the high-school drama group and the plan was to perform it throughout the fall and winter at any county library that expressed an interest.

"So my article in the *Advocate* will be a good advertisement for them," she concluded. "It will stay up online forever and they can include the link in their promotional material. And that's the kind of story, a nice local story about nice local things, that the *Register* won't scoop. Not like—" She stopped, made a sound like a backwards hiccup, and raised a carefully manicured hand to her lips.

"Not like what?" Pamela asked, puzzled, but only for a moment. The evening had been so pleasant—the meal, the Frasers' soothing company, their tranquil yard—that she had forgotten the events Bettina's invitation had been designed to help her forget. But now she remembered.

Her expression must have revealed that fact because Bettina transferred her hand from her lips to Pamela's forearm and squeezed. "I'm so sorry," she wailed. "So, so sorry." The cheer that normally plumped her cheeks and smoothed her brow had vanished and she looked a woeful ten years older.

"It's okay," Pamela said. "I can't hide from it. Even if I ignored the news, I'd hear about it anyway, from people."

"People like me," Bettina moaned and her head sagged forward until all Pamela could see was a tousle of bright red curls.

"Dear wife!" Wilfred bobbed up from his chair, leaning on the table to give himself a boost. In an instant he was standing behind Bettina's chair, his hands on her shoulders. "She didn't mean to bring it up," Wilfred assured Pamela. Pamela nodded and joined him in his comforting ministrations.

But the ice had been broken. (Wilfred's fondness for invoking old sayings was catching.) When Bettina raised her head and whispered, "I'm sorry," Pamela heard herself inquire, "When will you be meeting with Clayborn?"

Bettina looked momentarily blank, so she followed up with, "I'm sure the *Advocate* will be at least as interested in the . . . *event* . . . at Sufficiency House as in the drama group's *Hansel and Gretel*."

"I usually talk to him on Monday morning," Bettina said. "Just to see if anything is new, you know."

"Something *is* new," Pamela pointed out. "And as you've often said, even though the *Register* scoops the big stories, people like to read about local events in their local paper, even if it *is* just a weekly." She paused. "So will you be talking to him tomorrow?"

Bettina tipped her head in a slight nod, as if she wasn't sure how enthusiastic she should be about a meeting that was sure to include whatever details of the murder and its investigation Detective Clayborn wanted to release to the Arborville public.

"I know something he doesn't know." Pamela smiled a secret smile. "More than one person had reason to want Dr. Critter dead."

"Did you tell him that when he interviewed you?" Seeming to realize that Pamela was willing—even eager—to discuss the case now that the ice had been broken, Bettina was quite herself again.

"I told him that Dr. Critter's ex-wife jumped up after he gave his luncheon talk and accused him of stealing her good ideas for his book and polluting them with his bad ideas. Lots of other people probably told Detective Clayborn that too, because everybody at the conference came to the luncheon."

"Then a few hours later he has some kind of a spell after drinking a cup of coffee and that evening he dies." Bettina nodded, vigorously this time.

"*However*"—Pamela drew the word out slowly, enjoying the sense that both Bettina and Wilfred were paying rapt attention—"I didn't tell him about the conversation I overheard a bit later while walking to my car." She described the dialogue that reached her from behind the shrubbery near the dining hall door. "Definitely Dr. Critter," she concluded, "but not his ex-wife. Some other woman, a woman he'd misled into thinking he cared for her when he clearly didn't and who now feels betrayed."

"Seduced and abandoned." Bettina's sorrowful expression conveyed her sympathy for a woman in such a plight.

"So there are at least two suspects," Pamela said, "and maybe as Detective Clayborn interviews people close to Dr. Critter, somebody will mention his amours. I suspect there were many, and not just the woman in the shrubbery. And maybe Detective Clayborn will have a forensics report from the crime scene people by the time you talk to him."

"I'll be over tomorrow morning," Bettina said, "right after my meeting with him."

Wilfred began clearing away the plates, urging Pamela to remain where she was when she rose to help, and the conversation between Pamela and Bettina circled back to the gentle topics with which the evening had begun. As the sky began to redden in the west and a breeze sprang up, Wilfred appeared on the patio to suggest that dessert, raspberry-mango ice cream from the fancy ice cream shop in Timberley, be taken inside, accompanied by coffee and Pamela's cookies. As if the invitation wasn't appealing enough, the tantalizing aroma of brewing coffee wafted from the open doorway on the breeze.

CHAPTER 6

Pamela stared at her computer screen. Monday morning's email had brought a message from the alumni association of her alma mater, another coupon from the hobby shop, and a note from her bank saying her credit card statement was available. But there was nothing from her boss at *Fiber Craft*.

She'd finished a book review and evaluations of four articles the previous Friday and sent them off, and she'd been expecting a new batch of work to arrive with the beginning of the new week. Her boss seemed never to rest, and when there was work to be assigned it was generally waiting in her inbox first thing in the morning.

Well . . . she pushed back from her desk, spun her chair around, and rose. It probably didn't mean anything. The weekend had been busy. Perhaps her boss had fallen behind and was responding to her own email at this very moment, sorting through submissions to decide what looked promising enough for serious consideration. She'd been hoping for work though, hoping to lose herself in someone's interesting exploration of weaving technique, uses for hemp, or the history of the petticoat.

She crossed the hall to her bedroom, where she pulled on a fresh pair of jeans and a comfortable chambray shirt and traded her slippers for sandals. After a brief detour to the bathroom to comb her hair and secure it in a clip at the back of her neck, she returned to the kitchen. The *Register* was still spread out on the kitchen table, sharing the surface with an empty coffee cup and a plate dusted with a few toast crumbs.

She had hurried down the front walk as soon as she rose and seized up the newspaper in its flimsy plastic sleeve. But the front page had featured no dramatic break-through in the "Wendelstaff prof murder case." In fact, the story had been relegated to the "Local" section, where a brief article by Marcy Brewer merely reported that Arborville police had made no further statement.

Pamela collected the *Register* from the kitchen table and deposited it in the recycling basket in the entry, paus-ing to note that Catrina had already commenced her morning nap in the sunny spot on the thrift-store carpet. Feeling at loose ends, she wandered into the living room and plumped up the pillows ranged along the back of the sofa, taking special care that the needlepoint cat was front and center.

Her knitting bag waited on the carpet near the end of the sofa where she customarily sat. She could knit, though knitting was usually reserved for evenings. Surely work from the magazine would arrive soon. She wan-dered back into the kitchen. Bettina would be coming, and probably with a goody in hand. She could prepare by grinding a fresh batch of coffee and filling the cream pitcher.

But first, a tiny bit of coffee was left in the carafe and it seemed a shame to waste it. She lit the burner under the carafe and watched carefully until tiny bubbles formed at the edges of the dark liquid. She was just pouring it into her cup when the doorbell chimed.

Through the lace that curtained the oval window in the front door, a splash of bright orange garnished with a flourish of scarlet was silhouetted against the deep green of the lawn. Pamela had barely begun to pull the door back when Bettina sang out, "There's new information, more than he had when he talked to Marcy Brewer yesterday."

Once the door was fully open, Bettina stepped across the threshold and held out a white bakery box encircled with string. The splash of bright orange proved to be a fetching jersey wrap dress that contrasted dramatically with her scarlet hair. On her feet were kitten heels in a deeper shade of orange. She had accessorized the outfit with dangly earrings of amber set in silver and a matching necklace.

Pamela accepted the bakery box and led the way to the kitchen, looking over her shoulder to say, "I'll make coffee. It sounds like we've got things to talk about."

"The forensics report from the crime scene," Bettina said. "He got it first thing this morning."

"And?" Pamela set the bakery box on the table and turned to face Bettina.

"Coffee first." Bettina allowed a teasing smile to curve her lips. She stepped closer, slipped the string off the box, and folded back the flap that formed the cover. "Co-Op cinnamon rolls," she announced. "I don't know why we didn't discover these ages ago."

Resigned to waiting until they were both sitting at the table with steaming cups of coffee before them, Pamela filled the kettle and set it to boiling. She measured coffee beans into the grinder, pressed down on the lid, and for a few moments the small kitchen echoed with the rattle and crunch of the whirling beans.

Meanwhile Bettina fetched two small wedding-china plates from the cupboard, as well as a cup and saucer for herself, silverware, and napkins. She transferred the cut-glass cream and sugar set from the counter to the table and poured a goodly portion of heavy cream into the pitcher.

The kettle began to hoot, and soon the aroma of brewing coffee hinted at the pleasure to come. Pamela filled the cups and took her seat opposite Bettina, where a twirl of yeasty dough glistening with a dark, sugary glaze awaited her on a wedding-china plate.

"Okay," she said before she even took up her fork or sampled her coffee. "What did the forensics report say?"

"No trace of poison anywhere." Bettina's fork, bearing a morsel of cinnamon roll, paused midway to her mouth.

"What?" Pamela felt her forehead crease as she raised her brows. "So they don't suspect Dr. Critter was murdered after all?"

Bettina gestured to indicate she was chewing. After she swallowed, she said, "It's not that." As she continued talking, she spooned sugar into her coffee and, after an energetic spate of stirring, began to dribble in cream. "The problem is that too much time elapsed between when Critter was taken ill and when he died. Nobody expected him to die, and so the campus food service picked up the coffee dispenser and carried it away for washing. And Flo washed all the Sufficiency House cups."

Her coffee had attained the pale mocha hue that she favored and she raised her cup to her lips for a sample. Once the cup, with the print of her vivid orange lipstick on the rim, had been returned to her saucer, she went on.

"It was impossible to tell exactly which cup had been his, even though the Sufficiency House cups are a jumble of different patterns, so the forensics lab checked them all. And to make matters even more complicated, the Wendelstaff campus dining service owns ten of those coffee dispensers and had no idea which of them had been sent over to Sufficiency House. So they all had to be checked. But everything—cups and dispensers—had just been washed too thoroughly."

Pamela teased off a bite of her own roll and conveyed it to her mouth. The sweet, yeasty dough, with its hint of cinnamon, was the perfect vehicle for the glaze, with its rich brown-sugar overtones. She followed the bite of cinnamon roll with a sip of coffee.

"Nevertheless, he didn't die of natural causes," she said. "The hospital seemed sure of that, and he started gasping and twitching immediately after finishing his coffee, so it seems that something in the coffee carried him off." At the recollection of Critter's distress, she felt herself wince.

"The autopsy is still to be done." Bettina looked up from carving off a glistening morsel from what remained of her cinnamon roll. "So Clayborn might soon have more information. It would help to know exactly what it was that poisoned him."

"The whole thing is mysterious." Pamela sipped at her coffee, its bitterness a welcome foil for the sugary concoction on her plate. "Everyone drank the coffee, but only he was poisoned." She took another sip of coffee. "He helped himself, after all the knitters had been served—made quite a point of helping himself, in fact. Flo started for the kitchen to fetch him a cup but he said he was quite liberated, or something like that."

"So one empty cup was waiting there, by the dispenser?"

Pamela nodded. "I watched Flo fill the others and carry them to the dining room, one for each person who wanted coffee, and there was tea for the tea-drinkers. A cup and saucer stayed behind and Dr. Critter filled that cup for himself."

"There's that back door, the door the food service people used." Bettina tackled her cinnamon roll, probing at the twist to expose a pale, cinnamon-speckled curl of dough.

Pamela nodded again. "Are you thinking what I'm thinking?"

"That these cinnamon rolls are almost too big for just one person? You haven't eaten very much of yours at all."

Pamela laughed. "No—about the back door. The timing would have to be perfect, but someone who knew when Dr. Critter was going to be helping himself to coffee could have sneaked in the back door of Sufficiency House and added poison to the coffee dispenser just before he came in to fill his cup."

Bettina thought for a minute, then replied, "They'd have had to be sure nobody else was going to come back for a refill." Her lips parted and she inhaled sharply. "Or maybe they didn't care if somebody else died too—as long as they got Critter."

Bettina thought for another minute. A slight crease

formed between her carefully shaped brows. "Maybe the point wasn't to kill Critter specifically, but just to kill *someone* . . . or even many someones, random some-ones."

"Why would a person want to do that . . . unless they were some kind of psychopath?" Pamela's taste in enter-tainment veered toward the cozy—especially British mysteries, with their refined characters and beautiful houses and gardens. But she'd certainly watched the oc-casional thriller in which the murderer seemed motivated only by the desire to do evil.

Bettina leaned forward as if to speak confidentially, though no one was present except her and Pamela. "Clay-born stepped out of his office for a few minutes when I was with him this morning, and I overheard him talking to someone in the hall. Now I realize what they were talk-ing about could have had to do with the Critter case."

"And?" Pamela leaned forward as well.

"Some local developer has been trying for ages to buy Sufficiency House."

Pamela felt her eyes widen. She took a deep breath. "If Sufficiency House becomes a liability for Wendelstaff, the college might be more inclined to sell it. But poison-ing people is an awfully dramatic way to achieve a goal."

"It is." Bettina nodded and her amber earrings swayed. "And as far as Clayborn is concerned—at least as far as he wants the media to be informed—the Arborville police are investigating thoroughly but have no suspects."

"Not the ex-wife?"

Bettina shook her head no and her earrings continued to sway.

"And I guess nobody has told him yet about Dr. Crit-ter's womanizing ways." Pamela realized she had been neglecting both her coffee and her cinnamon roll. She took a sip from her cup, noticed her coffee had grown cold, and reached for her fork.

"Apparently not." Bettina had made further inroads with both coffee and cinnamon roll. Now she held out her coffee cup with a lift of the eyebrows that suggested she wouldn't say no to a refill.

Pamela said, "I'll warm what's left in the carafe," put her fork back down, and rose from her chair. As she stood by the stove watching for the small bubbles that would indicate the coffee in the carafe had reached drinking temperature, the conversation continued.

"Greed can be a motive for sure," she observed, "though killing random people that one doesn't even know in order to get one's hands on a piece of property seems extreme."

Bettina raised her cup again as Pamela approached the table carrying the carafe. "It does seem extreme," she agreed. "This developer is some local guy, but I didn't catch a name."

"Most murderers know their victims." Pamela returned the carafe to the stove and reclaimed her seat. "And they're angry about something."

"The ex-wife." Bettina looked up from stirring sugar into her fresh cup of coffee. "He stole her ideas—and who knows what other things he did to make her angry while they were still married?"

"And that poor woman talking to Dr. Critter in the shrubbery." Pamela shook her head sadly. "She gave him her love, and her . . . self. Then he broke her heart and just walked away."

"Revenge." Bettina returned her spoon to her saucer with a *clunk*.

"Yes, revenge—in both cases really. And I'd think Detective Clayborn could understand how a person whose ideas were stolen could have a motive to kill the thief, so I don't see why he isn't going after the ex-wife." Pamela nudged a morsel loose from her cinnamon roll.

"I don't either, though maybe she has an alibi. But if he talks to enough people somebody's bound to tell him about Critter's relationship with the woman in the shrubbery."

"I hope so." Pamela stabbed the morsel with her fork and raised her fork to her mouth. "Though I feel sorry for her. Maybe it would be better if she got away with the crime. Fairer even."

"Oh, Pamela!" The hand holding Bettina's cup paused midway to her lips and her eyes widened. "We can't be hoping people get away with murder!"

"No . . . no." Pamela sighed. "And I do hope Detective Clayborn gets to the bottom of this soon." She hadn't shared with Bettina her fear that her job at *Fiber Craft* might be in peril. She took a reflective sip of coffee and then went on. "Detective Clayborn is a detective, but he's also a man. I just don't know if a man could put himself in the mind of a woman who had been treated like that— seduced and abandoned. Even a very sensitive man . . . is still a man."

"My Wilfred isn't!" Bettina set her cup down with such vehemence that coffee splashed onto the saucer.

Pamela forbore pointing out that Wilfred was actually a man—she knew that Bettina was defending her husband's sensitivity, but she continued speaking. "And maybe Detective Clayborn doesn't understand how angry a person could be if their ideas were stolen. Maybe he sees things in more concrete terms—*male* terms, like lust for property."

And with that the conversation turned to less disturbing topics: Penny's reports on her first week back at school and the upcoming meeting of Knit and Nibble.

After Bettina left, Pamela tidied the kitchen, drying by hand the dishes that were usually left to dry on their own in the dish drainer and then mopping the floor. She was quite aware that the goal of this extra activity was to delay the inevitable moment when she would climb the stairs to her office and check her email.

Pamela was not normally a procrastinator. And when it came to work, she eagerly tackled whatever was set in front of her. Now, though, she was afraid that what she would discover when she sat down in front of her computer would be the absence of work—no email at all from her boss or, even worse, a message telling her that her editorial services were no longer required.

Upstairs in her office, she transferred Ginger from her keyboard to her lap and allowed her computer mouse to explore its keypad until her monitor came to life, holding her breath while she waited for the screen to brighten. As she had feared, her inbox held no messages from her boss. In fact, it held no messages at all. Clicking on SYNC raised her hopes by delivering two messages, but when she opened her inbox one proved to be spam. The other was from Dean Tate at Wendelstaff.

Dean Tate's message was not personally addressed to Pamela. She was one of many recipients in a large group, she was sure—a group that Dean Tate believed would want to know the details of Dr. Critter's upcoming funeral, scheduled for the next day at a church in Timberley.

Pamela stared at the screen, absentmindedly scratching Ginger's head as she did so. She should go to the funeral. There was no getting around it. She had been one of the conference organizers, Dr. Critter had been the keynote speaker, and she had been present when he was taken ill.

She left off scratching Ginger's head and swiveled her chair halfway around to reach for her office phone.

Bettina picked up on the first ring and her first words, even before Pamela identified herself, were, "Are you okay?"

"My phone knew it was you," she explained when Pamela was momentarily speechless.

"No worse than when you left." Pamela laughed, and she described the email from Dean Tate.

"You think you should go but you don't want to go alone." Bettina uttered the words as a statement rather than a question.

"I'd like company," Pamela said. "Moral support. It's in Timberley, ten a.m., to be followed by a reception at the Wendelstaff faculty club. I'll drive."

"See you tomorrow morning at 9:30," Bettina replied. "And wear something nice. Looking good will give you confidence."

No additional emails had magically appeared while she was talking to Bettina, so Pamela returned Ginger to her perch on the keyboard and headed downstairs.

It was too early for lunch, and eating a Co-Op cinnamon roll had guaranteed that she wouldn't be hungry for hours. The house was clean, the laundry had been done recently, and the larder was well stocked with food.

Organizing her time had helped Pamela stay calm through previous crises, so she made a plan. She would take a long walk, venturing down Orchard Street rather than up toward town, then she would check her email again. If there was still no work from *Fiber Craft*, she would sit down with her knitting and give herself over to the soothing rhythms of her needles.

CHAPTER 7

It was Tuesday morning. Half a slice of whole-grain toast remained on the small rose-garlanded plate. Pamela had barely managed to eat the other half. The morning's email had brought no word from Fiber Craft, and her fear that her job might be vanishing, along with apprehension about who she might meet at Dr. Critter's funeral and the reception afterwards had combined to take away her appetite, which was never that robust first thing in the morning anyway.

Then there was the article in the *Register*. The "Wendelstaff prof murder case" had once again been relegated to the "Local" section, reflecting the fact that not much progress had been made. The autopsy results confirmed what the doctors at the hospital had suspected: Critter had been poisoned. But the autopsy had not been able to reveal what type of poison—thus closing off a potential line of investigation. Other than that, police had nothing new to report on the case.

Pamela tucked the uneaten toast half into a ziplock bag, took a last sip of coffee, and washed her breakfast dishes at the sink, along with the cats' breakfast dishes. The cats themselves had long since retreated.

Upstairs, she pondered the contents of her closet. "Wear something nice," Bettina had said. "Looking good will give you confidence." It was too warm for the outfit she usually wore when serious clothes were required, the brown slacks and brown and black striped jacket she had bought long ago for a job interview.

She pushed a few hangers aside and pulled out one that held the black slacks she had worn for the conference. They would do, but what to wear on top? Maybe a plain white shirt—but did that qualify as a confidence-boosting "something nice"? She studied the stack of sweaters piled on her closet shelf. Most were too warm for a mid-September day, but she tugged out a light pullover she had knit from a cotton and linen blend. The color was pale amber, like autumn leaves. People didn't stick to dark colors anymore for funerals, and she decided the black slacks and the amber sweater would be suitable, with the addition of a paisley scarf in shades of amber, gold, and rust that Bettina had given her.

After dressing, she detoured into her office to check her email, but the only message was a note from the Arborville DPW reminding people that curbside leaf removal would start in two weeks.

She was sitting on the sofa knitting when Bettina rang the bell.

"The scarf looks nice with that sweater," Bettina commented as soon as the door swung back, "but surely you could tie it in a more interesting way."

Pamela sat in the chair that was the entry's main piece of furniture as Bettina untied the scarf and then redid it in what felt like a series of complicated loops and twists.

"Do you want to take a look?" she asked as she stepped back to survey her handiwork.

"I'm sure it's fine," Pamela said as she collected her purse.

Sunlight tinted shades of red, blue, and gold filtered through the tall stained-glass windows of St. Botolph's Church. Otherwise the interior was dim and chilly. It smelled faintly of incense and strongly of flowers, massed in profusion near the altar and adorning R. G.-G. Critter's sleek coffin.

The funeral service had been lengthy, and had involved standing, sitting, and kneeling, seemingly in waves as people farther back took their cues from those nearer to the altar. Now, after murmured words of dismissal on the part of the officiant, accompanied by a priestly gesture, the pallbearers took up the coffin and began their slow progress down the aisle. Within a few moments, the pews began to empty as mourners edged toward the aisle and fell into step behind the pallbearers.

Once Pamela's eyes had adjusted to the gloom, she had scanned the crowd discreetly, wondering if she would recognize any faces—or backs of heads, actually, since she was loath to turn around and make her staring obvious. Almost immediately she had realized that at least one person she knew was a fellow mourner: her boss from *Fiber Craft*.

The aggressively chic bun was hard to miss, jet-black hair smoothed straight back from the forehead and molded into a perfect oval just above the collar of a perfectly tailored black jacket. As she processed the sight, Pamela had felt her heart wobble and her throat constrict. Would there be an awkward confrontation in the church parking lot? One that would cause Pamela forever after to associate Gothic architecture with the day she lost her job?

She watched as pew after pew emptied and somberly dressed men, women, and children made their way down the aisle. One couple, among the first to fall in step behind the coffin, might be Dr. Critter's parents, she decided. Aged but elegant, they were leaning on one another for support and their faces spoke of the grief one would feel at burying a son. Other people walking close behind them, younger people, were also relatives, she decided, and the boys and girls in their suits and tidy dresses possibly nephews and nieces.

After those people came a group who didn't seem particularly grief stricken—colleagues perhaps. A man and a woman were even exchanging secret grins, as if sharing a private joke. Duty had brought them out, clearly, as it had brought her out.

While she was pondering this thought, she scanned the pews in front of her to estimate how much longer it might be until she and Bettina could escape from their pew and join the procession making its way to the exit. When her gaze returned to the procession itself, she found herself looking right into the eyes of her boss.

She swallowed hard while struggling to produce a smile suitable to the setting and occasion, but her smile was answered with only a curt nod as her boss swept by.

By the time Pamela and Bettina stepped through the church's heavy wooden doors onto the broad concrete porch, cars were already proceeding single-file from the parking lot and the hearse was in motion. She saw no sign of her boss as she and Bettina made their way to her car.

By the time Pamela and Bettina had parked at the cemetery and picked their way across the grass to where a deep rectangle had been carved into the earth, Critter's coffin had already been lowered into it. One of the pall-bearers, a young man who could have been a Wendelstaff student, was gently sprinkling a shovelful of dirt into the grave.

The crowd at the gravesite was considerably smaller than the crowd that had filled the pews at the funeral, though all the people Pamela had identified as family members were present, moving sadly across the bright grass as the ceremony concluded.

Ten minutes later, Pamela turned into the large parking lot at the north end of the Wendelstaff campus. The faculty club, where the reception was to be held, was in the student union building, which had its own lot, but that lot had been full.

"I guess we're in for another hike," Bettina said with a sigh as she stepped out onto the asphalt. She extended a foot and bent over to brush a few blades of wet grass from the toe of her elegant pump. She was all in navy blue today, a form-fitting navy sheath with a matching jacket that featured three-quarter-length sleeves, and navy pumps and a navy bag to match. She had accessorized the outfit with a sedate strand of pearls and pearl earrings.

They set off toward the Wendelstaff quadrangle and were just launching themselves onto one of the many paths that crisscrossed the well-tended lawn when a male voice hailed them with a cheerful "Hi, there!"

Hurrying down the steps of an ivy-covered building that faced the quadrangle was Brian Delano, waving with one hand and carrying a bulging leather satchel in the other. He was smiling the smile that gentled his wolfishly handsome features, and it grew wider as he neared them.

Bettina grabbed Pamela's arm and gave her a pleased but puzzled look.

"You're here for the reception, I suppose," Brian said when he reached Pamela's side.

Pamela nodded, remembered her manners, and performed the necessary introductions.

Bettina extended a carefully manicured hand. "Pamela has told me so much about you," she cooed, stressing every word. "I'm delighted to meet you at last." Tilting her chin and gazing into his eyes, she gave him her most dazzling smile.

Pamela bit her tongue. She had barely told Bettina anything about Brian Delano, except the few details Bettina had extracted. But contradicting her would be awkward. What would she say? *Actually I haven't told her anything?*

Brian glanced back and forth between Bettina and Pamela. "I'm on my way to the reception myself," he said. "After all, Critter was a colleague." He hefted the bulging satchel and added, "But I've just come from a class and I want to drop this by my office first." He took a few steps along the path. "Shall we walk together?"

Bettina fell into step beside him. They proceeded across the quad, with Bettina, viewed in profile by Pamela, smiling up at Brian and chatting happily as Pamela brought up the rear. After a few minutes, Brian veered onto a path that made a right angle with the one they had been following, heading toward an imposing brick building with white columns. But that wasn't their destination. A wider concrete walk led past the side of that building, and a modern building with a dramatic glass and steel façade came into view.

"Here we are," Brian said, "the home of Fine and Professional Arts—including photography." He gestured toward the concrete steps, bisected by an elegant steel handrail, which led up to heavy glass doors. "Shall we?"

Pamela opened her mouth to say, "Oh, we can just meet you at the reception," but Bettina was too quick for her.

"What a beautiful building!" Bettina exclaimed. "I'd love to see the inside."

And so Pamela found herself tagging along as Brian and Bettina climbed the steps. Brian pulled back one of the glass doors and in a moment the three of them were standing in a sunny foyer, where a pair of elevators flanked a wide hallway.

"Just down this way," Brian said, darting into the hallway. "This won't take a minute."

But when, after a few mazelike twists and turns, they neared the office he identified as his, they encountered a woebegone student lurking at the door, a young woman.

"Professor?" She brightened slightly and took a few steps toward them. "I wasn't sure I'd find you?" She had a curious vocal mannerism in which even statements sounded like questions. "That assignment you gave? I don't understand what you're really looking for?"

Brian pulled his keys out of his pocket and unlocked his office door. Speaking over his shoulder to Pamela and Bettina, he said, "Excuse me. I won't be more than a few minutes," and he gestured for the young woman to enter his office.

The door that Brian had entered was one of many doors ranged along both sides of a long corridor. But directly across from his office was an alcove with no door. From her vantage point Pamela could see rows and rows of pigeonholes—faculty mailboxes, she surmised—mounted on the wall, reaching from chest level to eye level. Below each was an embossed label bearing an initial and a last name.

Near the top Pamela recognized B DELANO, and directly next to it, R CRITTER. Most pigeonholes were empty, while others were overstuffed. Curiously, R CRITTER had received mail since his demise, one letter at least.

Pamela nudged Bettina, drew her across the corridor, and pointed to the pigeonhole. "Wouldn't you think whoever distributes the mail would have known Dr. Critter was dead?" she whispered.

Bettina shrugged. "Maybe some student office assistant was daydreaming while he did his work."

Pamela glanced toward Brian's office door. He had closed it behind him after joining the young woman inside. It was still closed. She darted into the alcove and snatched the envelope from the pigeonhole. Back out in the corridor, she checked the postmark and discovered the letter had been mailed Saturday, from Haversack.

If it had arrived the previous day, the police undoubtedly would have found it when they searched Critter's office and its environs for clues to his murder. But it must have arrived that morning, and Bettina was probably right. Whoever distributed the mail for Fine and Professional Arts had unthinkingly tucked it into the pigeonhole labeled R CRITTER, even though R CRITTER would never claim his mail again.

Pamela tucked the letter into her purse, and it was no sooner out of sight than Brian's office door opened. The young woman stepped out and, with a cheerful "Thanks, professor," skipped away. The next moment Brian rejoined them.

The student union building was a modern building too, at the very edge of the campus. Immediately inside the entrance was a sign welcoming people to the reception for Dr. Robert Greer-Gordon Critter and indicating, with an arrow, that they should proceed to the left.

"Follow me," Brian said, and he led them down a hallway to another hallway at right angles to the first and thence through an open door into a large, crowded, room.

The guests at the reception for Dr. Critter ranged from the soberly dressed and serious—among them the people Pamela had surmised were his relatives—to those whose unconventional garb and grooming marked them as students of an artistic bent. And the deportment of the latter suggested that the opportunity to browse at a sumptuous buffet (not to mention the free-flowing wine) had been the main draw. Between those extremes were academic types, older ones of the tweed jacket variety and younger ones in denim and flannel.

One whole wall of the room was windows, floor-to-ceiling windows that looked out on the Haversack River, with its grassy bank in the foreground and the ragged edge of downtown Haversack silhouetted against a bright September sky. Parallel to the windows was a long buffet table whose offerings were evidently so popular, judging by the dense crowd it had attracted, that it was difficult to see what those offerings actually were.

"I hope you're not starving," Brian said with a laugh. Actually, Pamela was feeling very hungry, and Bettina was bobbing her head this way and that, trying for a glimpse of what the buffet table held as the eager diners elbowed each other for advantage.

A young woman server who looked to be a student passed near them bearing a tray of glasses filled with wine, red and white. Brian spoke up, saying, "We'll take some wine here." The server turned, and in a moment they had each been provided with a glass of white wine. Pamela took a small sip, hoping that the crowd at the buffet table would ease up before the wine went to her head.

Brian raised his glass. Bettina did likewise, clinked his with a playful wink, and said, "I'm so happy we ran into you." She nudged Pamela. "Aren't you, Pamela?"

But they were interrupted. A young man with an unruly crop of blond hair corralled into a loose ponytail was approaching their small group, smiling broadly.

"Hey, professor!" he called. "What's doing?"

"Not much," Brian replied, matching his smile. "Waiting for a chance to grab some lunch. How about you?"

"Had some. It's good. Be sure to try the shrimp." The young man nodded toward the buffet table. "I've got a pal in food service and I got here early. But there's plenty more where that came from." He nodded toward the buffet table again.

Brian made an easy gesture that took in Pamela and Bettina and said, "Introductions are in order. Pamela . . . Bettina, meet Dermott Sparr. He's a graduate student in the Fine and Professional Arts department. Derm, meet Pamela Paterson and Bettina . . ."

He hesitated for a moment and Bettina supplied "Fraser."

"Friends of the Critter's?" Dermott inquired with a teasing lift of the brows.

"Not exactly, I was involved in organizing the conference," Pamela said, "so I thought I should . . ." Her voice trailed off and the voices reverberating in the large room suddenly seemed very loud.

Brian seemed to sense her discomfort. He'd been watching her face, but he raised his head and directed his gaze toward the buffet. "It looks like we can grab some plates and get started," he announced. He took leave of Dermott with a friendly shoulder pat and a "See you around the campus," and they made their way past groups of chatting people to the end of the buffet table, where a server was just depositing a new pile of plates.

Realizing that filling plates while they were encumbered with nearly full wineglasses would be difficult, not to mention the challenge of eating while ambulatory, they stared at the stack of plates for a moment and then stepped aside. The room had been set up for the reception and most of the guests were standing, having chosen to eat or drink but not both at once. But the room also contained comfortable lounge chairs along the walls, arranged in pairs facing small tables. Most were occupied, but not all.

"Let's grab a table," Brian suggested. He led Pamela and Bettina to the nearest unoccupied table and chair set, and tugged over a third chair. "I'll save seats and guard the wine," he announced, setting down his own wineglass and reaching for Pamela's and Bettina's. "Have some food, and be sure to try the shrimp!"

"He's cute!" Bettina exclaimed, grabbing Pamela's

arm when they were barely out of earshot. "Even cuter than his picture on the Wendelstaff website."

Pamela frowned. Bettina's interest in Brian's romantic possibilities and her efforts to learn more about him had led to an angry confrontation the previous spring. But oblivious to the frown, Bettina continued. "And such a gentleman! What a treat to get to meet him at last!"

Thankfully, Bettina was distracted then by the sumptuous array of finger food spread out before them, platters and trays and chafing dishes all precisely arranged on a starchy white linen cloth. She took a plate, as did Pamela, and they made their way along the edge of the long table.

A chafing dish held mini meatballs in a creamy sauce. Next to it was tray on which cheese in every shade from palest white to burnished gold formed a cubist design, with bright parsley tucked around the edges. Baskets presented crackers to complement the cheese. Platters offered tiny open-faced sandwiches garnished with sprigs of dill, grated horseradish, capers, or dabs of mustard. Other platters offered miniature quiches with delicately crimped pastry edges.

"These must be the shrimp!" Bettina crooned. They too were in a chafing dish, bathed in a sauce whose aroma hinted at sweet and sour. She speared one with a long toothpick and added it to her plate, which already held a meatball, an assortment of cheese, and three open-faced sandwiches featuring smoked salmon.

They returned to their chairs with heavy-laden plates, though Pamela's was less laden than Bettina's. Brian excused himself to fill a plate of his own, and when he returned they ate and drank in companionable silence for several minutes, though the room itself buzzed with chatter and even subdued laughter.

"Derm was right about the shrimp," Brian commented as he set down the long toothpick on which he had conveyed a shrimp to his mouth.

"Everything is delicious." Bettina smiled a smile that evoked the expression of a well-fed cat.

Pamela picked up the miniature quiche, the last thing that remained on her plate, and took a bite. The custardy filling suggested crab, and there was a hint of cayenne that added a welcome tang. Bettina and Brian had embarked on a lively discussion of ways to prepare shrimp.

Pamela knew he cooked but she hadn't realized how seriously until now, and she noted that this was yet another way in which he reminded her of Wilfred—a young Wilfred, to be sure, and a more dashing Wilfred—dark, with rugged looks that were quite dramatic. But he had Wilfred's genial self-confidence and the same openhearted manner.

After agreeing with Bettina that shrimp cocktail with spicy dipping sauce was a cliché but nevertheless delicious, Brian looked at his watch and climbed to his feet.

"Office hours, I'm afraid," he said with a bow. "Bettina, it was a pleasure and, Pamela, maybe this weekend . . . ?" He let the question hang.

"Well, he's certainly a keeper!" Bettina exclaimed, louder than Pamela might have wished, as Brian threaded his way through the crowd on his way to the door. "I could tell by the way he was looking at you that he's totally smitten . . . and so gentlemanly . . . and he cooks. I'm not sure Richard Larkin—"

Bettina closed her eyes, gulped, and clapped a hand over her mouth. Her head drooped forward until her face was hidden by a mass of scarlet tendrils.

"I didn't mean to say his name," she whispered. "It was just . . . I don't think he cooks. And Brian . . ."

Pamela heard herself growl and Bettina's head remained bowed. For a long minute they sat without speaking. Then Pamela took pity on her friend. She opened her purse and pulled out the letter she'd snatched from Critter's mail pigeonhole. A change of subject would do them both good.

Bettina raised her head in time to see Pamela slipping a folded sheet of paper out of the envelope and she watched as Pamela unfolded it and began to read, silently at first but whispering as she became aware of her audience.

"You made me see what I was capable of," the letter's final paragraph read, "coming back to school after so long. And when it seemed you wanted me, that we were a couple, I had to pinch myself. And I trusted you and I gave myself to you, but now I see I was just one of your conquests, one of many, and you laughed at me behind my back."

The letter was signed, "Someone who never forgets."

CHAPTER 8

"Oh, my goodness!" Bettina exclaimed. Her lips tightened into a stern line. "Another one, seduced and abandoned. What an unscrupulous person that"—she frowned
and shook her head as if censoring the words she'd been
about to use—"that Critter must have been! Speak no ill
of the dead, as Wilfred would say, but honestly!"

"Maybe not another one," Pamela said. "Maybe the
same one."

"Well, that's bad enough, one poor woman who trusted
him and was betrayed." Bettina's expression was as woeful as if she herself had been the victim of Critter's philandering. She thought for a minute, and then curiosity
brightened her mobile features. "But why do you think
it's the same one, the one you overheard talking to him
outside the dining hall?"

"She had to pinch herself," Pamela said. "She couldn't

believe he really cared for her and she had to pinch herself. That's exactly what the woman in the shrubbery said."

"I wonder if she's here." Bettina rose slightly from her chair and scanned the room. "Would you recognize her voice?"

"I might." Pamela nodded. The voice emanating from the shrubbery, with its nasal tone and unexpected diphthongs, had struck her as not typical of the world from which Dr. Critter might have been expected to select his paramours. And the hint of backstory in the letter— "coming back to school after so long"—suggested humbler origins and a midlife desire for self-improvement.

She rose and set out across the room, followed by Bettina, gliding among the clusters of people that crowded the floor of the faculty club. She moved quickly past groups composed of typical college-age students but lingered as she neared groups of more varied composition, listening carefully, especially when she spotted women nearing middle age.

As she wandered, she circled the buffet table and paused to eavesdrop on a tête-à-tête between two fortyish woman gazing out at the river. They were chatting about traveling in Europe with children, it turned out, and in cultured tones, so she moved on.

Bettina was eyeing the few shrimp left in the chafing dish as the man Pamela recognized as Bob from the maintenance staff gathered up the dirty plates that people had stacked here and there among what was left of the food.

"I do everything around here," he muttered in response to Bettina's sympathetic smile as he loaded the plates onto a wheeled cart.

"Any luck finding her?" Bettina asked Pamela as Bob headed toward the door. Pamela shook her head no.

"But I didn't check this side of the room." She nodded toward the right, where a particularly dense crush of people mingled, most standing but some sitting in chairs against the wall. "Shall we?"

She took a few steps as Bettina cast a glance back at the buffet table.

"They'll be bringing out coffee and sweets in a few minutes," said a voice behind Pamela. She turned to see Dean Tate, who had been conferring with one of the student servers but now stepped over to Pamela's side. Dean Tate looked surprisingly calm and rested, given the weekend's events and the fact that the college's response to Dr. Critter's death had obviously devolved upon her. She was wearing dark gray, somber but not quite funereal, a jersey knit dress that flattered her petite figure, and her pixie-cut hairstyle set off her bold silver earrings.

"How are you doing?" Pamela asked after introducing Dean Tate to Bettina and being encouraged to call Dean Tate by her first name, Louise.

Dean Tate sighed. "Looking on the bright side. Things are calming down, though the sooner the police get to the bottom of this, the better." She gestured toward the buffet table. "The head of food service feels terrible, as you might imagine, even though the police found no trace of poison in any of the dining hall coffee dispensers. Checking them all was an awful lot of extra work for them—but by then the dispenser from Sufficiency House had been washed and put away with the others. How could anyone have known to set that one dispenser aside untouched—when it wasn't until Saturday evening that Dr. Critter's death seemed anything other than some calamitous natural event?"

They were joined then by Flo Ransom. She was dressed for the occasion in a blue crepe skirt suit that, on a trendy young woman, would have looked like a lucky vintage find. On Flo it simply looked like a garment its owner had been frugally wearing for decades. Pamela conjured up a sympathetic version of her social smile, asked Flo how she was doing, and introduced Bettina.

"Getting along, getting along," Flo murmured, with a wan smile. "I try not to go into the living room . . . because that's where it happened. I can still see him gasping. And then there's the kitchen—where he got the coffee that . . ." She sighed and began twisting her hands so vigorously that Pamela was concerned for the state of her fingers. "I just hope the police figure out what happened, and soon. The college has paused the Sufficiency House programs for the fall."

Dean Tate nodded. "We didn't want to attract the curious." She shuddered. "There are people who make a hobby of visiting crime scenes, if you can imagine."

"Ghoulish," Bettina chimed in.

"But it's a shame," Flo went on, "because fall is one of our best times, with the vegetable harvest and the canning workshops."

Bettina's glance had been alternating between her conversation partners and the buffet table, and Pamela, whose back was to the table, had become aware from the aroma that coffee was being served nearby. She turned and as she turned, Dean Tate spoke.

"Yes," she said in a resigned tone, "that is one of the food service coffee dispensers. They're all perfectly fine—the police testified to that—and there's no other way to serve coffee to a large group. But I don't know if any of us will ever be able to look at one without remembering the events of the past weekend."

Nonetheless, in a few moments they had all joined the line inching past the platters of tiny tarts, miniature cupcakes, cream puffs, brownies, and lemon bars. Dean Tate discovered she was standing right behind the head of the architecture department and was drawn into a conversation about an upcoming curriculum change, and Flo lapsed into a mournful silence. Pamela was glad to think her own thoughts, soothed by the buzz of chatter and with her sociable friend at her side to respond if anyone seemed determined to converse.

Several minutes later they stepped away from the buffet table laden with cups of coffee and plates bearing sweets. Flo had wandered off, but Dean Tate was waiting for them and apologized for letting her colleague cut in.

"He's very conscientious," she explained, "and eager to get this curriculum issue settled."

They were then all faced with the quandary of having only two hands each, one holding a coffee cup and the other holding a plate of eatables, with no extra hand to convey the eatables to their mouths.

A few of the chair and table sets were free, but before they reached them, Dean Tate was accosted by another colleague, a tall and rangy woman dressed in black but for a much-worn denim jacket of the sort often paired with blue jeans. This colleague was seeking to discuss a topic more germane to the setting.

"Are we spending college money on this?" the woman demanded, flinging out her arm in a gesture that took in the buffet table and much of the room.

Dean Tate took a deep breath. "Pamela, Bettina," she

said, "let me introduce Shane Bennett from our Women's Studies department."

Pamela held out her hand and murmured her name, as did Bettina.

Shane nodded perfunctorily. "Well, are we?" she repeated.

"There's a fund." Dean Tate's voice was patient. Perhaps she'd had this conversation with other faculty members as well.

"Oh, here you are!" sang a voice behind Pamela, but a glance over her shoulder made her suspect that she was not the intended "you." She found herself looking at the woman who had risen from the audience to challenge Critter's luncheon talk, his ex-wife, Yvonne.

"I suppose you had to do this." Yvonne addressed herself to Dean Tate, who seemed relieved at the chance to focus on someone besides Shane Bennett. "Robert *was* a faculty member after all."

"We were just"—Dean Tate nodded toward her burden of coffee and goodies—"just looking to sit down so we could . . ." She took a few steps toward a grouping of chairs and a small table.

Yvonne followed her. Shane, meanwhile, had fastened onto Bettina, who had accompanied her self-introduction with a more genuine smile than the social smile Pamela had mustered. They too followed Dean Tate, and Pamela joined the procession. With not enough chairs for all, no one seemed inclined to sit. The table, however, usefully received the plates.

Pamela took her first sip of coffee and bent toward her plate to select a lemon bar. With two separate conversations in progress, one on either side of her, she found herself the odd person out and alternated between sipping her coffee and nibbling on the lemon bar.

To her right, Shane Bennett was railing about the fact that the conference organizers chose a man to give the keynote address at a conference about women's work—and Critter of all people. Bettina was also sipping coffee and nibbling on a lemon bar, but nodding frequently enough to convince Shane that she had an interested audience.

To her left, Yvonne was assuring Dean Tate that none of Critter's students would miss him and suggesting that any faculty she could press into service to cover his courses would be an improvement. Dean Tate was sipping her coffee too, but suddenly she lowered the cup to the table.

"Excuse me, excuse me," she said, tilting her head toward the room's exit. "I see that Dr. Critter's aunt and uncle are on their way out and I should say something to them before they go."

"Those aren't his parents?" Pamela asked. Dean Tate's head-tilt had been aimed at the elegant older couple Pamela had noticed at the funeral.

"His parents are long gone," Dean Tate said. She headed across the floor and Pamela found herself newly in demand as a conversation partner. As if aware that Pamela had overheard much of what she said to Dean Tate, Yvonne spoke up quickly.

"I was married to him, you see, and . . . so I knew him very well." She accompanied this statement with a smile. She was attractive in a lively way, with lines around her eyes and mouth as if she had spent a lot of time in the sun without sunscreen, but smiling more often than frowning.

Shane broke off in mid-sentence—something about an upcoming seminar—and turned away from Bettina.

"You're his widow?" she exclaimed, her bold features rearranging themselves to express amazement. "I had no idea, or I would have . . ." She paused and scanned the crowd as if seeking a clue to what she would have done. "He could be difficult, but I'm sorry he's dead, of course."

"I'm not." Yvonne's smile grew wider. "He was an idiot and the world is better off without him."

"Well, actually"—Shane gulped back a giggle—"I'm not sorry either."

As the two women bonded over their mutual dislike of Dr. Critter, Pamela and Bettina slipped into the chairs that faced the little table and devoted themselves to the remains of their coffee and the cream puffs, brownies, and miniature tarts that they had barely sampled.

Ten minutes later, their cups and plates were empty, Yvonne and Shane had departed—still deep in conversation—and the crowd had thinned considerably.

"Shall we go?" Pamela inquired. Bettina nodded and stood up, dusting a few crumbs from the skirt of her navy-blue sheath.

But there was to be yet one more encounter before they settled into Pamela's car for the ride home. Pamela had assumed her boss had gone home after the funeral because she hadn't seen her at the cemetery, and yet here she was now.

It was she who spoke first, looking as startled to see Pamela as Pamela was to see her. "I didn't realize you were here," she said. It was hard to tell from her expression what she would have done if their paths had crossed earlier. Her face, with its elegant but austere features, was difficult to read at the best of times.

"I, um, thought I should come." Pamela noticed that she was impeding traffic—many people were departing now—and backed up several steps.

"Yes, we do need to put in an appearance when these things happen, don't we?" Her boss's tone was dry.

"We do," Pamela murmured, nodding. Becoming aware that Bettina was still standing at her side, she drew Bettina forward and said, "I don't believe you've ever met my friend and neighbor Bettina Fraser."

Her boss extended her hand and provided her own name, Celine Bramley, but her next words were addressed to Pamela. "I'd just as soon *this* hadn't happened though. The magazine co-sponsored the conference and the conference will always be linked in people's minds with Dr. Critter's death. All the attendees have gone back to wherever they came from and what do you think they're telling people who ask how the conference was?"

Pamela knew the answer, but she decided a mournful expression would be a better response than words.

"It would help if the police were more efficient," her boss went on.

"Bettina is in close contact with Detective Clayborn of the Arborville police," Pamela said as Bettina nodded enthusiastically at her side. "She reports for the local paper. They're working very hard."

Bettina chimed in. "I'm sure something will break soon." But her boss paid scant attention. Her response was directed at Pamela.

"Oh, yes. Arborville. That's where you live, right? But we're not in Arborville now."

"Sufficiency House is just over the border," Pamela explained.

"And they're really working hard? There hasn't been much progress. Louise Tate has been keeping me up to date on what the *Register* is reporting."

"Something will break soon," Bettina repeated.

"Well, I hope so." Her boss lifted her wrist to consult an expensive-looking watch. "I've got to be on my way. I've spent the whole day in New Jersey." She turned toward the exit.

"Um"—Pamela reached out a hand but thought better of grabbing her boss's jacket—"just one thing before you go . . ."

"And that would be?" Her boss spoke in profile, still facing the exit. Pamela felt a scuffle in her chest as her heart sped up.

"I was wondering if there was some work I should be doing." Bettina's hand stole around Pamela's waist in a comforting gesture.

Bettina retracted her hand as Pamela's boss wheeled around. A vertical line had appeared between her brows. "I was busy all weekend, as you know, and since the conference ended—*abruptly*—I've had other things on my mind."

Pamela nodded meekly, but felt a jolt of relief when her boss added, "I'll get to it. Check your inbox tomorrow morning. You'll find some articles to evaluate."

"We should put the letter back," Bettina said en route to the car. "That way someone from the college might pass it on to Clayborn. I can't, because he'd wonder how I got it and he'd suspect I opened it."

Pamela nodded. Once that errand was done, they continued to the parking lot, comparing notes on their impressions of Shane Bennett and agreeing that they had a new suspect to add to their list.

CHAPTER 9

Nell Bascomb's house smelled of gingerbread, an aroma that complemented her homey décor. A comfortable sofa faced a natural stone fireplace, and the fireplace was flanked by loveseats upholstered in faded chintz. On this September evening, it featured a dried-flower arrangement, but in cooler months, logs provided a cozy fire.

Harold Bascomb had responded to the doorbell's ring and ushered Pamela and Bettina into the entry. The spacious living room, with its high, beamed ceiling, was just a few steps away. Their hostess appeared at the end of the long hall that led to the kitchen, her faded eyes bright and her voice warm as she greeted them.

"Something tells me we're having gingerbread tonight," Bettina responded, inhaling deeply and looking pleased.

"With whipped cream," called a more youthful voice

from midway down the hall. A moment later, Holly Perkins stepped up to Nell's side. "It's going to be amazing!" she exclaimed. "Another amazing recipe from our amazing Nell." She accompanied the statement with a smile that revealed her perfect teeth and brought her dimple into play.

Holly and Nell could hardly have been more different, in age and appearance—and even personality. Holly was a raven-haired twenty-something, bursting with exuberance, and Nell's white hair and restrained manner reflected her eighty-plus years. But when Holly joined Knit and Nibble, she had been captivated first by Nell's mid-century-modern kitchen, unchanged since the 1950s, and then by Nell herself.

The doorbell signaled another arrival, and Bettina turned to admit Roland DeCamp.

"You're all here," he announced, surveying the small group that crowded the entry and glancing toward the living room, where Karen Dowling sat on one of the loveseats chatting with Harold. He would retreat to his den once the knitting got underway, but he enjoyed keeping up with the club members' lives.

Roland was dressed as impeccably as if reporting to his job as a corporate lawyer, in a faultlessly tailored pinstripe suit and a well-starched dress shirt—white, of course. A luxuriant tie in muted shades of blue and gray finished off his ensemble. He carried the elegant briefcase that he used in place of a knitting bag.

"Yes, we're all here," Nell confirmed, "but you're right on time." With a gracious gesture, she invited them to advance toward the sofa and loveseats and get settled. Holly joined her friend Karen on the loveseat to the right of the fireplace as Harold excused himself and retreated. Pamela and Bettina claimed the other loveseat, and Nell lowered herself onto the sofa next to Roland.

From knitting bags, and Roland's briefcase, came colorful skeins of yarn and knitting needles from which dangled lengths of in-progress work. Pamela was just embarking on a new project, a bright red merino wool sweater that was to be a Christmas gift for her father. Next to her, Bettina was studying the directions for a new project of her own, a stylish burnt-orange tunic that was to be a gift to herself.

Holly had immediately lost herself in her work and a busy dance of crisscrossing needles and twisting, looping yarn was underway. She paused at the end of a row, however, to lean toward where Nell was sitting at the near end of the sofa.

"Something different!" she exclaimed. "It's an animal, but it's not an elephant."

Nell devoted her knitting efforts to projects aligned with the volunteer and do-good organizations dear to her heart. When she wasn't knitting caps for newborns, winter scarves for day laborers, or Christmas stockings for the children staying with their mothers at the women's shelter in Haversack, she busied herself with knitted animals for those children or for other groups that ministered to the needy. For as long as anyone could remember, the animals had been elephants. Her busy hands had turned out herds of them, in unlikely colors—lavender?—and textures—angora?—but destined to be cherished by their recipients.

The creature now taking shape, however, was sleeker in body and longer of leg.

"A donkey," Nell announced with a teasing smile. "Just for a change."

"Cute!" Holly focused once again on her own work, but after half a row she drew in her breath sharply and looked up. "Pamela!" she exclaimed, directing her gaze to where Pamela was sitting on the loveseat across the way. "Are you okay? I'm chattering on about elephants and donkeys and totally forgetting . . . what you've been through."

"Oh . . ." Pamela looked up from her knitting. "I'm fine. I was hoping we wouldn't . . ."

"I was too," Nell said firmly. "A very disturbing thing has happened in our little town and our own very dear Pamela has been caught up in it, and I don't think we need . . ."

Next to Holly, Karen was looking stricken, all the more touching given her delicate blonde prettiness. "Nell is right," she whispered.

But the whisper was too faint to reach Roland's ears. "I'm all for going after what you want," he declared, "but I certainly draw the line at murder."

"I hope so." Nell swiveled around to face him. "What on earth are you talking about?"

"Brad Scott, of course. Sufficiency House. Lawsuits."

With five startled faces gaping at him, Roland nevertheless maintained his poise. "The developer, Brad Scott. He's been angling to buy Sufficiency House for years— the land is what he's interested in, not the house. Wendelstaff has refused and refused."

"They should." Nell could look quite severe when she frowned, her eyes sharp in their nests of wrinkles. "Sufficiency House is a valuable resource." She paused and the frown turned from scolding to questioning. "What does this man, Brad Scott, have to do with"—she paused again—"with . . . what happened to that professor?"

But Bettina had been staring at Roland, and she spoke up now, her words almost overlapping with Nell's. "His name is Brad Scott?" she exclaimed. "And you know him?"

"I know *of* him." Roland glanced at the knitting in his lap as if he was longing to take it up again.

"It all fits together." Bettina nodded. "I overheard a conversation when I was at the police department yesterday. Clayborn and I were discussing Critter's murder and what the police are doing to solve it. Then he stepped out of the room for a minute to confer with somebody about a local developer who's been wanting to buy Sufficiency House. When he came back, he looked happier than when he left, but he told me that readers of the *Advocate* should be told that though the Arborville police are investigating thoroughly, they have no suspects at the moment."

"Ohhh!" Holly shivered. "It sounds like they *do* have a suspect. But I don't quite see why it would be this man who wants to buy Sufficiency House."

Next to Roland on the sofa, Nell let out a long sigh and closed her eyes. Bettina, on the other hand, was gazing at Roland with the same rapt attention she focused on her interview subjects.

"Underhanded, for sure," Roland intoned. "But people do underhanded things to get what they want."

"You must see a lot of that in your work," Holly cooed, raising a graceful hand to push an errant strand of turquoise hair behind her ear, where it rejoined the turquoise streak that accented her dark waves.

"A fair amount," Roland said, warming to his subject.

"The poisoning episode could be an effort to discredit Sufficiency House, or make it a financial liability to the college because of a lawsuit arising from the death—fortunately only one person succumbed to the poison. Or the intention could have just been to make a number of people ill."

From Nell's direction came a sound like a cross between and moan and a growl. She opened her eyes. "Murder is not a suitable topic for conversation at a meeting of a knitting club," she said. "I suggest we all tend to our knitting. And the fact that this . . . *dreadful* event took place at Sufficiency House makes it all the more . . . all the more . . ." She shook her head, and the locks of white hair that framed her face trembled. "Micah Dorset was a friend of my grandparents."

"Who's Micah Dorset?" Holly and Karen spoke at once.

"Sufficiency House was his house," Nell explained, suddenly calm, as if soothed by the recollection. Her eyes softened as she stared straight ahead, focusing on nothing in particular. "It was the Depression then, and he taught people how to make do with what they had—grow their own food, raise chickens, sew, knit . . ." She shifted her gaze to Holly and Karen and smiled. "Times were very hard, and he helped a lot of people."

"You were alive then?" Holly's wondering tone suggested that she had just now realized a person in her eighties would have been alive in the thirties.

"I was a little girl." Nell nodded.

"Was your family . . . ? Were you . . . ?" Holly's eyes grew wide. "Did you go hungry?" she whispered. At her side, Karen seemed on the verge of tears.

"*We* didn't," Nell said. "My grandfather was a doctor

and people always need doctors. But sometimes his patients didn't have money, so they paid him in food—eggs, vegetables, or something they had baked. My grandparents and my parents and I always had plenty to eat. And as far as clothes went, my mother sewed, and knit." She lifted her knitting needles to display the in-progress donkey. "That's how I learned."

"That is perfectly awesome!" Holly clapped—her knitting had sat disregarded in her lap for some time.

Even Roland seemed impressed. He too had been neglecting his knitting. Now he took it up again, but before resuming work on his half-completed row, he turned to Nell. "I never thought it would be a good idea to replace Sufficiency House with one of Brad Scott's projects," he said. "In fact I always thought it would be a very bad idea."

Roland's statement was greeted, unsurprisingly, with nods and murmurs of agreement. Looking pleased that his comment had resonated with his audience, he deftly inserted his right-hand needle in the loop of yarn awaiting at the end of his left-hand needle, caught up a twist of yarn with his finger, and embarked on the completion of his row.

The others took up their knitting again as well, except for Pamela, who took a moment to survey the works that were in progress around her. Facing her on the loveseat opposite, Holly was still engaged with the challenging project that had occupied her since the middle of summer—a pair of argyle socks.

Four inches of one sock dangled from a circular knitting needle, surrounded by bobbins wound with yarn in shades of orange, yellow, brown, and dark green. She had completed enough of the in-progress sock that the dis-

tinctive argyle pattern of diamonds overlaid with the out-
line of diamonds could be seen clearly.

Next to her, Karen was knitting something for herself—"for a change"—she had explained when she pulled
it from her knitting bag a few weeks earlier. Her previous
projects had mostly been destined for her daughter Lily,
born the Christmas before last. But this was to be a cozy
turtleneck in a creamy shade of white, hopefully to be
completed in time for winter wear.

The first section of Bettina's burnt-orange tunic, a
sleeve, was only several rows past the casting-on process,
but Pamela was already intimately acquainted with the
garment. She had accompanied Bettina to the fancy yarn
shop in Timberley and stood by with advice and encour-
agement as Bettina leafed through knitting magazines
and pattern books, and pondered shelves, tables, and cub-
bies heaped with yarn in every shade and texture before
finally making her decision.

Nell, of course, had taken up donkeys in place of elephants for her current do-good project, but next to her—
what was Roland working on? The same question had
occurred to Holly.

She leaned forward to get a closer look at the few
inches of ribbing dangling from Roland's needles. The
yarn was a striking choice—lavender shot through with
silver lurex threads. "You have a new project too!" she
exclaimed, as excited as if Roland's a new project was
the best thing that had happened all day.

"Yes." Roland spoke without looking up. "I do, because I finished the previous one last week and I don't
like to waste time." Roland's previous project had been a
charcoal-gray sweater for himself.

"Is it going to be another sweater?" Holly leaned closer.

"That looks like the beginning of a sleeve." Roland continued to knit without responding. Holly leaned closer still. "That's an awesome color, and the silver is amazing. Is it going to be for Melanie?" Melanie was Roland's fashionable wife.

"I'm trying to concentrate on this ribbing," Roland said, "but no, it's not for Melanie."

"For you then?"

Roland stopped knitting and raised his head, his lean face serious. "I come here to knit," he said, "not to engage in idle chitchat."

Pamela had scarcely been paying attention, but next to her she felt Bettina, who was sitting at the end of the loveseat closest to Roland, stir.

"Oh, for heaven's sake!" Bettina lowered her knitting into her lap. "Don't be such a sourpuss, Roland. Half the fun of Knit and Nibble is seeing what everyone else is working on."

"For you perhaps," Roland said primly. "I prefer to focus on my own work."

"You were happy enough to gossip about Brad Scott." Bettina swiveled around to face Roland.

"That wasn't gossip." Roland frowned. "And anyway, we were just getting settled. We'd barely started knitting yet."

"That's not true." Pamela couldn't see Bettina's face, but she could picture the tight-lipped glare that usually accompanied Bettina's indignation. "*You* were knitting."

"That's because I don't like to waste time, unlike some other people. And now, if you don't mind, I'll . . ." Roland took up his needles again and, with a murmured "knit one, purl two," embarked again on his ribbing. But before he even reached the end of the row, he froze. He raised his head, his lips parted in a sharp intake of breath, and he set his knitting aside to push back his immaculate shirt cuff and consult his impressive watch.

"Eight p.m.," he announced, looking flustered. "Actually, three minutes after."

Roland was anything but a glutton. His lean body attested to that. But he was a stickler for custom, and the Knit and Nibblers customarily paused for refreshments midway through their weekly knitting sessions. Lest anyone lose track of the time, particularly the hostess, it was Roland's self-imposed duty to announce the arrival of eight o'clock.

Pamela suppressed a smile at Roland's chagrin. A few minutes one way or another certainly didn't matter when it came to the Knit and Nibble agenda, but no doubt his attention to detail stood him in good stead in his corporate life.

Nell's kitchen was a long way from her living room, but Pamela could swear she already smelled coffee brewing, even though Nell, suppressing a smile of her own, was just now rising from her spot next to Roland.

Holly had already hopped to her feet. With a cry of "many hands make light work," echoing one of Wilfred's favorite sayings, she preceded Nell to the entry and from there disappeared down the long hall that led to the kitchen. Pamela set her knitting aside and joined the procession. Soon the three women were greeting Harold, who was monitoring the ancient aluminum percolator gurgling merrily away on the stove.

"I love, love, *love* your kitchen!" Holly surveyed the room, with its avocado-green appliances and pink Formica counters. The Bascombs' house predated the kitchen's midcentury style by several decades, but its kitchen had been newly renovated just before they bought it as young marrieds in the fifties and it had remained the same ever since.

"And Harold!" She aimed a dimply smile at him. "You started the coffee! What a sweet, thoughtful husband you are!"

A man would have been hard put to resist the enthusiasm that enhanced Holly's already radiant complexion, and Harold Bascomb was no exception. "Pleased to be of service," he beamed.

But Nell's attention had been drawn to another aspect of Harold's involvement in the Knit and Nibble refreshments. An oblong Pyrex baking pan rested on the pink Formica surface of the counter next to the stove top. The deep copper-brown hue and gingery aroma identified its contents as the gingerbread whose existence had been signaled the moment Pamela and Bettina stepped over the Bascombs' threshold. Its surface had been scored into a three-square by four-square grid. One square, however, was missing from the grid.

"Harold?" Nell turned away from the counter and faced her husband. Her face wore an expression of mock-puzzlement. "A piece of gingerbread is missing."

"Missing?" Harold feigned amazement. "No!"

Nell persisted. "Do you have any idea what happened to it?" she inquired, as her lips twitched in the beginnings of a smile.

He paused for a moment, controlling his own impulse to smile. Then he bowed his head and murmured, "I confess. I ate it." He looked up. "Nell, my dear, I have never been able to resist your gingerbread. And it was just sitting there, looking so tempting. I know I was wrong."

From the direction of the stove came an alarming sizzle as a trickle of coffee dribbled from the percolator's spout. Harold spun around, tugged the percolator off the heat, and turned off the burner.

"Tea water!" he cried, seized the kettle, which sat ready on a neighboring burner, and strode to the sink to fill it.

Everyone pitched in then. Harold scooped seven gingerbread squares onto seven china plates from a set that shared the kitchen's vintage pedigree. On them, wildflowers and wheat were sketched in faded shades of coral and gold.

"It's plenty sweet in its own right," Nell advised, "but I know few people will turn down a bit of whipped cream on top."

"I certainly won't," Holly said.

"It's in the refrigerator"—Nell nodded toward the hulking avocado-green appliance—"and the mixer and a bowl are on the counter by the sink. And you can pour a bit of cream into the cream pitcher too."

Pamela, meanwhile, had filled two of the wildflower and wheat patterned cups with steaming coffee from the percolator and was en route to the living room to deliver them.

Soon they were all settled in the living room once again, with coffee, tea, and gingerbread crowding the coffee table and people leaning forward from loveseats and sofa to add cream and sugar to their beverage of choice. Harold had joined the group, perching on the sofa between Nell and Roland.

Bettina was the first to taste her gingerbread and to comment, declaring it "perfect." Pamela agreed, to herself and then audibly. Nell's creation was luxuriously rich and dark, with a spicy bite to it that made the barely sugared whipped cream a soothing accompaniment.

Holly was the most voluble. "Only our Nell could

think of making such an amazing dessert as this," she declared. "It's like . . . it's like . . . something from a long time ago, something . . . nostalgic, from when people were . . ."

Nell laughed. "When people were pretty much like they are now."

"But they dressed up," Holly protested. "They didn't slouch around in public looking like they just got out of bed. And they had good manners, and men behaved like gentlemen, and children were polite. And women baked things all the time, things like . . . this gingerbread."

"Those clothes weren't all that comfortable," Nell said, with a fond look at Holly. "And the women might have wanted to be out earning their own money so they could be independent, instead of stuck in a kitchen all day."

"Well, still"—Holly gave a determined nod—"those times seem so *calm*."

"Only because we know everything turned out okay." Harold joined the conversation. "Things didn't seem calm then, the Depression, people waiting in line for food, and the war and young men going off to fight and leaving their sweethearts behind."

"Too sad!" Bettina spoke up. "Let's talk about something different, like . . . like . . ." She scanned the room, her gaze landing on Pamela.

"Don't look at me," Pamela whispered. Despite the fact that she apparently still had her job, the implications of Dr. Critter's murder were still weighing on her.

But as she was brooding on this theme, the conversation veered away from the topics Bettina had denounced as "sad." Roland's voice, uncharacteristically buoyant, intruded on her unhappy reverie.

"Yes," he declared, "a weekend getaway. Melanie's idea, but she's right: what's the point of working hard if you can't take a vacation once in a while?"

"Cape May will be beautiful this time of year," Bettina chimed in, with nods from Holly and Karen. "And it won't be crowded like in the middle of summer."

The discussion of Roland's travel plans took up just enough time for coffee and tea cups to be emptied and the last gingerbread crumbs and dabs of whipped cream to be scooped up.

Holly and Karen jumped to their feet and took charge of clearing away, and Harold excused himself to retreat to his den. Pamela took up her in-progress sleeve and drew a length of red yarn from the skein at her side, and had soon relaxed into the rhythms of looping yarn and crisscrossing needles. Around her, conversation returned to the theme of autumn travel, with New England leaf-peeping expeditions spoken of highly, but she was happy to knit in silence.

CHAPTER 10

Bettina's faithful Toyota waited at the curb, near the bottom of the steps that curved from the Bascombs' porch though a sloping yard lushly planted with azaleas and rhododendrons. Bettina seemed preoccupied as she drove, but as she turned onto Orchard Street, she suddenly said, "It would be better if Brad Scott did it."

The statement was unexpected and it took Pamela a moment to respond. When she did, it was to ask why.

"Because"—Bettina drew the word out—"if Roland is right and the intention was really to make everybody sick—or even kill them—for Brad Scott's own nefarious purposes, then that makes the murder not really about Critter and not really about the conference. So you shouldn't feel bad. Brad Scott could have struck any time Sufficiency House was hosting an event. He just happened to strike last weekend."

"I think the killer was really targeting Dr. Critter though." Pamela sighed. "Nobody else had any ill effects."

"Maybe the person Brad Scott enlisted to put the poison in the coffee—I'm sure he didn't do it himself—showed up late and didn't know everybody else had been served." They were nearing Bettina's house now and she slowed down.

"That's a good point." Pamela nodded. "But the killer could equally well have known that Dr. Critter would make his appearance after the others were served, so the poison goes in the dispenser then and nobody else has any ill effects, but Dr. Critter is dead. Mission accomplished."

Bettina pulled into her driveway and turned off the ignition. "He did have enemies," she murmured.

"At least three people could have wanted him dead." Pamela held up three fingers, silhouetted against the light coming from the Frasers' porch. She touched them one by one, saying, "His ex-wife Yvonne, his jilted paramour whose name we don't know, and—as we found out this morning—his colleague Shane Bennett."

"Maybe I should slip a word to Clayborn that there might be unclaimed mail waiting for Critter in his campus mailbox," Bettina said, "though he's sure to notice it's been opened."

"That is a problem," Pamela agreed. "But I know how we can figure out if Yvonne and Shane have alibis for the time the poison must have gone into the coffee dispenser." She opened the car door and started to climb out. "Come across the street with me and I'll show you."

"Sure!" Bettina pushed her own door open and lowered her feet to the asphalt. "I'll just run in and tell Wilfred where I'm going."

Pamela let herself into her house and hurried up to her office. There she opened a filing cabinet and extracted a manila folder. The folder was labeled "Fiber Craft/Wendelstaff Conference." Bettina rang the doorbell just as Pamela reached the landing on her way back down the stairs.

She welcomed Bettina, led her into the kitchen, and seated her at the table. Then she settled into the other chair and opened the folder. It contained correspondence leading up to the conference, printed emails to and from her boss, Dean Tate, Flo, and the campus food service. But most important, it contained a copy of the conference program. Disturbed as she'd been when she returned home after the banquet, she had tidily filed the program away with the other conference documents.

"If Yvonne and Shane were at conference workshops during the time that the coffee was served at Sufficiency House, they couldn't be guilty," she explained, leafing through the program as Bettina watched. "So"—she continued leafing—"here we are." She bent over the page. "Two workshops were scheduled for the three to four p.m. slot on Saturday: 'Home Ec Is Relevant Again,' led by Belle Rogers from Arborville High, and 'New Clothes from Old,' led by Callie Davenport from Wendelstaff College."

Bettina clapped her hands and smiled a bright smile. "We talk to Belle Rogers and Callie Davenport."

"Yes." Pamela nodded. "And if Yvonne or Shane—or both—were otherwise occupied during the time the poi-

son was being added to the coffee dispenser in the Sufficiency House kitchen, then we can cross Yvonne or
Shane—or both—off our list of suspects. And we won't
have to worry about whether Detective Clayborn will
ever get around to investigating them."

"Of course, then we'll be left with the jilted paramour." Bettina's smile faded. "And I don't want it to be
her. That poor woman!"

"Let's see what we find out about the whereabouts of
Yvonne and Shane first." Pamela closed the program and
slipped it back into the file folder. "What would your editor at the *Advocate* think about an article on the home ec
program at Arborville High?"

"He'd love it!" Bettina smiled again. "I understand
boys are signing up for the classes now." She pushed her
chair back and rose. "Lunch at Hyler's tomorrow? I'll get
in touch with Belle Rogers first thing in the morning and
we'll meet you there at noon."

No cats had been in evidence as Pamela and Bettina
were conferring at the kitchen table, but no sooner had
Pamela seen Bettina on her way, settled onto the sofa, and
taken up her knitting than Catrina strolled in from the
entry and snuggled up next to her. She was soon knitting
contentedly as, before her on the screen, a well-dressed
detective with a cultivated accent bent over a corpse
sprawled against a stone wall covered with climbing
roses.

Catrina was as startled by the ringing telephone as
Pamela was. The cat raised her head with ears on high
alert and stared toward the kitchen. Pamela set her knitting aside and paused the mystery unfolding on the screen,

stepping quickly through the entry and into the kitchen as the phone shrilled again and again.

But the voice that greeted her hello was pleasant—and welcome. "Brian Delano here," the caller said. "I hope it's not too late." Actually it was barely ten p.m., but telephone calls at any time were a rare feature of Pamela's daily routine.

"No, it's not." Pamela lowered herself into the chair nearest the phone.

"I just got home from class," he went on. "And I wanted . . . I wanted to check in. I hope you survived the rest of the reception."

"I did," Pamela said, "but I'm glad that's all over now—except for the police figuring out who killed Dr. Critter of course."

"So life is back to normal?"

"I feel normal."

"In that case . . ." Brian paused, then went on. "A buddy of mine has some pieces in a gallery show in the city, and the opening is this Saturday. Would you like to come with me? We could have dinner someplace interesting afterwards."

"That sounds like fun." Pamela nodded, though no one was present to see the nod except Catrina, who had followed her into the kitchen.

"Great!" The surprised enthusiasm in his voice suggested he'd been nervous about her response, though he'd seemed his usual confident self as he extended the invitation. "I'll pick you up at seven p.m."

Pamela returned to her knitting and her BBC mystery smiling to herself. She *did* feel normal. She still had her job at *Fiber Craft* and, though she'd implied to Brian that she trusted the Arborville police to solve the mystery of

Critter's death, the prospect of following up on two very definite suspects, even though the identity of the woman in the shrubbery remained elusive, had awakened her sleuthing instincts.

Pamela's boss had been hard at work while Pamela slept. Pamela had checked her email before she went to bed and found nothing of note. But now, at seven a.m. Wednesday, her inbox contained an email from Celine Bramley, its subject line adorned with the little stylized paperclip that indicated it bore attachments.

The message itself was terse: "Please read these and let me know by Friday which you think are suitable for *Fiber Craft*. Note that we have a special issue on quilts coming up and if the quilt one is suitable I'll need it edited asap. But let me know first."

Strung across the top of the email were three abbreviated titles, "Sheep to Shawl," "Jazz Quilts," and "Lyre or Loom." The first two seemed self-explanatory, but Pamela was curious about the third and opened the document to discover that the full title posed a question: "Calypso's Song: Lyre or Loom?" The question tantalized, and she determined to read that one first—as soon as she had fed the cats, who were standing in the doorway looking aggrieved, and had her own breakfast.

A few hours later, Pamela completed her evaluation of "Calypso's Song: Lyre or Loom?" by noting in her rejection that the article might find a more receptive home in a scholarly journal devoted to the classics. Calypso, the article had reminded the reader, was the sea nymph who enchanted Odysseus with her song as she worked at her loom. But observing that early handheld looms did not look all that different from Bronze Age lyres, the author had suggested that the Calypso episode in Homer's epic was based on a colossal misunderstanding. Couldn't the golden shuttle have actually been a pick?

After saving the file, she closed Word, raised her arms in a luxurious stretch, and climbed to her feet. She was to meet Bettina and Belle Rogers at Hyler's and was looking forward to the walk uptown on this bright September day. Bettina had suggested that she and Pamela feign a chance meeting at the luncheon spot rather than showing up together, since Bettina's stated premise in meeting with Belle was an interview for the *Advocate*, and what would Pamela have to do with that?

An expansive window facing Arborville Avenue gave people dining at Hyler's a chance to observe passersby and passersby a chance to observe them. Pamela's first impression on glimpsing Bettina and Belle through the window was that Bettina was talking to a slightly younger version of herself. A cheerful red-haired woman wearing a striking plaid shirt in autumnal hues faced Bettina across the table, gesturing with brightly manicured hands as her earrings, bold red stones set in silver, bobbed in time with her vigorous nods.

"Pamela!" Bettina's hand shot up as Pamela stepped through Hyler's heavy glass door. She beckoned and Pamela advanced toward Bettina and Belle's table with its conveniently empty extra seat. "Why don't you join us?" Bettina urged as Pamela drew near.

The large room buzzed with talk and laughter. The lunchtime rush that reliably filled Hyler's tables and booths had begun, as office workers, shopkeepers, hairdressers, manicurists, and all the other people who provided goods and services to the inhabitants of Arborville responded to their midday hunger pangs.

Bettina and Belle had been so deep in conversation that their menus sat unheeded before them. Bettina took a moment to make introductions and then said, "Belle was just telling me that she has more male students in her cooking classes than female."

Belle nodded, setting the earrings in motion again, and took up the theme. "And Bettina was just telling me about her Wilfred's mastery of the kitchen."

"Ahead of his time," Bettina added.

"Ladies," a voice cut in. It belonged to the server Pamela recognized as having worked at Hyler's as long as Pamela had lived in Arborville. "Have you made up your minds?" She handed Pamela a menu of her own, set placemat and silver before her, and gazed expectantly at Bettina and Belle. They quickly seized their menus.

"'The chef recommends?'" Bettina looked up with an amused smile. "Since when does Hyler's have a chef?"

The menus were the usual Hyler's menus—oversize folders on stiff, glossy stock listing item after item of traditional diner fare. But clipped to the menus was a printed card headed "The chef recommends" and listing a special sandwich for each day of the week.

"It's a new guy." The server shrugged. "The other guy retired."

Bettina studied the card. "Today's Wednesday," she murmured.

The Wednesday sandwich was provolone and sliced turkey topped with fresh pesto and served on a sourdough roll.

"I'll have the Wednesday sandwich," Pamela said with

a smile, "and iced tea." She handed over her menu as Bettina continued to ponder.

"Does the new guy make the Reubens?" Bettina inquired at last. "Like you used to have?"

"Of course."

"I'd like a Reuben then, and a vanilla shake." Bettina surrendered her menu and leaned across the table toward Belle. "And how about you?" she asked. "My treat, of course, to thank you for the interview."

"I've always liked the Reubens here," Belle said. "And the vanilla shakes."

Hyler's was filling up and soon tables and booths would be at a premium. The server's nod of satisfaction as she tucked the menus under her arm and made a few notations on her order pad reflected her eagerness to keep the lunch crowd moving, Pamela was sure.

"Now where were we?" Bettina resumed. "Home ec isn't what it used to be, with boys wanting to cook, and . . ."

"Less emphasis on baking," Belle said.

"Well, that's a shame." Bettina looked as disappointed as if a treat had been offered and then snatched away. "Pies are one of my Wilfred's specialties. What *do* your students want to cook?"

"Some of them are vegetarians." Belle smiled. "All to the good, really. They're very concerned about the fate of the planet."

"They'll have to live on it long after we're gone." Bettina nodded, setting the scarlet tendrils of her hair in motion. "But I do like my steaks on the grill . . . and my Reubens."

She and Belle chatted on until they caught sight of their server, making her way among the close-packed tables with a large oval platter in one hand and two more balanced on her other arm.

The server lowered the platters onto the waiting place-mats, announced that the drinks were coming right up, and departed. The Reubens were impressive—two slices of rye bread grilled to burnished perfection, with driblets of melted cheese and slivers of rosy-pink pastrami peek-ing out between them. They were accompanied by long pickle spears, pale green and glistening, and pleated paper cups of coleslaw.

Pamela herself had enjoyed a Hyler's Reuben on many occasions, but now she examined her own sandwich. The sourdough roll was plump and crusty, sliced laterally and with its top set aside to display the layered cheese and turkey, which had been anointed generously with pesto. Tucked alongside the sandwich were a clutch of cherry tomatoes and several Greek olives the color of ebony.

The milkshakes arrived in tall frosted glasses, along with the iced tea. Bettina and Belle resumed their conver-sation, praising the meal and then returning to the home ec theme.

Pamela sampled her sandwich and was delighted with the juxtaposition of the sharp provolone and the mild turkey, and the way the pesto with its essence of basil and olive oil both soothed the bite of the aggressive cheese and perked up the unassertive turkey. From time to time she joined the conversation, particularly when it veered from food to the domestic arts involving fabric and fiber.

In those realms, Belle reported, girls outnumbered the boys in classes at Arborville High. Knitting was newly cool, which Pamela already knew, and sewing was a way to personalize one's wardrobe. And some students had their sights set on careers in the fashion industry, which beckoned from right across the Hudson.

Bettina was making very good on her stated premise for meeting with Belle. She was even recording the proceedings on her phone. But when would she get around to the real reason for the meeting, Belle's conference workshop and its participants? At the moment, Bettina was making encouraging sounds as Belle described a foray into ice cream production.

"You don't need one of those special machines," she was saying, "but you have to take it out of the freezer every once in a while and stir and stir and stir."

"Could you do it with fresh peaches?" Bettina inquired. "My Wilfred came home from the farmers market in Newfield with a whole bag of them."

Their platters were all but empty now, and a few people standing near the entrance were eyeing their table. The server had taken note and was approaching. Bettina tipped her glass and angled her straw to slurp up the last melted bit of milkshake, and Pamela grabbed up her last olive. But before popping it in her mouth, she took advantage of the break in the conversation as the server began to collect their dishes.

She turned toward Belle and, willing her voice to convey surprise, said, "I know why you look familiar. You were at the Wendelstaff conference last weekend."

"Oh, my goodness!" Belle's surprise was real. "So were you! I was asking myself, where have I seen that woman before?" She frowned slightly and stared at Pamela for a long minute. "In fact . . . didn't they introduce you at the group session Saturday morning?" She paused and seized Pamela's arm. "You were one of the organizers. You poor dear—what a stressful event for you!"

"And you . . ." Pamela frowned in what she hoped was a convincing imitation of someone struggling to remember. "Belle Rogers!" she exclaimed. "I knew I'd heard that name before. You were in the program. You did a session on . . . on . . ."

"'Home Ec Is Relevant Again,'" Belle supplied with a pleased expression.

"Of course!" Pamela exclaimed. "And it sounds like you're well-positioned to make that point."

"I focused on teaching basic sewing techniques. Can you imagine that some students don't even know how to thread a needle?"

"What were your workshop participants like?" she asked. "Did you have a good crowd?" (Like Yvonne Graves or Shane Bennett, she added to herself.)

"Home ec teachers." Belle nodded and her earrings swayed. "From all over the state. And they were very enthusiastic."

Pamela nodded too. "No Wendelstaff faculty, I guess."

"No." Belle shook her head and her earrings changed direction. "Not even from the ed department. Nobody but high-school home ec teachers."

Bettina looked up then—the server had appeared—and held out her hand for the bill. She caught Pamela's eye and gave a very subtle wink accompanied by a sly smile. She insisted on paying for Pamela's lunch too, and after the bill was paid, the three women stepped out onto the sidewalk. Belle, with a cheerful "so nice to have met you both," headed toward her car.

"Delightful person," Bettina commented as they watched

her walk away. "So attractive and I love her hair. I felt like I'd known her forever."

"And we found out what we wanted," Pamela said. "Neither Yvonne nor Shane was at her workshop—nobody but home ec teachers."

"I'm going to try that freezer ice cream with some of Wilfred's peaches." Bettina's eyes had a faraway look as if she was mentally savoring the result.

"Did you drive?" Pamela asked as, with a jaunty wave, Belle climbed into her car and they turned away.

"Of course! I'm not the walker like you." Bettina extended a foot to display a delicate kitten-heel shoe in a tangerine shade that coordinated with her tangerine jersey wrap dress. "Do you want a ride home?"

"I do," Pamela said, "but do you mind if we stop by the Co-Op first? I haven't shopped for food since before the conference and if I'm getting a ride I can really stock up on cat food too."

CHAPTER 11

They continued down Arborville Avenue. In a few minutes Pamela had collected a shopping cart from the neat rows lined up on the sidewalk and they were gliding through the automatic door, a recent addition to the Co-Op, which otherwise revealed its age as an Arborville institution. Aisles were narrow and the worn wooden floors creaked, but the produce department was bounteous, the butcher stocked meat from local suppliers, the fish were always fresh, the cheese selection was vast, and the bakery goods were made in-house.

"I hardly ever come here anymore, except to buy goodies," Bettina commented as Pamela steered the cart toward the produce section. "What a treat it was for me when Wilfred retired and took over the cooking duties. And speaking of that"—they had reached a bin in which avocados had been stacked in a careful pyramid—"why don't you come to dinner Saturday night? Wilfred is longing to do something more elaborate on the grill than the burgers we fed you last weekend."

Pamela had been in the act of reaching for an especially promising avocado but her gesture stalled in midair. She turned to Bettina.

"I'd love to," she said, "but I . . . I made other plans."

Bettina let out a whoop of delight. "You did?" she squealed. A woman browsing among the root vegetables glanced cautiously in Bettina's direction. "It's a date with Brian, isn't it?" Bettina added, thankfully at a lower volume.

Pamela nodded and picked up the avocado, observing, "From California or Mexico, I suppose. They certainly don't grow in New Jersey."

But Bettina was not to be distracted. "Where is he taking you?" she inquired, her features as animated as if she herself had received the invitation.

"Some kind of gallery opening in the city." Pamela deposited the avocado in her cart and moved on to the aisle where green and leafy things were displayed.

"Gallery opening in the city? You can't wear just any old thing. Let me think . . ."

And as Pamela maneuvered her cart through produce, past meat and fish, up the cat food aisle and down the cleaning products aisle, picking out items as she went, Bettina proposed and then rejected several ensembles concocted from her recollection of Pamela's existing wardrobe.

At last they reached the bakery counter. Though Pamela always bought the same kind of bread, she enjoyed surveying the many choices, which ranged in shape from baguettes to plump rounds and in color from toasty golden to deepest brown. She requested her usual whole-grain loaf. As she waited for it to be sliced and bagged, Bettina, who had been quiet for the past few minutes, spoke up.

"There's no getting around it," she declared. "We'll have to go to the mall." Apparently taking Pamela's silence for acquiescence, she let the topic rest.

"So," Bettina said after she had backed her faithful Toyota out of its parking space and they were cruising south on Arborville Avenue, "now we have to find out whether Yvonne or Shane or both were at—what was it?—'Old Clothes are New.'"

Pamela laughed. "'New Clothes from Old'—Callie Davenport teaches design classes where the students remake thrift-store finds into fashionable garments. I went to one of her class's fashion shows last spring." In fact, that had been the occasion of Pamela's meeting Brian Delano—not at the fashion show but in the Wendelstaff parking lot while waiting for Triple A to help with a dead battery.

"That's our entrée then!" Bettina reached out to squeeze Pamela's arm and smiled with glee. "Another article for the *Advocate*—or maybe the same article."

"They're called 'refashions,'" Pamela explained. "It's a step beyond Penny and her friends simply shopping for vintage clothes and wearing them as is."

"Young women using their sewing skills to create fashionable one-of-kind garments," Bettina mused. "We'll talk to Callie Davenport at Wendelstaff tomorrow and I'll weave that in with what Belle told me today. I should be just in time to get my article into this week's *Advocate*. And the most important thing"—she lifted a hand from the steering wheel to shake a determined finger—"after meeting with Callie we'll know whether to cross Yvonne and/or Shane off our list of suspects."

Neither of them spoke again until Bettina turned onto their block. As they neared the spot where her house and Pamela's faced each other across Orchard Street, Bettina said, "I'll track Callie Davenport down and make an appointment for an interview. Watch your email tonight— I'll let you know what time to be ready."

At home, Pamela put away her groceries, including the bountiful supply of cat food that would free her on-foot errands from that burden for the next few weeks. This afternoon was to be devoted to *Fiber Craft* work, but before she opened the Word file for "Sheep to Shawl," she sent off an email to her daughter. The conversation with Bettina about Callie Davenport and her refashion initiative had made her think of Penny.

"Hi, Penny," she wrote. "I hope you are doing well and settling into the new semester. Things are fine here. Love, Mom."

She wouldn't say anything about the murder case. She'd told Penny on the phone that she would let the police handle it and there was no point in raising the topic anew.

The full title of "Sheep to Shawl" turned out to be "Sheep to Shawl: Shearing, Spinning, and Weaving History in a Reconstructed Colonial Village." The village was situated in Connecticut and the author was a docent there, which struck Pamela as a fine credential for the topic. But the article itself turned out to be more about curious interactions with visitors to the village and the lamentable behavior of students on high-school field trips than about the technicalities of colonial-era wool production.

Pamela closed the file and composed a rejection for "Sheep to Shawl," suggesting that the author downplay her criticism of high-school students and submit a revision of the article to a publication dealing with history and tourism in her region.

Two messages popped up in her inbox as soon as she had closed Word and switched over to email. The first, from Bettina, simply said, "I'll be at your door tomorrow at two thirty." The other was from Penny. It read, "You didn't say anything about the murder case and that makes me think you are hiding something from me. Please do not do anything dangerous."

Pamela hated to lie to her daughter, so she would have to think about how to respond. In the meantime, it was close to dinner time.

Hungry cats were waiting at the bottom of the stairs, Catrina and Ginger enthusiastic in their greeting and Precious, befitting her lean elegance, more aloof. Soon the three were feasting on fish medley (including shrimp!) and Pamela was waiting for a slice of salmon to steam on a bed of mustard greens while a pot of brown rice simmered on a back burner.

It was Thursday morning. The cats had been fed, toast eaten and coffee drunk, and the *Register* skimmed on the off chance that Marcy Brewer had ferreted out some new details on the Critter murder that Clayborn had kept hidden from Bettina. (She hadn't.)

Catrina had retreated to the entry, where she was lounging in the spot of sun that appeared every morning to make the colors of the thrift-store carpet glow. Ginger was playing with her new toy, a plush fish weighted in such a way that it seemed to undulate when batted across the floor. And Precious was watching the proceedings from the top platform of the cat climber, an elegant pale streak against the dark blue of the carpeting that covered the platform, with her long sable tail draped gracefully over the edge.

Pamela climbed the stairs. In her bedroom she exchanged her robe and pajamas for jeans and a casual blouse and her slippers for her comfortable old Birkenstocks. In the bathroom, she combed her dark hair and smoothed it into a clip at the back of her neck.

Her computer waited in her office, awake and ready for its day since she had paused for a quick email check before descending the stairs an hour earlier. One article remained of the three her boss had sent the previous morning, "The Jazz Quilts of Ida Rae Thomas." The instructions had been to evaluate all three and, if "Jazz Quilts" was suitable for the upcoming issue devoted to quilts, to copyedit it. Evaluations and copyedited article, should it pass muster, were due the next day.

The jazz quilts, it appeared, were not literally jazz quilts. Pamela had imagined figural quilts with appliquéd scenes—saxophone players brandishing instruments clipped from yellow cloth as pianists fingered tiny keys delineated with embroidery, and bass players stroked basses as tall as they were.

Instead, the quilts were old—very old—and many were in the possession of a collector who was also the author of the article. While traveling in Alabama, she had met the quilts' creator, Ida Rae Thomas, in the latter years of

Ida Rae's life and recognized her talent. The collector had arranged gallery exhibits for Ida Rae's quilts, where they had been purchased by other collectors and even ended up in museums. In her final years Ida Rae had been financially comfortable and, more important, recognized for her artistry.

The article included photographs of several quilts, and the text described how they illustrated Ida Rae's development as an artist. The application of the term "jazz" to the quilts, the author explained, referred to the fact that the viewer's eye was drawn into a rhythmic dance as it moved over the surface of the quilts.

Colors and shapes were juxtaposed seemingly at random, but in a way that evoked the most sophisticated abstract art. Stripes started, stopped, and started again, jagged and syncopated, constantly surprising. Pamela had lingered over the photographs before reading the text. Then she had studied the photographs again, delighted by the way the quilts' patterns led the eye here and there, balancing order against chaos.

Pamela quickly sent off a note to her boss with an enthusiastic assurance that the article would fit perfectly into the upcoming issue on quilts and then set about copyediting it.

It was just two thirty, and Bettina was always punctual. But even if she hadn't been expecting Bettina, Pamela would have recognized her through the lace that curtained the oval window in the front door. Bettina, garbed in a striking shade of magenta and with bright scarlet hair, fairly glowed against the late-summer green of lawn and shrubbery.

Pamela collected her purse from the chair in the entry and they set off down the walk toward where Bettina's faithful Toyota was parked at the curb.

"Still nothing new in the *Register* about the murder case," Bettina commented as Pamela climbed into the passenger seat. "And Marcy Brewer is even better at getting information out of Clayborn than I am."

"Thankfully, my boss hasn't been asking me if there's been any progress," Pamela said. "Still, it would be a relief to get this all behind us—though nobody at that conference is ever going to forget that the author of *Spinning Civilization* was murdered at a conference sponsored by Wendelstaff College and *Fiber Craft* magazine."

Bettina made a soothing sound and patted Pamela's hand. "We'll see what Callie Davenport has to tell us." She summoned a cheerful tone. "Let's be off!"

"She's in that building where Brian's office is," Bettina said as they neared the campus. "So maybe we can park in that little lot by the student union. It's closer than walking all the way from the big lot by the river."

Five minutes later, Bettina was nosing into a parking space between a Jeep and a jaunty sports car. The student union building loomed off to the right and the quadrangle was behind them. It bustled with students hurrying this way and that, many of them dressed as if for a summer outing in denim cutoffs and tee-shirts, with only their bulky backpacks and their purposeful walks indicating that learning rather than recreation explained their presence.

Pamela and Bettina followed the narrow path that cut across the end of the quad and then they veered onto the walkway that skirted the brick building with white columns. They headed toward the glass and steel façade of the modern structure that lodged Fine and Professional Arts, where students flowed up and down the concrete steps as if suddenly possessed by the need to be somewhere else, and quickly. Pamela checked her watch. It was nearly three—obviously classes had just gotten out and others were about to commence.

Inside the building, the lobby was equally crowded. Callie Davenport had given Bettina specific directions to her office, and Bettina led Pamela toward one of the elevators, where they joined a small group watching the lighted buttons that indicated the elevators' whereabouts and progress. The elevator to their left glided to a stop and, with a whisper, the doors slid open. The people waiting stood aside as the elevator emptied and its cargo scurried to exit through the heavy glass doors that led to the concrete steps. Then the waiting crowd surged forward, carrying Pamela and Bettina along with them, and the elevator, once again full, sealed its doors and rose to the floor above.

The hallways on this floor were as mazelike as Pamela remembered from the visit to Brian's office on the floor below. They were not, however, as empty as they had been that day. Conversation and laughter reverberated as students popped in and out of classrooms, dodging around each other and darting past slower-moving groups.

Pamela and Bettina had reached a spot where the hallway dead-ended into a T-intersection when Pamela suddenly grabbed Bettina's arm and whispered, "Listen!"

"What?" Bettina swiveled her head to stare up at Pamela, looking more curious than alarmed.

"Down this way." She tugged Bettina to the right.

"But Callie's office is the other way." Bettina tugged back. A young man in a tee-shirt with the image of a space alien on it veered around them.

"I heard her!" Pamela whispered, but urgently. "The woman Dr. Critter seduced and abandoned."

A voice had suddenly risen above the cacophony echoing around them, a voice piercing in its nasality and marked by unexpected diphthongs. "I'll call you tonight," the voice had said.

Abandoning the effort to pull Bettina along with her, Pamela released her friend's arm. The voice had seemed to come from the right, where knots of people jockeyed around each other near the doorways of classrooms, some exiting the rooms as others hurried to enter them. Pamela eased her way into the crowd, pushing forward as she listened intently, scanning faces and bodies in search of a woman well past the traditional age of a college student.

As she moved along the corridor, the crowd thinned, students either dispersing to go their separate ways or vanishing into classrooms. By the time she reached the end of the corridor and turned around, the only people in sight were professors closing their classroom doors and Bettina, standing where Pamela had left her.

"No luck," Pamela said as she drew near. "But I could swear that was her voice."

"All is not lost." Bettina's voice was cheerful. "We'll come back after we're finished talking to Callie. The classes in session now will probably get out in about an hour."

CHAPTER 12

Callie Davenport's office was the second door along the corridor that led off to the left. She opened the door as soon as Bettina tapped and waved them inside with a cordial gesture.

"You must be Bettina," she said, correctly identifying her interviewer and adding a friendly smile, "because"—she turned her gaze to Pamela—"I know you're Pamela Paterson from *Fiber Craft*." She waved them toward two molded plastic chairs arranged near a brightly painted wooden table that served as a desk. "I was at the conference," she explained, "and you were introduced at the group session Saturday morning."

"We're neighbors," Bettina said. "Pamela told me about some of the sessions and I knew readers of our town newspaper would be interested in the fascinating classes being offered at Wendelstaff. Refashioning—so timely."

It had occurred to Pamela many times that her friend bought many more clothes than she needed, but perhaps the fact that Wilfred wore the same thing nearly every day balanced things out.

Callie's office featured a bookcase filled with books whose titles, visible on their spines, alluded to famous designers, eras notable for distinctive styles, sewing techniques, costume history, and the like. A huge bulletin board was crowded with sketches, clippings from magazines, photographs, fabric samples, and handwritten notes, all overlapping in a vibrant collage.

Callie herself was a petite woman, almost birdlike, with a smooth swoop of auburn hair that just reached her shoulders. She was wearing a garment that appeared to be a testament to her refashioning prowess.

It looked like it had started life as a man's dress shirt, fine crisp cotton in a tiny blue and white check. But it had been transformed into a sleeveless tunic, buttoning down the front with the original buttons and buttonholes intact. The original collar was intact too. The fact that it seemed slightly oversized in its new context added to the garment's quirky feel. The tunic reached nearly to Callie's knees—she was small and the shirt had been very big. Perhaps fearing that legs bared up to the thigh would seem inappropriate in work attire, she had added a pair of mid-calf-length leggings in navy blue. A pair of sleek navy-blue mules finished off the ensemble. Callie looked to be in her fifties, but her delicate build, her pretty skin, and her wide hazel eyes gave her a youthful air.

"That must be one of your creations!" Bettina smiled with delight. "It's adorable!" Her admiration seemed genuine to Pamela this time, in contrast with the not-so-genuine flattery that Bettina was capable of when she was determined to get an interview subject to talk.

"Why, thank you!" Callie smiled in return. She rolled a swivel chair from its location behind the painted table to a spot nearer where Pamela and Bettina sat. "It's the project I demonstrated at my conference workshop. It starts with a cast-off men's shirt."

"I can see that," Bettina said. "Such a good idea—the fabric is often such good quality."

Callie nodded. "And they're easy to find in thrift stores. Sometimes the collar is frayed, but a collarless version is cute too. I handed out instructions for the participants to reproduce and use in their own workshops or classes, and I did a show and tell with this dress." She gestured at the dress she was wearing. "There wasn't time to demonstrate making the whole garment—though it goes together very quickly—but I brought in a shirt similar to the one I used for this one and explained how to measure and cut based on the size of the person who's to wear the dress."

She pushed off with the toes of her mules and her swivel chair rolled back toward the painted desk, where she rummaged in a folder and came up with two printed sheets of paper. She rolled back and handed one to Bettina and one to Pamela. The paper was headed, "Simple Shirt to Tunic Refashion."

Pamela had been about to ask Callie if she could have a copy of the instructions for the shirt-turned-tunic. She hadn't sewed seriously in ages, but Penny would love this idea. Thrift stores *were* full of men's shirts, often cast off with nothing very seriously wrong with them, and they deserved to be rescued. Perhaps she could revive her sewing skills and pass them on to her daughter. Penny had already requested lessons and taken up knitting. Pamela thanked Callie, folded the paper, and tucked it into her purse.

Bettina did likewise, and then she inquired about the sorts of refashioning ideas Callie's students came up with on their own. Callie scooted her chair back toward the painted table to pick up her phone. She fingered the screen briefly and handed the phone to Bettina. Pamela leaned over to watch as Bettina scrolled through photos that Callie said were projects created the previous term.

As Bettina oohed and aahed at everything from jackets that might once have been coats to form-fitting dresses that might once have been voluminous, Callie veered off onto another topic, a topic less benign than the stated purpose of the interview.

"Yvonne certainly put Critter on the spot at the luncheon," she commented in an off-hand way. "Or did it only seem that way to me?"

"I . . . uh . . ." Pamela looked up from the phone, where the small screen showed a young woman garbed head to toe in faded denim. Clearly, Callie's comment and question were aimed at her, since Bettina hadn't been at the conference. "He did seem rattled," Pamela said after a bit, "and he was definitely eager to get away."

"I didn't blame her at all," Callie said. "Yvonne is a writer too, and I suspect it's true that all the good ideas in Critter's book are hers. She's not a professor, but she's got a strong background in anthropology, Central American to be exact. And she knows more about spinning and weaving than Critter could ever hope to. I know I'd be furious if a man stole my ideas—and I'd be happy to put him on the spot any chance I got."

"Would you kill him?" Bettina inquired suddenly, the phone forgotten in her hand.

Unexpectedly, Callie laughed, a delighted rippling laugh that faded to a chuckle but left her smiling. "Probably not," she said, "but I'd fantasize about it."

"Do you think Yvonne could be the person that poisoned Dr. Critter?" Pamela wouldn't have launched the topic as bluntly as Bettina had, but now that it *was* launched . . .

"The poison was in that coffee they served at Sufficiency House, wasn't it?" Callie said.

"Probably," Bettina said, and added parenthetically that she had been meeting with Detective Clayborn of the Arborville police department in connection with her reporting duties for the *Advocate*. "Was she by any chance at your workshop?" Bettina went on. "That would give her an alibi."

"No." Callie shook her head and the tips of her hair swept her shoulders. "Her interests run more to spinning and weaving, that sort of thing. She imports textiles from a women's collective in Guatemala and sells them at the Newfield farmers market."

"So it sounds like you know her . . ." Pamela knew that Bettina's expression of rapt interest was one of her most potent tools as an interviewer.

"The split between her and Critter was fairly recent," Callie said. "Before that, Yvonne came to a lot of campus events with him. I like her and I'd hate to think she could be a murderer—even if she had a good reason."

Pamela and Bettina nodded, Callie nodded back, and with that point settled no one said anything for a few minutes. Pamela took a surreptitious peek at her watch. There was still plenty of time before classes would get out and she would have another chance to listen for the voice of the woman Dr. Critter had seduced and abandoned. And so far they had only learned that Yvonne didn't have an alibi for three to four p.m. on Saturday. What about Shane?

Callie didn't seem in a hurry to cut their visit short, and had seemed as happy to discuss the Dr. Critter case as she had been to talk about refashioning. In fact, she was the first to speak again.

"His book got some positive reviews," she observed thoughtfully, as if she had spent the few minutes of silence mulling over the pros and cons of her deceased colleague. "And it reflected well on his department, and on the college." She gestured toward the bookcase. "That's it up there. He gave me a copy."

Pamela glanced in the direction of the gesture. Wedged between *Sew It Now* and *Style for the Masses* was a large book with a bold orange spine. Angular black letters spelled out *Spinning Civilization*.

"The choice of him as keynote speaker for the conference was controversial though." Callie twisted her lips into a curious knot and gazed first at Bettina and then at Pamela. "What did you think?"

"Well . . . the fiber arts and crafts are in large part women's arts and crafts," Pamela said. She was about to elaborate when Bettina cut in.

"I know one person who thought it was a terrible idea," she declared. "That . . . what's her name? Shane something. I was talking to her at the reception after Critter's funeral and she gave me an earful."

"Oh"—Callie laughed her rippling laugh again—"now there's another person I wouldn't blame if she murdered Critter!"

"Really!" Pamela and Bettina both spoke at once.

"Oh, sure." Callie's tone implied absolute certainty. "He was a thorn in her side almost from the day she was hired. He served on the college grants committee and she was convinced he was the reason her proposals were always turned down. He was a pompous fool, if you ask me, and terrified of smart women, but somehow I got along with him."

"I suppose she wasn't at your workshop either," Pamela said.

"No interest at all in fashion." Callie flung out a hand as if to mime Shane's dismissal of the very concept. "Not even refashion. She thinks women waste time dressing up to please men when they could be changing the world."

"They can't do both?" Bettina ventured in a small voice. "People have to wear clothes."

"Of course they do, and clothes are fun. So are men." Callie glanced at her watch. "Oops," she said. "I've got a class at four. It's hands-on, with sewing machines, and it's in a studio way across the quad, so I've got to get moving."

After a few rounds of thank-yous and goodbyes, she was on her way, and Pamela and Bettina were once more standing in the corridor outside the classrooms that had emptied and then quickly filled an hour ago. It was crowded again, and becoming more crowded by the minute, as students clustered near the doors of the classrooms where their four o'clock classes would meet.

One door opened, and another, and backpack-laden students swarmed out as others swarmed in. A youngish male professor with a canvas messenger's bag slung over his shoulder paused to respond to a student who said she would be leaving class early. An older woman professor greeted him as she slipped out through the door he was poised to enter.

Pamela glanced this way and that, focusing on the faces of the female students. Most faces were unworn, evoking Penny's youthful glow, but she peered intently, seeking a face closer in age to the one that looked back at her from her mirror every morning. And she listened, seeking to isolate that distinctive nasal intonation from the random din reverberating around her.

Bettina had edged her way farther along the corridor. She hadn't heard the voice, either emanating from the shrubbery outside the dining hall or an hour ago when Pamela had thought she recognized it. But she too was scanning faces.

The corridor had begun to empty out, as the classrooms refilled and the students who had occupied them previously drifted away. The older female professor, pleasant looking in a casual shirt and slacks outfit and with an attractive salt-and-pepper bob, had lingered to speak with a young male student. When he went on his way, with a muttered, "I guess I get it," she noticed Pamela and Bettina.

"Are you lost?" she inquired. "This building is like a maze."

Pamela was about to say they weren't lost. They clearly had not succeeded in their objective, but she was sure they could find their way back to the elevators. But Bettina was never one to lose an opportunity.

"Just snooping around," she said with a flirtatious wink. Pamela had noted that her friend's charm was as effective with women as with men. "I'm Bettina Fraser, from the *Arborville Advocate*." She extended a graceful hand and the woman professor took it.

Pamela didn't know what Bettina was up to, but she thought it best to be unobtrusive.

"I'm doing a story on older women returning to school," Bettina went on. "It's timely, since the fall semester is just getting underway. I'd love to talk to some older students, and just a few minutes ago I thought I saw one. But then I lost track of her."

"That must have been Bitsy Daniels," the female professor said. "She's not one of mine this term but I've seen her up here a few times since the semester started. She works part-time in the Fine and Professional Arts office and takes classes as part of a free tuition program for employees."

Bettina gave Pamela a sidelong glance and a victorious but subtle smile, then she thanked the woman, who headed off down the corridor and disappeared into an office near Callie's.

"Next stop, the Fine and Professional Arts office?" Bettina asked as they headed down the long corridor that led to the elevators.

"Absolutely!" Pamela nodded. "I think it's on the first floor near those faculty mailboxes."

They had the elevator to themselves, given that classes were in session, and its doors glided open onto a nearly empty foyer. Pamela remembered the route they had followed with Brian the day of Critter's funeral and reception, and they retraced the twists and turns that had led them to his office.

Just before they reached his office and the alcove with the faculty mailboxes, they came upon a door with a plaque larger than those bearing the names of individual professors. It read "Office of Fine and Professional Arts." She tried the doorknob and it turned.

Responding to her gentle nudge, the door swung back and they stepped into a white-walled room furnished with a streamlined metal desk and a few streamlined metal chairs. The walls were decorated with large abstract prints in eye-catching colors. Through an open door to the right of the desk Pamela could see a larger office. The décor was similar but included well-stocked bookcases.

A young man with impressive tattoos on his arms met Pamela's gaze from behind the computer monitor that shared the desk's surface with a cactus in a pottery bowl. "Dr. Baldwin has gone home for the day," he said. "Can I help you?"

"I was hoping to find Bitsy Daniels." It was Bettina who spoke, perhaps to preserve the fiction that it was she who sought Bitsy, and with the goal of an interview.

"She's gone home too." The young man glanced toward a large clock on the side wall, as if to gauge how much longer he was going to have to work. "She's part time," he added. "Won't be back till Monday."

"Will she be here Monday morning?" Bettina asked.

"Probably." He nodded. "I won't."

As they approached the sunny foyer once again, Pamela said, "I doubt there's much point in looking for Shane now. It's getting on toward five."

"Tomorrow then, and let's take a drive out to the New-field farmers market to visit Yvonne." Bettina slipped her phone out of her purse. A few benches whose lines complemented the modern feel of the building flanked the glass doors. Bettina perched on a bench and Pamela joined her as she fingered the screen of her device.

After a minute or two she held it out so Pamela could see the screen as well. She had located the website where Yvonne offered her Guatemalan imports for sale and where she posted details of her farmers market stall.

"The stall is open Tuesday through Saturday," Bettina murmured.

"She was at the conference last Saturday," Pamela said, "at least during the luncheon. But if she hurried out to Newfield right afterwards she'd have an alibi."

"Maybe she has an assistant." Bettina scrolled down and images of colorful hand-woven fabrics appeared in quick succession. "Beautiful things," she added.

"Maybe," Pamela agreed. "She was here last Tuesday too, for the funeral and reception."

Bettina continued scrolling. "Uh-oh," she said. "She'll be at the music and arts festival in Stilesborough, Pennsylvania, Friday through Sunday. Back in Newfield Tuesday." She clicked her phone off and tucked it back in her purse. "We can look for Shane Bennett tomorrow though." She turned to Pamela. "I've got to cover a story for the *Advocate* at eleven—a dog that summoned help after its owner locked himself in his garage is being given an award by the humane society, but right after lunch we'll come back here and track down Shane Bennett. And Monday we'll talk to Bitsy. And Tuesday we'll drive to Newfield."

They stood up and moved toward the doors.

"Wilfred used up all those peaches he brought home the last time he was at the farmers market," Bettina said clutching the elegant steel handrail as they descended the concrete steps. "He made three pies and gave two of them away. So if I'm going to try fresh peach ice cream, I'll need more."

"Two birds with one stone then," Pamela said with a laugh.

It was five thirty by the time Bettina pulled into her driveway and parked the faithful Toyota next to Wilfred's ancient but lovingly cared-for Mercedes. She and Pamela chatted for a few minutes about their plans for the next day and then Pamela crossed the street to her own house. She was greeted in the entry by three hungry cats. They prowled around her ankles in a tangled blend of black, ginger, and cream as she tried to head for the stairs, but when she changed direction and aimed for the kitchen they trotted happily ahead of her.

After cans had been opened and servings of tuna-liver medley scooped into fresh bowls, a large one for Catrina and Ginger to share and a smaller one for Precious, Pamela opened her refrigerator. She'd eaten her Co-Op salmon the previous night, but the organic chicken from a local farm awaited. Roasted with a few sprigs of rosemary from the pot on the back porch tucked inside, it could be ready in an hour, and the leftovers would provide many meals to come.

Once it was in the oven, Pamela climbed the stairs to her office, where she pushed the buttons that brought her computer and monitor to life. After a few moments and a brief concert of clicks, chimes, and whirs, the monitor brightened and she summoned up her email.

Three new messages popped up, but only one was of interest. She quickly deleted the offer of a 20% off coupon from the hobby shop and the note from the power company reminding her that chilly weather was approaching.

The interesting message was from delanob@wendel-staff.edu. It read,

Hi, Pamela,
Looking forward to Saturday night. Here's a pre-view (attachment).
Brian

She clicked on the attachment, which was labeled "Taggart Show." It was a flyer from the Stone Gallery on Broome Street advertising the upcoming exhibit of paintings by Stretch Taggart. Most of the flyer's surface was taken up with a dramatic portrait of a woman posing as if for an update of a portrait Pamela recalled studying in art history. The subject of that portrait had been someone named Madame X, she thought, and the portrait had showed a slender, elegant woman with exceptionally pale skin wearing a revealing black gown that must have been very shocking at the time.

The update seemed tongue-in-cheek. Stretch Taggart's subject was slender and elegant and her skin was exceptionally pale. But instead of replicating Madame X's haughty demeanor, she was winking at the viewer, and the revealing gown had been replaced by a black bikini top and a black sarong loosely wrapped around her hips.

Pamela replied with a quick thank-you to Brian, then she clicked on NEW and entered Penny's email address. "Keep on the lookout for men's shirts in good condition when you go thrifting," she wrote, and she went on to describe Callie Davenport's shirt-to-tunic project. "I have the directions," she added, "and we can try making one when you're here at Thanksgiving."

The aroma of roasting chicken, made more seductive by the hint of rosemary, had begun to drift up the stairs. But before descending to launch a pot of rice and slice the tomato she had harvested when she picked the rosemary sprigs, Pamela stepped across the hall to her bedroom. She opened her closet and stared at the contents. A few pairs of jeans and several casual blouses and shirts occupied most of the hangers. A few other undistinguished items lurked in the closet's darker recesses. The shelf above held sweaters, mostly hand-knit, in a range of colors more interesting than the rest of the closet's offerings.

But what on earth would she wear to the gallery opening? Broome Street was in SoHo, she thought, where fashionable people lived, and then Brian had said they would go to dinner, probably somewhere chic. She pushed her closet door closed and descended to the kitchen.

A few hours later, just in time for her favorite British mystery, Pamela settled at her customary end of the sofa and picked up her knitting. The cultured accents of the detective and even the suspected evildoers were as soothing as the chorus of soft purrs emanating from the three cats who soon joined her there.

Pamela spent Friday morning checking over the jazz quilts article, making sure she had caught every deviation from *Fiber Craft* style and that the article's tone was appropriate for a magazine that served not only fiber aficionados and hobbyists but also the academic community. The author had been effusive in her praise of the quilts, which in Pamela's view was highly justified, but she had tried to tame some of the more florid language. As she had explained in her evaluation of the article, thanks to the excellent photographs the quilts nearly spoke for themselves.

Satisfied that her work on "The Jazz Quilts of Ida Rae Thomas" was complete, Pamela skimmed her evaluations of the other two articles, attached them and the copy-edited manuscript to an email, and sent it off to her boss. After a quick grilled cheese sandwich, she crossed the street to Bettina's house.

CHAPTER 13

"You have to have some pie," were Bettina's first words as she pulled back her front door. She seized Pamela's hand and led her through the living room and then the dining room into her spacious kitchen, where a homey scene greeted her. Woofus, accompanied by the ginger cat, Punkin, was lounging against the wall, and Wilfred, wearing an apron over his bib overalls, was standing behind the high counter that separated the working area of the kitchen from the eating area.

"Have some pie," he greeted her, echoing Bettina's invitation.

Half a pie, its crust flaky and burnished gold, waited atop the counter in a deep pottery pie dish. Its cut edges revealed chunks of peach in a deeper shade of gold. They were enveloped in a syrup so thick as to imply the presence of much sugar. Rivulets of the syrup had oozed onto the now-vacant portion of the pie dish, where they glistened against the pottery surface.

Before Pamela could answer, Wilfred produced a small plate from Bettina's sage-green set. He placed it on the counter next to the remains of the pie and turned away to fetch a knife and spatula.

"You have to try it," Bettina urged. "It's one of his best." She turned her attention to Wilfred and said, "I might have a bit more too, just a tiny slice."

"Dear wife"—he beamed at her, his ruddy face the very picture of cheer—"your wish is my command." He turned away again and returned with two more plates, as well as three forks. "Food shared is enjoyed all the more," he commented as he cut and served the pie. When he was finished, only one bare sliver was left in the pie dish.

In a few moments they were all seated at the scrubbed pine table, carving off bites of pie and conveying them to their mouths.

"Umm." Bettina's lips curved up and she closed her eyes. "Late summer peaches are the best," she sighed. "I hope we can find some more at the farmers market Tuesday."

The pie was a masterpiece. Despite the sugary implications of the syrup, the sweetness didn't overpower the peaches, whose flavor came through with a slight but distinct acidic tang. Wilfred's piecrust resisted the soggy-bottom effect that sometimes afflicts juicy fruit pies, and the top crust was light and delicate, the perfect foil for the intensity of the filling. Even Pamela's last few bites of the pie, which consisted of the scalloped edge where top crust met bottom, were a flaky treat.

"Well, that was just delicious," Bettina said, setting down her fork, which chimed against the empty plate. "I don't know if I'll even try to make the peach ice cream—

I don't know what could be a better use for them than these amazing pies."

"It was a treat." Pamela aimed a smile at Wilfred, then tilted her head toward Bettina. "Shall we be off?"

Bettina rose. Her purse, which today was a pale blue quilted Chanel-style bag, was hanging from the back of her chair, as if she'd gone directly to the kitchen for lunch after her morning errand. Her phone was lying on the scrubbed pine table.

She picked it up and reached for her purse, but before she tucked the phone away, she said, "I was showing Wilfred before you got here. This dog—the dog that got the award—was the most beautiful creature you can imagine." She fingered the phone and handed it to Pamela when the screen lit up. "A chocolate lab! Have you ever seen anything more gorgeous? There are more pictures—just use your finger to scroll sideways."

Bettina circled the table to stand behind Pamela, who was still sitting, as she studied the images on the phone's screen. The dog *was* a noble creature, with its finely modeled head, its muscular body, and its gleaming chocolate-brown coat. In the photo taken after the awards medal had been hung around its neck, it stared straight ahead with a gaze that implied humble acknowledgment of its own magnificence.

At the edge of the room Woofus lifted his shaggy head, but no one noticed him until a sound escaped from his throat, like a faint whimper. Pamela spoke up first.

"I think he hears us," she said, "and he knows we're talking about another dog."

Wilfred had stepped away from the table, carrying the plates and forks to the counter next to the sink, but he quickly hurried out to where Bettina was already kneeling at Woofus's side.

"You are a special, special doggy," she was crooning as she stroked the spot between the dog's floppy ears. "Looks are not everything, not everything at all." Wilfred joined her there, a bulky figure in bib overalls with an apron tied about his ample waist.

A few minutes later they had bidden goodbye to Woofus and Wilfred and stepped out onto Bettina's porch. As they proceeded down the driveway toward the faithful Toyota, Bettina happened to glance across the street. A compact bundle sheathed in flimsy plastic was lying on the strip of grass between the curb and Pamela's sidewalk.

"I guess you didn't bring in your copy of the *Advocate* yet," Bettina commented as she unlocked the car's passenger-side door. "My interview with Belle is in it, but this issue had gone to press before I turned in the interview with Callie. And there's nothing new from Clayborn. I called him a few times but he said there was no reason to meet."

The *Advocate* generally arrived on Friday morning, but not always. Pamela had noticed it lying there when she checked for the mail but hadn't felt like walking to the end of her front walk to retrieve it.

Both its admirers and detractors characterized the *Advocate* as containing "all the news that fits," and Bettina could be sensitive about the weekly's humble place in the news ecosystem. Even she, however, admitted that it wasn't difficult for the *Register* to scoop the *Advocate* given that the *Register* came out every day.

"There's a nice article about the Boy Scout field trip to Ellis Island too," Bettina said as Pamela settled into her seat.

"I'll be sure to pick it up when we get back from our errand," Pamela assured her friend. "And I know Belle will appreciate the nice spotlight on the high-school home ec program."

Sitting in her car in the Wendelstaff parking lot, Bettina had checked her phone for the location of the women's studies department. It was in the red brick building with white columns, the oldest building on the Wendelstaff campus. All the college's older buildings ringed the grassy quad, creating a setting unchanged since the era when coeds wore pleated skirts, saddle shoes, and bobby socks. Instead, however, the young woman students scurrying along the narrow pathways that crisscrossed the quad at random angles wore jeans or even shorts, and boots or sandals.

Pamela and Bettina passed between the columns that framed the building's heavy wooden doors and entered a shadowy foyer. A staircase straight ahead served the second floor, which was their destination.

Bettina paused at the top of the stairs to catch her breath. "Down this way, I think," she said, pointing to the left. They made their way over creaky wooden floors, past wooden doors opening off on either side of the paneled corridor. They were nearly at the end of the corridor, Bettina lagging a few yards behind, when Pamela halted and turned. The door she was standing in front of bore a placard that read "Women's Studies." Facing it across the corridor was a door with a placard that listed Shane Bennett, Lex Ransome, and Del Marcus as the office's inhabitants.

"It's weird that such a modern subject as women's

studies should have its offices in this ancient building, don't you think?" Bettina commented when she reached Pamela's side. "With the white columns and the wood paneling and all you'd expect subjects like history."

"Yes, you would," said a voice behind them.

They hadn't heard the door open, but at the very end of the corridor a bookish-looking woman was stepping over the threshold. She drew close, regarded them through rimless glasses, and added, "Or classics."

"Yes," Bettina said brightly, "or classics."

With an expansive gesture that took in nearly the entire corridor, the woman sighed. "This all belonged to the classics department once," she explained. "Now there aren't that many people who want to study the ancient Greeks or Romans."

Pamela had bent forward to ponder the chart of office hours below the placard.

"Are you looking for one of them?" the woman asked.

"Shane Bennett," Pamela replied. "It looks like she's not in at all on Friday, but Saturday is"—Pamela looked up—"Feminar at the Women's Collective Workspace?"

The woman nodded. "I'm not opposed to women's studies actually. In fact the Amazons, the ancient female warriors, are one of my research topics. So sometimes our disciplines overlap."

Everything was intertwined, Pamela knew. She had read articles for *Fiber Craft* that drew on history, biology, chemistry, so many different fields. And women's studies, of course, given the women's work aspect of the fiber arts and crafts.

Her mind had wandered but Bettina's hadn't. "Is the Women's Collective Workspace here on campus?" Bettina was asking as Pamela's mind returned from its musings.

The woman shook her head. "Haversack," she said. "Somewhere in Haversack. I think it has a website."

"You're not busy tomorrow, I hope," Pamela said as they crossed the quadrangle on their way back to the parking lot.

"I'm as curious about the feminar as you are." Bettina was hurrying to keep up with Pamela's long-legged stride, and her pace wasn't helped by her footwear—delicate kitten heels in a pale blue that matched her purse. "I need to find out whether the Arborville children will be leaving the grandchildren with Wilfred and me tomorrow, but we'll see what the website for the Women's Collective Workspace has to tell us. I'm sure I can get away for a bit."

Pamela looked at her watch. "It's not very late," she said, "and while we're in the neighborhood, there's something we never thought to check on and we should have."

"What?" Bettina asked. They had reached the edge of the quad. "Does it involve more walking?"

"Not much." Pamela laughed. "It has to do with Sufficiency House and we can drive most of the way."

As they continued on toward the main parking lot where Bettina's car waited, Pamela explained.

"We've been thinking that whoever put that poison in the coffee dispenser was able to pop unnoticed into the Sufficiency House kitchen, after all the knitters had been served but before Dr. Critter arrived and served himself. But we never poked around behind Sufficiency House to see what the route to the kitchen door is like, and we never checked to see if somebody could park nearby without being visible from the living room."

"Maybe the person liked to walk," Bettina said. "Like you."

"Maybe," Pamela agreed. "But is there shrubbery behind the house, along the sides of the house, where someone could hide and wait?"

As they pulled out of the Wendelstaff parking lot, Pamela directed Bettina to head for County Road. But instead of turning onto the block where Sufficiency House was located, she told her to continue on to the next cross street and turn there. That street featured a large apartment building on the corner, and then two shabby little wood-frame houses. The rest of the block was a kind of park, not very well maintained, but including a pond with a few wild ducks bobbing in it. A gravel road separated the park from the northern end of the county-owned nature preserve that marked Arborville's western border.

"We'll park along here," Pamela said, "and see what it's like to approach Sufficiency House from the back rather than the front."

Bettina pulled over in front of the wood-frame house closest to the park. There were no sidewalks on this block, or curbs, and the shaggy lawns of the two houses trailed off as they met the ragged edges of the street's asphalt.

Bettina joined Pamela, who stood a few yards from the car and was staring in the direction of Sufficiency House, or at least where she imagined it to be from this angle.

"Look"—she pointed between the two houses—"I think I see an apple tree, and beyond it something green, something painted green. Sufficiency House is green." She turned her gaze on Bettina as if to check for agreement. "I believe we're looking at the backyard of Sufficiency House," she said. "So let's go."

"Let's go?" Bettina extended a foot to demonstrate the unsuitability of her footwear for tramping over untended terrain. "And besides, we can't just cut through these people's yards."

"It doesn't look to me like anybody's lived here for a long time," Pamela said. "At least in this house." She nodded toward the house they'd parked in front of. "But we could circle around by the pond and creep up on it that way."

"That would be worse." Bettina shuddered. "If I'd known you were going to want to do this I would have worn my sneakers—and a different outfit."

Bettina's shoes and purse had been chosen to complement a pale blue linen pantsuit accessorized with a triple strand of pearls.

"I'll wait in the car," she said. "You go ahead."

So Bettina headed back to the car, and Pamela picked her way over the uneven ground aiming toward the gap between the two houses. Along the foundations, straggly iris plants and gray-green peony foliage that had succumbed to late-summer mildew testified to someone's long-ago interest in gardening. But the yards of both houses were sadly neglected.

It was startling, then, to gaze across untended backyards at a vision of nature cultivated and tamed. The boundary between the land owned by Sufficiency House and the land Pamela was standing on was unmarked, except that the tangle of crabgrass and weeds all around her suddenly gave way to garden plots devoted to useful crops.

A gravel walkway leading to the back porch of Sufficiency House bisected the yard. In a stand of corn off to the left, heavy ears trailing hanks of silk hung from stalks. Beyond the corn, a row of poles supported bean tendrils weighed down by bulging pods. To the right, beyond the apple tree, huge fuzzy leaves sheltered the vivid orange and yellow squash that lay among snaky vines. The grid-like layout of the garden was interrupted nearer the house by a small garden shed whose weathered wood contrasted with the green-painted exterior of the house itself.

Pamela made her way along the gravel path, enjoying the silence, which was interrupted only by the soothing chirp of an insect and the slight crunch of the gravel underfoot. As she neared the garden shed, however, an additional sound was added to the mix, a human sound, like rhythmic grunting or panting. Or two humans, one grunting and the other panting. The panting rose to a crescendo and then a voice, definitely human, shouted, "Yes, yes!"

Pamela was not a nosy person. It was clear that the shed was being used for more than the storage of garden equipment, and so she quickly sped past it. Her errand had revealed that it was possible to approach Sufficiency House from the back, and that if one came by car one could arrive and park unnoticed by anyone who might be looking out the living room windows. But she still wanted to sneak along the side of the house to check if the person bearing the poison could have looked in windows to confirm that all the knitters had been provided with coffee.

She was studying the first window she came to, noticing that it was a little high for a normal-sized person to see much of the room beyond it, when a familiar voice called, "Here you are!"

Startled, she stepped away from the window. Bettina

was advancing from the front yard, treading carefully in her delicate little shoes.

"I was getting worried," Bettina added. Her expression underlined the sentiment with a wrinkle between her carefully shaped brows and slight quiver to her brightly lipsticked lips.

Before Pamela could answer, a competing voice reached her from the other direction.

"Pamela Paterson?" the voice said. "Were you looking for me?"

She turned to see Flo Ransom, looking uncharacteristically flushed and with the buttons up the front of her much-washed housedress misaligned with their buttonholes. She hadn't been looking for Flo, actually, but before she could think of how to explain her presence, Bettina darted around her.

"We were just in the neighborhood," she said brightly. "And Pamela mentioned what a wonderful job you've done with the gardens here. Harvest season is upon us and"—Bettina edged past Flo to survey the backyard—"are those heirloom tomatoes?"

Pamela looked where Bettina was pointing. In one of the carefully laid out plots near the house were eight sturdy tomato plants barely contained by their wire cages. Dangling among their dark leaves were tomatoes of various shapes and hues, from pale yellow to mahogany. Beyond the plot, a man carrying a shovel was just disappearing around the side of the house.

"They, uh, yes . . ." Flo seemed flustered. "But here's something even more interesting." She grabbed Bettina's arm, spun her around, and led her along a narrow path that cut between plots. Pamela followed.

The destination was a bed notable for the variety of plants it contained. Some were woody shrubs, others were low bushes with leaves that were fernlike or blade-like or lobed in curious ways, and still others bore flowers in golden clusters or daisy-like on long stems.

"This is the section of the garden where we grow our dye plants," Flo said. "All part of the Sufficiency House do-it-yourself ethos."

Each plant was identified with a small marker listing its Latin name, and many of the markers also noted what colors could be achieved by using parts of the plant as dye.

"Yarrow," Flo explained, pointing at the plant with the striking golden flowers. "And this one is indigo." She pointed at the plant with the fernlike leaves. "Or *Indigofera tinctoria* to be more precise. It doesn't do so well in this climate but I've been able to coax it along."

"This one is cute," Pamela said, stooping toward a plant with unusual seven-lobed leaves.

"*Sanguinaria canadensis*," Flo said. "It gets the most beautiful flowers in the spring, white with lots of petals, sort of like daisies."

Talking about the dye plants had restored Flo's composure and banished the flush that had reddened her complexion. She would realize soon enough that her haphazardly rebuttoned dress hinted at dressing in haste, and without a mirror at hand, but by that time her visitors would be gone and she could blush in private—or perhaps viewed only by the person for whom she had removed the dress in the first place.

"Very nice person," Bettina commented as she led Pamela around to the front of Sufficiency House, where her faithful Toyota was now parked. "But did you think she seemed a little flustered? And she certainly doesn't take any interest in clothes at all. Worse than you. That dress must have been older than she is. And she hadn't even bothered to button it correctly."

Pamela bit her tongue, but the minute they were sitting in Bettina's car with the doors closed, she burst out laughing. Bettina watched, puzzled, until Pamela managed to control herself by dint of taking several deep breaths.

"Did you notice that Flo wasn't alone in the garden?" she asked and then bit her lips to contain the giggle that threatened.

"The man hurrying away with a shovel?" Bettina squinted and tightened her lips into a quizzical knot. Pamela nodded. Then she described the sounds she'd heard emerging from the garden shed.

"Oh, my goodness!" The expression on Bettina's face was curious. Not amused, not disapproving, but . . . delighted, in a way that brightened her hazel eyes and rosied her cheeks. "Everyone deserves love," she said at last. "It's wonderful when people find each other. As Wilfred says, for every pot there's a lid."

Bettina was right, Pamela reflected, as Bettina inserted her key in the ignition and the Toyota's engine grumbled and then caught. They were silent for a bit, but once they were back on County Road and heading toward Orchard Street, Bettina began to speak again. Imagining Flo finding happiness had apparently reminded her of a romantic pairing in which she took a more personal interest.

"Have you decided what you're going to wear tomorrow night?" she inquired. Pamela had been gazing out her window at the nature preserve, with its trees still the deep green of late summer and bright wildflowers dotting the untamed grasses at the sunny edge of the woods.

"Um?" She turned, not yet grasping the significance of the question.

"Hello?" Bettina shifted her attention from the road to Pamela and Pamela resisted the urge to squeal. "Your date with Brian Delano? The gallery opening? Dinner in the city?"

"I'll think of something." Pamela raised a finger to her brow to rub away the beginnings of a frown. "I've never dressed up specially for our dates in the past."

"This is different." The Toyota lurched as Bettina braked to avoid hitting a car that had slowed for an unexpected turn. "This is a date in the *city*, meeting chic people, his artist friends. You have to—"

Pamela laid a hand on Bettina's arm. "Bettina," she sighed. "Please just drive. I won't be in any state to go anywhere tomorrow night if we have an accident."

"I'm sorry I brought it up." Bettina's tone was prim. She straightened her spine, lifted her chin, and said no more for the rest of the trip.

When they reached the spot halfway up Orchard where Bettina's and Pamela's houses faced each other across the street, Bettina nosed to the curb near the end of Pamela's driveway.

"Well," she said, not looking at Pamela, "here you are. Home."

Pamela pushed the car door open. But before getting out, she said, "Would it be okay if I wore my amber sweater?"

"He's already seen you in that." Bettina's manner had thawed a bit. "You were wearing it at the reception after Critter's funeral. But suit yourself."

"Do you still want to come to that place in Haversack with me tomorrow?" Pamela asked as she lowered one foot to the ground.

"Do you want me to?" Bettina could be coy.

"Aren't you curious?" Pamela pulled her foot back in and turned toward Bettina.

"A little."

"Two p.m. then? And I'll drive." Pamela pushed the car door open further and swung both feet around.

"No, no," Bettina said. "I will. I don't mind."

Once inside her house, Pamela felt at loose ends. It was too early for dinner, and preparation would be simple anyway, since there was still plenty of chicken left from Thursday night. Precious was lounging on the top platform of the cat climber but Catrina and Ginger were nowhere in sight. Clearly Pamela's housemates weren't longing for dinner yet either.

Upstairs, she checked her email. While she was gone, she had received a note from the alumni association of her alma mater, a notice that her recent order of ink cartridges for her printer had been shipped, and a message from her boss. A stylized paperclip next to the subject line meant attachments, and attachments meant a new work assignment.

"Please evaluate these articles," her boss had written, "and get back to me by Thursday morning." The abbreviated titles for the attachments referred to the articles as "Bayeux Tapestry," "Pueblo Textiles," and "Seeing Red." What could "Seeing Red" mean? Something about dye perhaps? She'd read that one first.

CHAPTER 14

"It seems they don't want to be found," Bettina complained the next day. She and Pamela were scanning the list of names ranged opposite a row of buzzers in the foyer of an apartment building several blocks from the Haversack commercial district.

"These are all just people." She pointed to a tiny strip of embossed plastic that read R JAMES. "And this is just a normal apartment building, and an unprepossessing one at that."

Yet an internet search for "Women's Collective Workspace, Haversack NJ" had led them to this address.

"Women's Collective Workspace, Women's Collective Workspace," Pamela murmured, leaning close to the buzzer panel. "Women's Collective . . ." She paused, then pointed at a spot near the bottom of the list, where a buzzer was labeled WCW. "It must be this. Three B."

She pushed the buzzer. The response was a startlingly loud buzz and then a click, as the lock on the door that separated the foyer from the building's lobby disengaged.

The lobby had once been grander than it was now. A floor paved with tiny octagonal tiles was partly covered by a frayed rug. The walls, painted an institutional shade of green, were cracked in spots. A few steps at the lobby's far end led to a landing where two elevators waited, one with open doors. Pamela and Bettina entered.

A few minutes later, the elevator announced with a low chime that it had reached the third floor and they stepped out into a short hallway.

"Let's try this way," Bettina said, and she took off to the right. In her bright yellow shirtdress she made a colorful figure against the walls and carpet, which were a bland shade of tan. "It's down here," she called after she had turned the corner.

There was no need to check the apartment number. The door was already open and Shane Bennett, in olive-green cargo pants and a long-sleeved olive-green tee-shirt, was standing on the threshold. The ensemble suited her lean body and lent her a kind of guerrilla chic.

"Was that you who buzzed?" she inquired with an inquisitorial stare that suited the outfit, as did the dark, untamed curls that surrounded a face free of makeup.

Before either Pamela or Bettina could answer, Shane advanced toward them. "I know you," she said. "I know you from somewhere."

"The reception for Dr. Critter." Pamela mustered her social smile. "We met you there." She mentioned her name and Bettina's.

"Why are you here?"

"The Feminar?" Pamela ventured.

"That was this morning." Shane backed up until she stood on the threshold again.

Bettina stepped around Pamela. "It was actually my idea to come," she said, pointing at herself. "You have a workspace."

"We do." Shane nodded.

"I need a workspace. I'm a writer."

Shane's gaze traveled from the top of Bettina's scarlet-tressed head, past the bright yellow shirtdress, and all the way down to the matching ballet flats. She wrinkled her nose and said, "Is that a fact?"

"Yes, a reporter. For the *Arborville Advocate*." Bettina smiled cheerfully, ignoring the implied snub. "And I need a place to work in peace. It's hard to work at home with a husband retired and underfoot, and a dog, and a cat."

"I can see how it would be." Shane nodded.

"I'd be happy to pay my share." Pamela couldn't see Bettina's face but she could picture the eager expression that so often won people over to Bettina's point of view.

"Take a look then, if you like." Shane backed through the open door and gestured for Pamela and Bettina to enter.

They found themselves in an apartment living room with windows in the far wall. Instead of a sofa, coffee table, and occasional chairs, however, the room was furnished with long tables, like a library reading room. Women were seated here and there at the tables, pecking at the keyboards of laptops, or staring at and scribbling on pads of paper. Though there were no easels in evidence, a slight odor of oil paint hung in the air.

"The art room is through there." Shane nodded toward a closed door. She was silent for a few moments while Bettina surveyed the room, then she spoke again. "Why were you at the reception for Critter anyway?" she inquired.

"Oh, because Pamela . . ." Bettina's voice trailed off as Shane shifted her attention to Pamela and her eyes widened.

"That's right," she exclaimed. "You were one of the people who organized the conference where he met his end, so I guess you thought you should be there. I hope it wasn't your idea to make him the keynote speaker at the conference."

"No!" Pamela hadn't meant to shout, but Shane didn't seem to find the reaction out of line. "I mean," Pamela went on, "the college arranged that part."

"Did you read his book?"

Pamela shook her head no.

"Don't bother!" Out of the corner of her eye, Pamela noticed that the women at the long tables had stopped work and were glaring at Shane. One of them made a shushing sound, but Shane ignored it. "Of course the spinning wheel wasn't the first wheel," she said, sounding as angry as if Pamela and Bettina had suggested the idea. "And anyway the spindle—duh!—came before the spinning wheel. And women probably invented the wheel anyway. Who did all the work? And kids to haul around? Just because a man writes something everybody takes it seriously. Even women. *Some* women. Not me. A woman without a man is like a fish without a bicycle."

"I guess you weren't at the luncheon then," Pamela offered.

Shane snorted. "I had better things to do than listen to that pompous idiot. I wasn't even at the conference. I imagine you think I'm glad Critter is dead and I am. I only went to the reception because the food is usually good at faculty club affairs." She pushed back the edge of her tee-shirt sleeve and glanced at her watch. "So"—she gestured toward the long tables, ignoring the irritated glares of the women working at them—"what do you think, Bettina? Better than a husband and a dog and a cat underfoot?"

"I'm sure I could concentrate much better." Bettina nodded and set her earrings, bright Murano glass baubles, to swaying. "I'll confer with my editor about whether the *Advocate* can find some money in the budget."

"Whatever." Shane shrugged. "Let me know." She saw them off with firm handshakes and they retreated to the hall.

"Did we learn anything?" Pamela asked as they headed back toward the elevators.

"She *said* she wasn't at the conference," Bettina replied as she pushed the button that would summon an elevator, "but she could be lying—and besides she wouldn't have had to be at the conference to creep up on Sufficiency House from the back and poison what was left of the coffee in the dispenser."

A low chime alerted them to the elevator's arrival. As the doors open and they prepared to step in, a voice called, "Hold it, please."

Hurrying around the corner was a woman who had been sitting at one of the long tables in the workspace. She was carrying a pack of cigarettes. Pamela reached out to hold the elevator door.

"Horrible habit, I know," the woman said as she joined them in the elevator. "And I'm just as glad we can't smoke in there, but sometimes you just need a cigarette, even if you have to go outside."

Bettina offered a sympathetic smile, which encouraged the woman to further conversation.

"Shane's a pain in the neck," she said, "but Critter shot down every grant proposal she ever submitted—just because she's a woman, I'm sure. She's made it pretty clear she couldn't be happier that he's dead. The next person in line to head that committee has got to be an improvement."

They reached the first floor and the elevator doors began to open. But before the woman, who had already extracted a cigarette from her pack, stepped out, Bettina suddenly blurted, "Maybe she killed him."

"Not a chance," the woman replied. "She was otherwise occupied last Saturday afternoon. If you want to know how, ask the super." She winked and looked at her own watch, then she sped across the lobby.

The elevator doors began to close and Pamela reached for the button that would open them. But as she did so she noticed that next to the button labeled B for basement was an embossed plastic strip that read SUPER'S OFFICE.

"Shall we?" Pamela said.

Bettina nodded. Pamela pushed the button for the basement and the elevator doors whooshed closed again. When they opened, Pamela and Bettina stepped out into a linoleum-floored hallway with many doors. One was labeled FURNACE, another LAUNDRY, and some were unmarked. Straight ahead, however, was a door labeled SUPER.

"Ask the super," the woman had said. But how to phrase the question?

As Pamela was mulling this over, the super's door opened

and a man who resembled a heavily tattooed Viking emerged, brawny and monumental, with blondish-red hair and a matching beard. His lips parted in a genial, wide-mouthed smile and he bowed slightly.

"I don't see laundry," he chuckled, "so I don't think you're looking for the laundry room. And I don't think you're from the exterminator, though I can't be sure. Women can do anything they want these days, can't they?"

Pamela barely had time to murmur yes before he continued.

"My mom was a tough woman. I guess that rubbed off on me. She's still tough, down in Mexico right now, on her own in an RV. I'll make it down there someday myself. Have to learn the language first." He raised a huge hand, stroked his beard, and chuckled again. "Come to think of it, the exterminator sent a lady once. She did a good job too, very careful. But that's not surprising. Women like things to be clean, cleaner than men. I'm a slob, I confess."

He paused for an instant, reiterated that he was a slob, then said, "I talk too much too. I know that. It gets lonely down here though, and I'm a friendly guy, as you can see. I was raised that way. And I . . ."

Pamela hated to interrupt people, but perhaps this man was used to being interrupted. How would the apartment building's inhabitants resolve their difficulties with clogged drains, balky windows, or toilets that refused to stop running unless they were willing to cut into one of his monologues?

She took a deep breath, but just then a chime indicated the arrival of the elevator. Before the doors were fully open, a voice cried, "Take me, lover man!" and a moment later Shane Bennett was revealed. She had flung off a long smock that now dragged on the floor, and she was wearing only thong panties and a lacy bra, bright orange.

Catching sight of Pamela and Bettina, she scurried through the super's door. He followed and closed the door behind him.

"I guess she has an alibi," Bettina observed after she managed to stop laughing. They were standing on the sidewalk in front of the building. "He *was* kind of hunky, I must say, though he certainly liked to talk." En route to her car, she added, "I could never see how those thong panties could be all that comfortable."

Soon they were approaching one of Haversack's main thoroughfares, Water Street, which met up with the east-west route that would take them across the Haversack River and back to Arborville. Bettina maneuvered into the left lane as they neared the intersection and clicked on her turn signal.

Pamela had been mulling over their recent adventure, not really paying attention as Bettina drove through a neighborhood of apartment buildings similar to the one they had just left and then past a cluster of storefronts that included a dry cleaner, a nail salon, and restaurant offering pizza slices for one dollar. But she spoke up when the light changed to green and Bettina swung the Toyota's steering wheel to the left.

"Isn't Arborville the other way?" she said. "Where are we going?"

Bettina waited until she had made the turn and merged

with traffic speeding along the bank of the Haversack. "You'll see," she responded, her eyes on the road but her teasing smile obviously meant for Pamela.

Up ahead, an overpass routed Water Street over an expressway, but instead of remaining on Water Street, Bettina swerved toward the expressway's west-bound entry ramp.

"Bettina!" Pamela stared at her friend. The teasing smile had not abated. "Where are we going?"

"You'll see," Bettina repeated.

The answer became clear soon enough, as Bettina braved an encroaching van to make a daring lane change and Pamela realized they were en route to the mall.

"An early Christmas present," Bettina explained as, several minutes later, she pulled into a space in the multi-level parking garage closest to the mall's fanciest department store.

"*Very* early," Pamela murmured.

"Humor me." Bettina reached around to collect her purse from the backseat, opened her door, and climbed out of the Toyota.

"Are you coming?" she inquired as she opened the passenger-side door and waited for Pamela to join her in the cavernous parking structure. They walked past rows and rows of cars, footfalls and revving motors echoing around them, toward the bank of heavy glass doors that opened into the mall.

Once they were inside, Bettina veered to the right and they found themselves among counters bathed in a fluorescent brightness, offering perfumes and cosmetics packaged like priceless treasures. A hint of fragrance hung in the air. Bettina lingered for a few moments to examine a display of lipstick, like glossy crayons in colors from palest pink to deep burgundy. Then they were on their way again, heading for the escalator to the second floor.

The ride gave a birds-eye view of departments devoted to handbags and shoes, and it delivered them to a space dominated by racks—racks of trousers, of jackets, of blouses and shirts. Interspersed with the racks were tables, stacked with neatly folded sweaters in the subtle tones that implied natural fibers. Underfoot, carpeting muffled the sounds of browsing shoppers.

"We want 'Better Dresses,'" Bettina announced, steering Pamela past a trio of mannequins garbed in wide-legged wool pants and matching cashmere turtlenecks. In a few moments, Pamela was watching as Bettina scooted hangers along a metal rack, examining one dress after another and occasionally glancing toward Pamela.

"Size 10, I suppose," she commented at one point, "but different labels fit differently. You can't know for sure until you try it on."

She continued examining dresses, now and then lifting a hanger from the rack and raising it aloft to study a dress more closely. Pamela so far had not seen anything she could imagine wearing. Some dresses featured large and colorful prints, while others had curious details like over-size collars, sleeves that puffed out at the shoulders, or peplums.

"Maybe black," Bettina murmured as if talking to herself. "It's a good color on her and she can use it for funerals."

She backed away from the rack that had been occupying her attention and turned around to survey the other possibilities offered by "Better Dresses." A circular rack rather like a carousel was hung with garments in more sedate hues. Without consulting Pamela, she darted across the carpeting and seized a hanger near the plastic ring showing that dresses in that section of the rack were size 10.

Pamela reached her side as she held the dress out to study the front. Before speaking, she twisted the hanger around to show the back. It was a simple sheath in a medium-weight fabric, black, with a V neck and sleeves that were neither long nor short.

"You could really wear it all year round." Bettina turned toward Pamela and lifted the hanger so that the dress's shoulders lined up with those of its prospective wearer. "Except maybe in the middle of summer."

Pamela reached for the price tag but Bettina swatted her hand away. "An early Christmas present," she said. "Remember?" She took a few steps toward a doorway with a sign that indicated it led to dressing rooms. "Let's go try it on."

The dressing room was carpeted and spacious, with three mirrors, hooks for garments waiting to be tried on, and a small upholstered bench. The dress fit, and Pamela found herself contemplating the image, reflected from three different angles, of an attractive woman in a chic black sheath that seemed made to order for her slender but shapely figure.

Bettina's voice reached her from the hallway that served the dressing rooms. "I want to see," she called. "Come out."

Pamela emerged, feeling self-conscious, to be greeted by Bettina's enthusiastic applause.

"We'll get it," she said, "but you have to . . ." She approached Pamela and seized a few locks of hair in each hand. "You have to put your hair up to show off your long neck." She tried to lift the hair she had seized and pile it atop Pamela's head, but she wasn't tall enough. "You do it," she said, letting go of the hair and stepping back.

A very large mirror at the end of the hallway gave shoppers an additional chance to study their selections. Pamela turned toward the mirror and obediently gathered her hair into a loose ponytail, then held it atop her head with one hand while she let the other fall to her side.

"Very glamorous," Bettina said with a satisfied smile.

The figure in the mirror did look glamorous. The simple dress was a far cry from Madame X's ball gown, with its daring bare-shouldered décolletage, but Pamela's skin seemed paler and almost luminous, set off as it was by the dark hair and the darker dress. And the upswept hair and deep V-neck emphasized the elegant contour of cheek and chin.

"Yes," Bettina repeated. "Very glamorous. Merry Christmas!"

Pamela returned to the dressing room, slipped the dress off, and handed it out to Bettina. By the time she had changed back into her jeans and blouse and joined Bettina among the racks and tables of the sales floor, the dress had been paid for, swathed in tissue, and tucked into a large shopping bag bearing the name of the department store in flowing script.

"Come for dinner tomorrow night," Bettina said as she handed Pamela the shopping bag, which she had retrieved from the trunk of the Toyota. They were standing in Bettina's driveway.

Pamela laughed. "So you can cross examine me about my date?"

"I *will* be curious, of course. In fact, I might drop by tomorrow morning." Bettina accompanied the admission with a teasing close-mouthed smile. "But besides that, we have things to discuss. About the case."

"I think we've established that Shane didn't do it." Pamela set the shopping bag on the asphalt and grasped the pinkie of her left hand with the thumb and index finger of her right.

Bettina nodded, setting the tendrils of her scarlet hair in motion. "The Saturday afternoon tryst with the hunky super appears to be a regular thing, based on what that woman in the elevator told us."

"There's still Yvonne." She moved on to grasp her ring finger.

"Who won't be back at her farmers market stall till Tuesday," Bettina added. "But Bitsy"—she reached out to touch Pamela's middle finger—"works in the Fine and Professional Arts office at Wendelstaff and will be there Monday."

Pamela stooped to retrieve the bag. "Thank you," she murmured as she pulled Bettina into a one-armed hug.

"Be sure to put your hair up," Bettina reminded her as she set out across the street, "and wear those sparkly earrings I gave you a few years ago."

CHAPTER 15

"What's the occasion?" Brian Delano spoke from the porch, surveying Pamela from head to toe as she stood in the doorway of her house.

"I . . . we . . ." Pamela felt an unaccustomed blush rising. Was she overdressed? Had she allowed Bettina to talk her into an outfit completely unsuited to the evening Brian had planned?

The next thing she knew, he was laughing. "Pamela," he said, "you look terrific! I was teasing and I shouldn't have."

He wasn't a tease, actually, and that was one of the things she liked about him. And he wasn't a flirt either, not even with her, at least if flirting implied something you did to call attention to how opposite the opposite sex was.

Catrina had ventured to the threshold to inspect the caller and Brian stooped to give her a sociable head-scratch. "Shall we be off?" he asked when he was once more upright. A few minutes later they had taken their seats in his well-cared-for Saab and were heading for Arborville Avenue.

"Things getting back to normal?" he inquired as he waited for a break in the traffic to make his turn.

"Pretty much." Pamela nodded. She had followed Bettina's instructions and worn the earrings—dangly, sparkly creations that reminded her of miniature chandeliers— and the unfamiliar sensation of earrings brushing against her neck was curious. She had put her hair up too, happy that messy buns were in fashion, because the best she'd been able to manage was to gather it, twist it, fold it back on itself, and secure it with a big clip.

"On the campus too—though there are still people who want to rehash the whole thing at the drop of a hat. Mostly people who are glad he's gone—it's like they feel justice has been done. Somebody put a stake through the monster's heart." Brian chuckled, pulled forward, and made a swift left turn. They were heading for the big intersection by the Co-Op, where the cross street led to the ramp for the George Washington Bridge.

"Was he really a monster?" Pamela asked.

"Critter could be a very cruel guy." Brian's tone had become more serious. "I was surprised Dermott Sparr came to the funeral—he's that grad student I introduced you to at the reception. Of course, maybe he just wanted to make sure Critter was really dead."

"What had he done to Dermott?" Pamela asked.

"Completely demoralized him, last spring when the design students presented their end-of-term projects. The projects are critiqued by panels made up of faculty, other grad students, professionals from the design world. Critter was assigned to the panel for Derm's presentation. He tore the project to shreds in this kind of snotty, witty way of his. He even had the rest of the panel laughing. Derm told me he almost didn't come back this term."

"What was Derm's project like?"

"His work is kind of unusual," Brian said. "He does weird things with food, like woven spaghetti and blue mashed potatoes. He wanted to do a workshop on woven food for the conference, but Critter shot that down too. Derm's an industrious guy though, and really committed to his ideas. Some of our grad students are at Wendelstaff on fellowships and some have rich parents. But Derm is working his way through as a resident advisor in the dorms."

They had reached the ramp for the bridge, and Brian was silent as he joined the small procession creeping toward the ramp's head. Once there, he waited for a break in the traffic and after a minute slipped in behind a convertible. Soon they were in one of the many lanes hurtling toward the gaping row of toll booths. Brian edged leftward and then leftward again, aiming for another ramp that veered off to the side and up.

"I like the upper level," he said by way of explanation. "The view is much better."

It was true. Once they were through the toll booth, the sensation was almost like flying, with the roadbed an arcing curve ahead and the darkening sky above. The view upriver was of the river widening between bluffs and green shores. In the other direction, pinpricks of light had begun to decorate the jagged skyline of the city.

The view of the city, mutually enjoyed, led to recollections on Brian's part of growing up in New Jersey with Manhattan so close—pilgrimages at Christmas with his parents and then the heady fun of taking the bus in with his high-school friends. Pamela's recollections led inevitably to mention of the husband with whom she had shared her first experiences of the city. They had moved there together after college.

"I'm so sorry," Brian said. "I can't imagine . . . and . . ."—he paused as if the sudden tightness that had seized her throat was afflicting him too—"well, I just can't imagine."

Silence seemed appropriate for a bit then. It was Pamela who broke it, lest Brian worry he had been responsible for awaking a memory that would cast a pall over the evening to come.

"I liked the painting your friend's gallery used for the flyer," she said. "Madame X, I think, but in a black bikini."

"You got the joke!" Brian sounded pleased. "I don't know if everyone who sees his work knows what he's up to."

"Two semesters of art history in college," Pamela said. "From the Egyptians to Andy Warhol. Do all your friend's paintings in this show make secret references to old, and not-so-old, masters?"

"I don't know." Brian laughed. "We'll find out. If so, we can have a contest to see who recognizes the most."

"The loser pays for dinner?" Pamela laughed too.

"No. That's my treat."

By this time, the Saab was cruising slowly down one of the narrow streets that led into the heart of SoHo, bumping over cobblestones and stopping at every corner to check for cross traffic. Darkness had fallen, and bright shop windows beckoned. In some, mannequins modeled clothes whose simplicity testified to their expense, while other windows displayed artful arrangements of gourmet food or luxurious items for the toilette.

Brian leaned forward, peering not at the shop windows but at the unbroken row of parked cars lining the curb. "Sometimes," he muttered, more to himself than to Pamela, "sometimes there are places around this corner at night because the block is reserved for deliveries till six." He swung the steering wheel to the right and whispered "Hurrah!" as a long stretch of empty curb came into view.

A few minutes later, he had eased the Saab into a spot a few feet from the corner and joined Pamela on the narrow sidewalk. "Down this way," he said, directing her with a gentle hand on her back.

The destination was clear once they reached the end of the block and turned once again. People were converging on an entrance several doors down, couples and groups walking across the cobbled street into the cone of light cast by the streetlamp that illuminated the bold sign: Stone Gallery.

Inside, people milled about in a large space whose pale wood floor and pale walls upstaged neither the art nor those contemplating it. Ensembles ranged from studiously rumpled to aggressively chic, often styled so as to show off tattoos. Grooming choices involved eye-catching hairstyles or hair colors, or sometimes no hair at all.

The art was more colorful than the clothes, which tended toward black. Even a cursory glance from the doorway indicated that Stretch Taggart's current show focused on portraits of women. Conversations punctuated by laughter echoed around the room as a ragged procession made its way from one painting to another.

"Hey, Bri!" a hearty voice called from amid a cluster of people standing near a bar in an alcove off to the side. The owner of the voice detached himself from the cluster and advanced toward them, edging around a newly arrived couple. He was a burly man with shaggy hair and a shaggy beard, both ginger-colored but laced with gray.

"Stretch!" Brian reached out to grasp the offered hand and then clapped the man on the shoulder for good measure. He glanced around the room and added, "You got a good crowd." Reaching out to draw her forward, he said, "Pamela, this is Stretch Taggart. Stretch, Pamela Paterson."

"Well, well, well." Stretch studied her for a long moment and she felt the social smile she had mustered begin to falter.

Brian noticed her discomfort and interceded with a quick, "How are sales?"

"Not bad, not bad. A few are spoken for already. Interested?"

"I can't afford you." Brian said good-naturedly.

"We could make a deal." Stretch winked at Pamela. Then, with a "Great to meet you," he was off, shouldering his way through the crowd to greet another new arrival.

"How about a glass of bad wine?" Brian asked after he was gone. "That's always part of the gallery experience when a new show opens."

Pamela nodded and started to follow him as he took a few steps toward the alcove that housed the bar.

"There's kind of a mob," he observed. In fact the bar itself was barely visible, hidden by the press of bodies. "No point in both of us getting squashed," he added. "White?"

Pamela nodded again. Left alone, she edged toward the wall. A lively group of viewers had just moved away from the nearest painting, making it possible to get a good look, and she swiveled around to focus on it more attentively.

"*Girl with a Pearl Earring*," she said to herself. "Maybe." The image was of a lovely woman, very fair, with her head turned at a sharp angle to stare out from the canvas. She looked startled and wary, as if her attention had been summoned from an unexpected direction.

But whereas Vermeer's subject wore a headdress of elegantly draped silk, this young woman's hair, which was pale blonde, had been shorn into a buzz cut that made it nearly invisible. And the pearl earring had become a disturbing fang-like object that seemed to impale her ear lobe.

Pamela was trying to recall other details of Vermeer's painting when a voice behind her said, "Pamela Paterson?"

She turned to find a woman staring at her, a very attractive woman. The deep burgundy hue of her slender dress set her olive complexion aglow, and her hair was pulled back and up in a style that accented the fine modeling of her cheekbones.

She leaned closer. "It is Pamela, isn't it? I almost didn't recognize you."

Pamela *did* recognize *her*. The woman was Jocelyn Bidwell, the love interest to whom Richard Larkin had turned after Pamela spurned his advances—spurned them for reasons Pamela herself still didn't quite understand.

"Jocelyn," she said, trying for a smile. "Yes, it's me." Her encounters with Jocelyn had usually taken place when Pamela was doing yard work in her oldest pair of jeans or, even worse, collecting the newspaper in robe and slippers. No wonder the woman had been puzzled. "I guess you're a friend of Stretch?"

"Not me, exactly." Jocelyn smiled the smile that revealed her perfect teeth.

She twisted her head to glance toward the bar. Pamela followed the glance. A man had detached himself from the tangle of people seeking wine and, bearing a glass of wine in each hand, was making his way toward where Jocelyn and Pamela were standing. He was taller than almost everyone else in the room, a striking figure in narrow, dark pants and a dark shirt.

"I'm here with Richard," Jocelyn said.

Pamela and Richard had waved occasionally, as neighbors do, in the months that had passed since he had taken the hint and looked elsewhere. But now, seeing him so close, in the bright room, she struggled for a casualness befitting an unexpected encounter with a neighbor.

He noticed her when he was still halfway across the room. His face could look so stern, beneath the crop of dark blonde hair that was more often than not in need of a trim. For a moment, his expression was sterner still. Then, as if an inner voice had reminded him that a social encounter called for sociability, his features softened into a smile and he sped up to join them.

"Pamela," he said, focusing on her even before he delivered Jocelyn's wine. "You're here. Do you know Stretch?"

"No, I . . . my friend does." She glanced toward the bar, but there was no sign of Brian.

"You look . . . well." Richard's gaze was so intense that being its object was almost a physical sensation, and Pamela felt herself flush. After a long moment, he realized he was holding two glasses of wine and turned away to hand one to Jocelyn. He stared at the other, seeming flustered, then extended it toward Pamela. "Would you like this?" he inquired. "I remember . . . I think . . . you like white."

Pamela took a step back. "No, I . . . my friend went to the bar. It's, uh, very crowded."

"Yes, yes." Richard was studying the floor now. "Stretch got a good turnout. The gallery, uh . . . the gallery . . ." Looking a bit desperate, he raised his eyes to survey the room. "What do you think of the art?" he asked suddenly.

"I've only seen a few so far. It's so crowded . . ."

"Very." Richard nodded. "Yes, it is."

At this point, Jocelyn spoke, but not to either of them. "Why, Brian Delano," she cried. "What brings you here?"

Brian was advancing across the floor, dodging around chattering groups, intent on steadying the two glasses he carried. He raised his head when Jocelyn's greeting reached him.

"Jocelyn Bidwell!" he responded, his face transforming as his gentle smile eased the wolfishness of his handsome features. With a few long steps, he reached Pamela's side and handed her one of the glasses with a tongue-in-cheek bow. "Jocelyn Bidwell," he repeated. "How long has it been?"

"Two years, at least." She reached for Richard's arm, smiled up at him when he tipped his head in her direction, and said, "Richard, it seems Pamela and I both know Brian Delano." She waved a graceful hand toward Brian. "Brian, meet Richard Larkin."

Hands were shaken and pleasantries exchanged, Brian tilting his head to make eye contact with Richard, who towered over all three of his companions.

With glasses of wine in hand, conversation seemed the next logical step. As Pamela ransacked her brain for a topic suitable to the occasion and the company, Jocelyn came to the rescue—though it was with a question that Richard had already posed.

"What do you think of the art?" she inquired brightly.

Her eyes were on Pamela, so it was Pamela who responded. The gallery *was* crowded, with knots of milling people obscuring most of the paintings. But she'd seen one—or two if you counted the flyer.

"Stretch paid attention in art history class," she said. "His update of *Madam X* was on the gallery flyer, and I think *Girl with a Pearl Earring* is over there"—she pointed—"behind that woman in the purple caftan."

"You're one ahead of me!" Brian chuckled, then he explained the contest he had proposed on the drive over.

"Now that you mention it, I think I noticed *Naked Maja*—with her fleece bathrobe on the floor." Jocelyn chuckled too. "Stretch doesn't exactly glamorize his subjects." She paused for a sip of wine then went on, aiming the question at Brian. "Speaking of artistic impulses, how's your photography going?"

"I'm into poison ivy and garden pests," Brian said.

"His photos are good," Pamela contributed, and soon the conversation was flowing easily. It veered from photography to gardens, with Richard joining in to say that he'd had a lot to learn about gardening when he became a suburbanite and he was grateful to Pamela for her guidance. Brian asked Richard what he did for a living and for a few minutes the two men discussed architecture while Jocelyn inquired after Penny's likely career interests.

The crowd had begun to thin out and their wineglasses, now empty, had been collected by a young woman circulating with a tray. "Pamela and I still have pictures to look at," Brian commented. "Now's our chance." He glanced toward the wall to their left, where only a few people still lingered in front of paintings.

"We've done the circuit." Jocelyn rested one hand on

Richard's arm and seized Brian's hand with the other. "This was a treat," she said, "catching up. Let's not lose touch again." She leaned forward and kissed him on the cheek. "And Pamela"—she turned and tilted her head at a pretty angle—"you're right next door to Richard. We should chat more often."

Brian and Richard ended their encounter as it had begun, with a handshake, but Richard's parting words were addressed to Pamela. "I'm right next door," he said, the expression in his eyes hard to read. "Don't forget that, if you ever need anything." He and Jocelyn made their way toward the exit and joined the small procession flowing out onto the cobblestoned street.

"Interesting guy," Brian commented as he and Pamela turned in the other direction and advanced toward a large portrait whose subject resembled an unkempt *Mona Lisa*.

"He's my neighbor," Pamela said. "I guess you got that. And my daughter is friendly with his daughters, though they don't live with him. Where do you know Jocelyn from?"

"We moved in the same circles." Brian's expression suggested he found the phrase a bit silly. He shrugged. "It was a long time ago."

Half an hour later they had completed their circuit of the room and were standing on the sidewalk outside the gallery comparing notes on the Old Master lookalikes they had identified. "The restaurant I have in mind is just around the corner," Brian said after a bit, and they set out down the block.

It was nearly midnight by the time Brian pulled into Pamela's driveway. Dinner had been lovely, in a restau-

rant decorated to resemble a Parisian bistro, complete
with the day's menu specials listed on an expansive mirror that filled nearly the whole wall behind the bar. Afterwards they had walked and walked, enjoying the mild
September night and ending up in the Village for cannoli
and coffee at a small café.

In their end-of-date ritual Brian always circled around
the back of the car to open the passenger-side door and
reach for her hand. Now she waited, expecting to see him
bend toward her door handle. Instead, she heard his
voice, from the sidewalk, calling, "Hey! You look familiar!"

She waited a few moments, then pushed the door open
on her own and joined him on the sidewalk. He was facing Richard Larkin's driveway, where Richard Larkin's
olive-green Jeep Cherokee had apparently just discharged
its cargo. Richard and Jocelyn were standing behind the
Cherokee, cheerfully waving at Brian in the light from
the streetlamp.

"Pleasant evening?" he inquired.

"Very!" Jocelyn called back.

"Us too!" Brian reached out and drew Pamela close.

"Funny coincidence," Brian observed, "them getting
back at exactly the same time we did." With more waves,
Richard and Jocelyn headed for Richard's porch, where
Richard unlocked the door and they both disappeared inside.

Like Pamela's other dates with Brian, this one ended
with a kiss on Pamela's porch.

CHAPTER 16

The light was different. Unless the day was overcast, the white eyelet curtains at Pamela's bedroom windows usually glowed as the morning sun lit them from behind. But today, though the sun was shining, the curtains' glow was subdued. And from the hallway came a plaintive wail. Pamela rolled over to consult the clock on her bedside table. As she did so, two furry presences sharing the bed with her stirred.

She was shocked to discover that it was nearly ten a.m. So the sun was higher in the sky, rather than at the angle that set the curtains aglow. And the wail must be coming from Precious, who preferred to sleep alone, downstairs. She flopped onto her back. Why Catrina and Ginger hadn't made their desire for breakfast known was a mystery, unless they too had spent a restless night and been unaware of how late it had become.

At the very moment this question occurred to her, she found herself looking into a pair of amber eyes. Catrina's head, lustrous with black fur, had popped out from beneath the bedclothes and her gaze was accusing. In a moment Catrina was joined by Ginger.

With a groan, Pamela eased the bedclothes aside, sat up, and swung her feet onto the floor. One would have thought that a bedtime well past the usual time would have resulted in a sleep rapid of onset and refreshingly deep. But the reverse had been the case. She had been haunted by the vision of Richard matter-of-factly escorting Jocelyn through his front door.

Of course she had known that Jocelyn often spent the night. She had even seen Jocelyn retrieving the Sunday morning *Register* in robe and slippers infinitely more fetching than her own. But somehow, the juxtaposition—a goodnight kiss with Brian on the porch and then he was on his way—rankled. She suspected, and had suspected for a while, that Brian would be happy to make their relationship more . . . *intense.*

What was she waiting for? For Richard to realize that he'd made a mistake giving up on her so soon? Those looks he'd aimed at her in the gallery suggested he still felt something. And she'd felt something too, seeing him there.

She realized she'd been staring at the floor as two hungry cats milled about her feet and another complained from the hallway. She blinked a few times, shook herself, and rose. Slippers on feet and robe tugged over pajamas, she opened the door and proceeded, trailing cats, down the stairway.

Cats were the first order of business. Murmuring apologies, she opened a large can of crab-salmon medley. A double portion went into the large bowl that Catrina and Ginger shared, and a single portion went into the small bowl that belonged to Precious alone. Once they were contentedly eating, and provided with fresh water, she stepped into the entry.

Peering through the lace that curtained the oval window in the front door, she scanned the sidewalk. Sunday morning meant people arriving for services at the church next door. An eight a.m. dash for the newspaper in robe and slippers was an accepted suburban ritual, but now it was past ten. No one was in sight, however, so Pamela opened the door, dashed across the porch, hopped down the steps, and sped toward the grassy strip between sidewalk and street where the paper lay.

Before she reached it, however, her attention was captured by a voice calling, "Pamela! Pamela!"

Bettina stepped off her porch, waving. She rushed down her driveway and darted across the street, greeting Pamela again when she reached her side. Surveying her from head to foot and then studying her face more closely, she said, "It's not like you to be in robe and pajamas this time of day." The beginnings of a teasing smile appeared. "I guess you had a late night."

Bettina herself was already dressed, in leggings and a tunic, both a vivid shade of turquoise.

"It was a lovely evening," Pamela responded primly. She stooped to collect the newspaper.

"I'll bet you haven't even had breakfast yet." Without waiting for an answer, Bettina went on. "Wilfred's already been out, and he came back with crumb cake. Get the coffee started—I'll be right over. Leave the door open."

Returning to her kitchen, Pamela set water boiling in

the kettle, measured coffee beans into the grinder, set the plastic filter cone atop the carafe, and fitted the cone with a paper filter. The clatter of coffee beans whirring in the grinder blotted out the sound of Bettina's arrival, and Pamela turned in response to the kettle's whistle to find Bettina standing by the table. In the center of the table, next to the *Register*, which was still sheathed in its plastic wrapper, was a white bakery box fastened with string.

While Pamela tipped the kettle over the filter cone and inhaled the coffee-scented steam, Bettina fetched wedding-china cups, saucers, and plates from the cupboard and arranged them on the table. As the coffee brewed and the rich aroma spread through the kitchen, Pamela transferred the cut-glass sugar bowl and cream pitcher to the table, and Bettina supplied the pitcher with a large dollop of heavy cream from the carton in the refrigerator. Forks, spoons, and napkins were added, and moments later the two friends took their seats opposite one another with steaming cups of coffee before them.

"Tell me everything," Bettina commanded, leaning toward Pamela. So eager was she for details of the date with Brian that she hadn't even added sugar or cream to her coffee yet, or opened the box containing the crumb cake.

"The art was very interesting," Pamela said, "but the gallery was incredibly crowded. Afterwards we walked around the corner to a restaurant that was like a Parisian bistro and I had lamb chops. Then we walked up to the Village for coffee and cannoli."

Bettina slapped the table and the coffee cups clattered against their saucers. "That's not what I mean!" she exclaimed. "What did he say? What did he do? Did he like your dress?"

Pamela reached for a bit of string that trailed from the bow on top of the bakery box. She tugged and the string loosened.

"Are you ready for crumb cake yet?" she inquired, lifting the flap that formed the box's cover and peering inside. "It's been ages since we had any." She jumped up. "I'll get a knife."

Bettina sighed and pulled the sugar bowl closer. She added sugar to her coffee, and then cream, until she had achieved the desired sweetness and pale mocha shade. Meanwhile Pamela cut portions from the generous square of crumb cake in the box and transferred them to the plates.

Bettina was, thankfully, silent as they sampled the crumb cake, breaking the silence only to comment that it was as good as ever. Pamela agreed. The buttery cake layer, with its slight hint of lemon, was perfectly accented by the rich and even more buttery cinnamon crumble topping. And she enjoyed the way her own coffee, which she preferred black, enhanced the sweetness of the sweet treat.

After several bites of cake, interspersed with sips of coffee, Bettina set down her fork. She watched for a long minute as Pamela continued to feast, teasing off bites of crumb cake and raising them to her mouth, following up with swallows of coffee. Finally she said, "That's all you have to say then? The art was interesting and the gallery was crowded and you ate lamb and cannoli? What about the dress? No compliments?"

Pamela set her fork down too. "I think we have a new suspect," she said.

"What?" Bettina leaned forward, her eyes widening.

"Remember that graduate student Brian introduced us to at the reception? Dermott Sparr?"

"I do." Bettina nodded.

"Brian said he hated Dr. Critter."

"Hmmm." Bettina's eyes grew wider. "Why?"

Pamela recounted what Brian had told her about Critter savaging Dermott's end-of-term presentation, to the point that Dermott almost dropped out of his graduate program. "So Dermott definitely has a motive," she concluded.

"I would say so." Bettina nodded again, more forcefully. Her earrings were turquoise pendants set in silver and they continued swaying long after her head was still.

"And not only does he have a motive"—Pamela raised a finger, like a lecturer making an important point—"he also does weird things with food."

"Like what?" Bettina wrinkled her nose.

"It's part of his art, Brian said. Things like woven spaghetti and blue mashed potatoes." Pamela shrugged. "There actually *are* blue potatoes, so all he would have to do is mash them but the effect could be artistic. I suppose he researches the foods he works with. So maybe he knows about poison foods—rhubarb *leaves* are poison, for example, but not the stems."

Bettina chimed in. "He's a student at Wendelstaff so he's probably familiar with the layout of Sufficiency House and its grounds."

Her coffee was getting cold, but Pamela was growing more and more excited as she realized how likely it was that Dermott could be the person responsible for Critter's death.

"And one more thing"—she raised her finger again—"Brian said Dermott wanted to offer a workshop at the conference, but Dr. Critter turned his topic down."

"Awful man," Bettina interjected.

"Dermott probably had a good sense of the conference schedule though—since he had wanted to be part of it," Pamela said. "So . . . motive, means, and opportunity." She raised three fingers.

Bettina pulled the bakery box toward her and raised the flap. "I'd have a little more," she murmured. "How about you?"

"No—but help yourself." Pamela pushed the knife across the table.

"And . . . is there . . . ?" Bettina peered into her coffee cup.

"Yes, there is"—Pamela rose—"but it needs to be warmed up."

As Pamela stood at the stove watching the carafe for the tiny bubbles that would indicate the contents were enjoyably drinkable again, Bettina sliced off another portion of crumb cake and settled it onto her plate.

A few minutes later, Pamela was back in her seat. Bettina's coffee cup had been refilled and the dregs in her own revived with a large splash of steaming brew.

"So," Bettina said, pausing a forkful of crumb cake halfway to her mouth, "we definitely have to figure out what Dermott Sparr was doing the afternoon of the conference. If he has an alibi, we cross him off the list. If not . . ."

"If not, what?" Pamela regarded Bettina over the rim of her coffee cup.

"I'll slip a word to Clayborn. I know the police interviewed a lot of Critter's Wendelstaff colleagues, but I doubt Clayborn's suspicions extended to the student body." The crumb cake continued on its trajectory, Bettina's lips parted to receive it, and for a few moments she was occupied with chewing.

"We should follow up with those other people too," Pamela said, "starting with Bitsy Daniels in the Fine and Professional Arts office tomorrow. And while we're on the campus, we'll see if we can track Dermott down. Brian said he's a resident advisor in the dorms."

Bettina reached for her coffee cup. "And Tuesday we talk to Yvonne at the Newfield farmers market."

"What if we've decided Dermott or Bitsy is definitely the killer by then?" Pamela asked.

"We'll go to Newfield anyway," Bettina declared. "I want to get more of those good New Jersey peaches for my homemade ice cream."

"Speaking of New Jersey produce . . ." Pamela swiveled around to wave toward the bowl of tomatoes on the counter behind her.

"Beautiful," Bettina sighed.

"And I've still got a lot of them out there, a few new ripe ones every day. So you'll take some, I hope."

"I certainly will."

Bettina was on her way soon after, carrying a small bag of Pamela's home-grown tomatoes. "We'll see you tonight at about six," she said before descending the steps and setting out down the front walk. "It gets dark earlier now but we'll have plenty of time to grill."

"I'll bring dessert," Pamela said.

Bettina turned. "Wilfred is getting more of that Timberley ice cream."

"I'll bring cookies then." Pamela waved her on her way.

It was getting on toward noon. After the crumb cake, she wouldn't want lunch for quite some time, and articles to be evaluated for *Fiber Craft* awaited upstairs on her computer. Pamela wasn't one to lounge in pajamas all day even though her home was her office, so before sitting down to work she changed into jeans and a casual blouse.

Seated at her computer, Pamela opened the Word document identified as "Seeing Red." The abbreviated title had titillated, suggesting perhaps a discussion of dyes or pigments. Now the full title, "Seeing Red: The Natural History of a Color," revealed that her supposition had been correct.

The author, who was a chemist by profession, surveyed the various means by which the color red had been achieved before the invention of aniline dye revolutionized fields as diverse as cloth-making, printing, and woodworking. Discussions of alizarin crimson, cochineal, cinnabar, rose madder, bloodroot, and much else were accompanied by drawings and photographs.

A detailed drawing showed the cochineal beetle—responsible for the distinctive magenta that enlivened so many Central and South American textiles—several times larger than life. Accompanying the drawing were photographs of the process by which the dye was extracted.

The next page contained photographs of plants—not as engaging as the beetle, but Pamela found herself staring at one photograph in particular: a low-growing plant with unusual seven-lobed leaves and pretty, multi-petaled white flowers. "*Sanguinaria canadensis*," the caption read, "Bloodroot."

It was one of the dye plants Flo had pointed out in the Sufficiency House garden, the dye that—as Pamela recalled—Flo had said she used to dye the yarn she was working with at the knitting bee. The plant hadn't had flowers when Flo pointed it out in the garden, but she had mentioned that when it bloomed in the spring the flowers were white and daisy-like.

Pamela scrolled back to reread the discussion of *Sanguinaria canadensis*. The dye is extracted from the plant's rhizome, the author had written, and—Pamela heard herself gasp—is highly poisonous. Had Dr. Critter's killer been able to source the poison from the garden of Sufficiency House itself?

CHAPTER 17

"What a coincidence Rick and Jocelyn were at that gallery show last night!" Wilfred had stepped away from tending the grill to greet Pamela, and now he lingered on the patio to chat before returning to his duties. Bettina was just emerging from the kitchen after depositing Pamela's gift of more oatmeal cookies on the pine table.

The sliding glass doors had been left open on this mild evening and Bettina paused in the doorway, her expression changing from relaxed sociability to amazement. "What?" Her voice scaled an octave. The next instant she was at Pamela's side, gripping her arm. "You and Brian ran into Richard and Jocelyn on your date?" She tilted her chin and stared into Pamela's eyes with an intensity that was startling. In the same piercing tone, she continued. "Why didn't you tell me?"

Pamela backed away—but Bettina required answers

when she got like this. "It appears you know," she said at last, "*now*. Or at least Wilfred knows."

"Oops!" Wilfred raised a hand to his mouth. "Have I let the cat out of the bag?"

Pamela nodded, trying not to frown. It was hard to be angry with Wilfred and, anyway, the damage had been done. It was water over the bridge, as he would say, in his characteristic garbling of that old saw. Clearly he hadn't seen the information as particularly noteworthy or he would already have told Bettina.

"I didn't know it was a secret," he said, looking so crestfallen that Pamela reached out to stroke his back.

"How did you even know?" Pamela tried to keep the irritation out of her voice.

"Rick was out in his yard when I was walking Woofus this afternoon. He mentioned it, just in passing. Not like it was a big deal."

"It wasn't," Pamela said. "It wasn't a big deal at all."

"Then why didn't you tell me?" Bettina wailed. The excitement that led to her outburst had faded, leaving her pale and mournful.

"It wasn't that interesting, really." Pamela reached for Bettina's hands and bent to look into her eyes, with their careful application of shadow and mascara. "They were there and we were there, and it turns out that Brian and Jocelyn know each other and—"

Bettina's eyes widened and she seemed on the verge of speaking, but instead her lips tightened as if by the sudden action of a drawstring. "I won't say it," she mumbled.

"Anyway"—Pamela stepped back—"I have something exciting to tell you." As Bettina's eyes grew even wider, Pamela hastened to add, "Not about my *date* . . ." (she couldn't help but find the term silly when applied to the activities of people in their forties) ". . . but about something I discovered this afternoon while I was reading an article for *Fiber Craft*."

Wilfred had crept away during this exchange. Now he stepped through the doorway between patio and kitchen bearing two tall glasses of beer, glowing golden and topped by an inch of creamy foam.

"Pamela"—he tipped his snowy head in a slight bow—"and dear wife, please have seats. The coals are ready and the shrimp will take barely any time at all."

Pamela accepted a beer but instead of sitting said, "Please let me help with something."

"The salads are made and the table is set," Wilfred responded, back to his genial self. "And too many cooks spoil the broth," He delivered the other beer to Bettina, who had already taken a seat, and returned to the kitchen.

Indeed, the table was set. Tonight Bettina had chosen a cloth that evoked the French countryside, pale green in the center but featuring a wide border patterned with fruit in tones of dark green, orange, and maroon. Atop the cloth were plates from her sage-green pottery set, accented with linen napkins that picked up the maroon of the cloth's border. A bowl of mixed nuts awaited nibblers.

"Come, Pamela." Bettina gestured toward the chair across from her. "Tell me the exciting thing. And have some nuts. They're not a fancy appetizer but they go so good with beer."

Wilfred emerged, followed by Woofus and carrying his own beer and a tray on which lay long skewers threaded with jumbo shrimp. He headed for the grill as Pamela told Bettina about "Seeing Red: The Natural History of a Color."

"And why is this exciting?" she concluded.

"Why?" Bettina asked obediently.

"Bloodroot!" Pamela said triumphantly. "Bloodroot is a dye plant. The root—or rhizome, technically—yields a red dye. It grows at Sufficiency House garden. We saw it there the day Flo gave us a garden tour to distract us from the fact that she had just emerged from a tryst in the shed."

Pamela paused for a refreshing sip of beer.

"She was knitting with red yarn at the knitting bee and she told me she had dyed it herself with bloodroot from the Sufficiency House garden. I didn't think anything of it at the time, but now that I've read the article . . ."

"Umm?" Bettina looked up from the nuts, to which she had been devoting her attention. "And this is exciting because . . . ?" She licked a bit of salt from her fingers.

"Because bloodroot is poisonous." Pamela smiled to herself as Bettina's bored expression transformed. "And Flo has access to it. And she's the one who served the coffee at the knitting bee."

"So she crushed the bloodroot rhizomes and put the juice in the coffee dispenser after it was delivered by the Wendelstaff food service people . . . ?" Bettina uttered the words slowly, as if figuring out the details as she spoke.

Pamela nodded. "But not until all the knitters had been served."

"But then what if somebody wanted a refill?" Bettina asked.

"I don't think anybody did, but anyway she could have waited till everyone had as much as they wanted and then put the juice in just before she knew Critter was going to show up."

"That all really makes sense." Bettina raised her beer glass in a toast.

Pamela raised her own. "Much more sense than someone coming in from outside at just the right moment." They both drank.

"There's just one thing." Bettina set her glass down. "Why would Flo want to kill Critter?"

The aroma of grilling shrimp, pungent with a marinade of lemon juice and garlic, had begun to drift across the lawn. "It's getting close," Wilfred called.

Bettina rose. "Wait till you see the beautiful salads he made," she said as she headed for the kitchen. Pamela started to get up. "No, no." Bettina waved her back. "Stay right here. Relax."

The Frasers' backyard was a relaxing spot. The patio, decorated with plants in colorful ceramic pots, looked out on a broad lawn bordered by exuberant shrubs and shaded by an ancient maple tree. Woofus lounged on the grass as Wilfred, wearing his apron and wielding his tongs, monitored the progress of his grilling shrimp.

After a few minutes, Bettina returned, bearing a bowl in each hand. Pamela moved the nuts aside and Bettina deposited the bowls in the center of the table. "You'll recognize your beautiful tomatoes," she said, pointing toward a clear glass bowl that Pamela knew was a piece of Bettina's favorite Swedish crystal.

"And corn!" Pamela exclaimed. "What a perfect combination!"

"Sweet corn is still in season," Bettina said. "Wilfred found some at the Co-Op. He was going to grill it, but we had corn on the cob last week when you were here. So when I came home with your tomatoes, he got this idea."

She pointed toward the bowl again. "There's avocado too, and some black beans. And those lacy little leaves are cilantro."

"And the other salad?" Pamela edged forward in her chair and bent toward an oval sage-green bowl. "Orzo?"

Bettina nodded. "With feta and Greek olives."

They were distracted from the salads by Wilfred's cheerful voice summoning them to the grill. "Bring the plates," he called. Pamela looked over to see him holding aloft a skewer threaded with a row of sizzling shrimp.

Pamela was the first to be served, but she waited on the grass as Wilfred coaxed shrimp off a second skewer and onto Bettina's plate. Woofus had risen from his napping position.

"Dear ladies," Wilfred said, after two now-empty skewers had been set aside, "please take your seats. I will be there shortly."

He lifted another skewer from the grill and slid two shrimp from it onto the tray that had transported the skewers from the kitchen before he turned to supplying his own plate.

"Yes," he said to Woofus. A subtle change in the angle of the dog's shaggy ears indicated his interest in the proceedings. "Yes, I think they're cool enough now."

He lifted a shrimp from the tray and extended it toward Woofus, who accepted it delicately and devoured it with a wuffling sound. The process was repeated with the second shrimp, and then Wilfred joined them at the table after a detour to the kitchen to fetch more beer.

Bettina urged Pamela to help herself to the salads, and after the pleasant hubbub of bowls and serving spoons passing from hand to hand, the three of them surveyed plates on which shrimp, seared rosy, nestled side by side with piles of olive-flecked orzo and the colorful medley of corn, tomatoes, beans, avocado, and cilantro.

Wilfred, in his element with ruddy cheeks and genial smile, bid them "Bon appétit!"

The shrimp were perfect, sweet and moist, tangy with lemon and garlic, but hinting at char from the grill. Though Pamela's reaction to her first bite had been a very audible "mmmm," Bettina was the first to speak.

"You have outdone yourself, Wilfred!" she exclaimed, spearing a whole shrimp with her fork and raising it aloft as if to display evidence of her claim. "And Pamela"— she shifted her gaze to Pamela—"the tomatoes are outstanding."

Each of Wilfred's salads was an inspired creation. The tomatoes balanced the sweetness of the corn kernels with a refreshing acidity, while the beans added a hearty texture. The avocado, which had been chosen at its peak of ripeness, felt buttery in the mouth. The orzo salad exploited the sharp and salty feta and the Greek olives to enliven the rice-like pasta shapes.

As they ate they chatted about town doings: Bettina would soon be writing her annual article for the *Advocate* on harvest time in the community gardens. The life drawing course the rec center had just begun offering was attracting controversy, given that it involved nude models. The grammar school attended by the Frasers' grandsons was recruiting a new principal to replace the thirty-year veteran retiring at the end of the spring term.

But as their hunger subsided and the act of eating required less focus, the conversation veered toward more demanding topics. When Wilfred announced from the grill that the shrimp were nearly done, Pamela and Bettina had set aside the question of why Flo might have wanted to kill Critter. Now Bettina revisited the issue, first summarizing for Wilfred what Pamela had told her about bloodroot, Flo's access to it, and her role in serving the coffee at the knitting bee's afternoon break.

"So," she concluded, "Flo had means and opportunity. But as far as we're aware, no connection with Critter that would make her want him dead."

"On the other hand," Pamela chimed in, "we know of two other women who had definite motives."

"The ex-wife and the ex-girlfriend," Wilfred supplied, and Pamela recalled that the three of them had sat at this same table exactly one week ago and discussed these two possible suspects. "Hell hath no fury like a woman scorned," Wilfred observed sagely.

"No definite access to bloodroot," Pamela noted, "though we don't know that that was the poison the killer used. But we think we've figured out the identity of the ex-girlfriend—"

"Not really girlfriend," Bettina corrected her, looking up from the plate on which she had just deposited a dollop of orzo salad. They'd long since emptied the other salad bowl. "More like seduced and abandoned. From what you overheard it didn't sound like Critter ever really cared for her at all." Her expression was as mournful as if she knew the woman and had been privy to her woes through the whole sad experience.

"I'm looking forward to talking to Bitsy tomorrow," Pamela said. "Once I hear her voice, I'll know for sure if she's the 'seduced and abandoned' we're looking for."

"And if she isn't?" Bettina inquired.

Pamela shrugged. "We'll keep looking. But we've got Yvonne to follow up with too, and now we've got Dermott, the blue mashed potato guy."

Always interested in new recipes, Wilfred raised his eyebrows and leaned forward. Pamela summarized what she knew of Dermott's food explorations.

"Sounds like fun," Wilfred said. "But what did he have against Critter?"

"Dr. Critter apparently didn't have as broad a sense of what constitutes food—or art," Pamela explained. "He was on the critique panel for Dermott's end-of-term project last spring. He tore the project apart in a very cruel way, and he rejected Dermott's proposal to do a workshop at the conference."

Wilfred smiled sadly. "Wounded pride could be a strong motivator, especially if the young man's academic success is at stake. But money is the root of all evil." He tipped his head toward Bettina. "Has Clayborn said anything more about that developer?"

"He hasn't said anything more to me about anything because he hasn't been taking my calls or responding to my emails," Bettina sighed. "I'm sure he's hiding from me because he hasn't figured anything out."

"You said you thought he was following up with the developer angle though . . ."

Bettina shrugged. "Perhaps there was no evidence to connect the developer with Sufficiency House on the day it happened." She scooped up a forkful of orzo salad, the last dab left on her plate.

Sitting on the patio as dusk fell and eating dessert by candlelight had provided a lovely climax to many a summer barbecue hosted by the Frasers. "Shall I clear away?" Pamela asked, rising. She smiled at Wilfred. "Bettina said there would be ice cream for dessert . . ."

Bettina's smile was directed at Pamela. "And cookies." She joined Pamela in the task of clearing. But as they worked, the pleasant evening breeze stiffened. Woofus lumbered across the grass and disappeared indoors, and after a brief debate, the three humans followed him.

A short time later, they had decamped to the Frasers' living room, Wilfred and Bettina on the comfy sofa and Pamela in one of the comfy armchairs that faced it across the coffee table. Bright cushions covered in hand-woven textiles accented the room's sage-green and tan color scheme. The room's welcoming atmosphere was enhanced by the aroma of the coffee Wilfred had brewed while Bettina was spooning out ice cream and Pamela was arranging her oatmeal cookies on a pretty tray.

"They do make delicious ice cream at that shop," Bettina commented, cradling a small bowl in one hand and plying a spoon with the other. "I don't know why I'm so determined to make my own, but I just think it would be fun to start with fresh peaches and see it come together."

The ice cream Wilfred had brought home from the Timberley shop this time was pineapple—not like sherbet though. It was rich and creamy, pale yellow with strands of fresh-tasting pineapple running through it.

Pamela set her empty bowl on the coffee table and reached for another cookie. She'd ignored her coffee while she ate her ice cream. It had been steaming fresh from the carafe when Wilfred served it and now it was just the right temperature for pleasant sipping.

Bettina and Wilfred had reached the stage of sipping coffee and nibbling on cookies too, and for a bit the three friends sat in contented silence.

Wilfred raised his coffee cup to his lips and tipped his head back to drain the last drops. As if the small jolt of caffeine had stirred something in his brain, he suddenly spoke.

"I drove past the turnoff for Sufficiency House on my way to the ice cream shop," he said. "That's a very tempting piece of land there along County Road, and the two houses near the corner whose yards back up to the Sufficiency House property are completely derelict. Judging by what else is along there, the zoning permits large apartment buildings. I can see why a developer would be interested."

The following morning, Pamela's doorbell chimed at exactly ten a.m. She hurried down the stairs, collected her purse from the chair in the entry, and stepped outside to join Bettina on the porch.

"My car or yours?" Bettina inquired. She had dressed for their visit to the Wendelstaff campus in a linen fit-and-flare dress, summery in its fabric and style, though its color evoked the rusty amber of autumn leaves. She had accessorized it with a chunky gold necklace and matching earrings, and on her feet were wedge heels in a burgundy tone.

"I pictured us trudging all over the campus," she explained, extending a foot to display one of the shoes.

"They look very comfortable." Pamela nodded. "But why don't I drive, so you don't have to walk back across the street?"

"Are you teasing me?" Bettina was en route to the steps, but she glanced over her shoulder to see if Pamela's expression betrayed a lack of seriousness.

"Of course not," Pamela assured her.

"Just because I don't tramp all over town wearing Birkenstocks . . ." Bettina muttered in her own version of a tease as they made their way toward Pamela's service-able compact.

Soon they were on their way, cruising toward County Road at the bottom of the block and then heading north, skirting the nature preserve to the west and chatting about the previous evening.

"I'm thinking maybe we inquire about Dermott first," Pamela said as they neared the cross street that would lead to the campus. "We might not find him right away, but since he's a resident advisor he probably has to post a notice somewhere saying when he's available."

"Where do we inquire?" Bettina asked.

"There are dorms at both ends of the campus," Pamela said. "Those low buildings south of the student union and that newer tall building by the main parking lot. But there's probably an office somewhere that handles the de-tails that go into managing them."

"Maybe it's in the tall building," Bettina suggested. "That would put it closer to where most of the students are. Those buildings at the other end don't look like they hold very many people."

"Good point," Pamela agreed. "We'll start there."

They were approaching the neighborhood where Suf-ficiency House was located, coming up on the street with the two derelict houses whose lots backed up to it. Bet-tina bent her neck and looked past Pamela to study the passing scene.

"There's that big apartment building," she observed, "facing County Road. And I can see how if that devel-oper, Brad Scott, was able to get his hands on those two run-down houses around the corner—probably easy—and then buy Sufficiency House, he'd have a nice big par-cel of land to build more apartment buildings."

"But you don't think Clayborn is following up on him as a suspect," Pamela said.

Bettina shrugged. "No evidence he actually did anything. You know, those crimes where somebody just sets out to harm random people are the hardest to solve. Like those people who put poison in jars of whatever and then put the jars back on store shelves."

Dermott Sparr, they learned from the campus housing office, would be on call in his dorm room from two to four p.m. that afternoon, and every Monday, Wednesday, and Friday afternoon for the rest of the term. And his room was not in the big new residence hall but rather in one of the older buildings by the student union, Room 4, Unit 3, to be exact.

It was now ten thirty. Accordingly, Pamela and Bettina set out across the campus to address the other item on their to-do list: determining whether Bitsy Daniels was indeed the seduced and abandoned woman they were looking for.

CHAPTER 18

They strolled across the quad, nearly deserted now with most students in class, and past the brick building with the white columns. A turn to the right and a few steps along a concrete walk brought into view the modern façade of their destination. They continued along the walk, climbed the building's broad stairs, crossed the sunny foyer, and entered the wide hallway that led into the building's heart.

Pamela recalled the route they'd taken with Brian and then again on their own, and she led them through the twists and turns that delivered them to the door with a plaque reading "Office of Fine and Professional Arts." The office they stepped into was just as Pamela recalled it—the white walls were hung with abstract prints and it was furnished with a modern-looking metal desk and chairs.

But in place of the slender young man with tattoos they had spoken with on their last visit, they found a woman, far from slender and well advanced in middle age. The desk chair had been pushed aside and she was standing. Just visible from Pamela's vantage point near the doorway, a foot wearing a red sock and a sneaker protruded from beneath the desk.

"Okay, Bitsy," came a man's voice, "the printer should work now. I think you kicked the power strip with your foot, but I plugged everything back in."

The woman—Bitsy Daniels, evidently—stepped aside and the man crawled out from under the desk. He stood up and Pamela recognized Bob the maintenance man.

"I'm getting too old for this," he complained, but cheerfully. "Anything else you need?" He held up a hand to count on his fingers. "Power strip, phone jack, fixed the blinds. And I set the mouse trap in Baldwin's office. Tell Baldie if he didn't eat lunch at his desk he wouldn't attract vermin."

He nodded toward Pamela and Bettina, but Pamela wasn't sure if it was because he recognized them. "Jack of all trades," he said. "I do everything around here—electrician, handyman, exterminator. At least this building is new. That red brick monstrosity is full of carpenter ants, all kinds of pests in their hidey holes."

As he spoke, Pamela studied Bitsy Daniels. Could this be the unfortunate woman Dr. Critter had seduced and abandoned? Perhaps. Some men felt more comfortable with women whose looks suggested they would be grateful for attention.

But then Bob picked up a metal toolbox from one of the other chairs. He advanced jauntily toward the door, where he turned and said, "See you soon, Bits."

"Not if I see you coming," she responded in the voice of a long-time smoker. She punctuated the joke with a braying laugh.

He laughed too and was on his way.

The minute Pamela heard Bitsy's voice she knew they hadn't found the right person. She was about to tell Bitsy that they had wandered into the wrong office, take Bettina's arm, and retreat. But Bitsy spoke first, in raspy tones that made Pamela even surer the woebegone voice emanating from the shrubbery hadn't belonged to the woman before them.

"What can I do for you ladies?" she inquired genially, pushing her desk chair back into place and lowering herself into it. She wasn't actually unattractive. Her eyes were a startling blue, and her carefully waved hair and bright nails suggested she put some effort into her grooming, though her smock-like dress seemed chosen with concealment in mind.

Bettina stepped forward. "Bettina Fraser from the *Arborville Advocate*," she announced. "I understand you're not only an employee but also a student, thanks to Wendelstaff's free tuition for employees program. I'm doing an article on older students returning to college"—Bettina winked—"not that you're that much older."

"Well, hon, you've come to the right place. Have a seat."

Bitsy seemed happy to have an audience and was so voluble that Pamela found herself hoping Bettina would repay her cooperation and really write the article. As Bitsy wound down, Bettina took the opportunity to change the subject.

"The college is so close to Arborville," she said, "and Arborvillians take a lively interest in campus events—

even tragic ones." She modulated her cheerful expression and tone to reflect the direction she was steering the conversation. "The Department of Fine and Professional Arts must be reeling from the loss of Dr. Critter."

"Not really," Bitsy said matter-of-factly. "Nobody liked him very much. The cops have been all over the place, and everybody told them the same thing." She shrugged. "I guess they followed up where they wanted to follow up, but they sure haven't caught anybody yet."

"People didn't like him . . . ?" Bettina feigned surprised, and Pamela bit her tongue, though she had to agree Bettina's acting in this instance was more convincing than usual.

"He was pretentious, and silly." Bitsy affected a mincing tone. "Dr. Robert Greer-Gordon Critter—and heaven help you if you left out the hyphen. Or forgot to call him 'Doctor.' He'd have a fit."

"I guess he thought he deserved respect," Bettina commented, "with the book and all. The college sent a press release to the *Advocate* when it came out."

"Oh, yeah, the book. He was bad even before the book. Afterwards he became hopeless." As if she had just noticed Pamela, Bitsy suddenly exclaimed, "Hey, you were at the conference. I thought you looked familiar."

"I was." Pamela nodded. "Did you enjoy it? I mean, until . . ."

"I was only at the luncheon. Critter made sure all the department staff got tickets. Wanted everybody to hear his talk, I'm sure." She paused. "His moment of glory, until his ex-wife . . ." A braying laugh, so long it brought tears, completed the thought. When the laugh subsided, she wiped her eyes. "He was actually kind of good-hearted though, in his own weird way." She pointed toward the door through which Bob had recently departed. "He got that guy his job."

They thanked Bitsy and set out to retrace their steps back to the building's entrance. When they reached the foyer, Bettina consulted her pretty watch.

"It's just coming up on noon," she said.

Pamela nodded. "And Dermott won't be in his room till two."

"But there's no point in going home to Arborville and then driving back here all over again." Bettina lowered herself onto one of the benches that furnished the foyer. "What shall we do?"

"We could have lunch," Pamela suggested. "Haversack is just across the river, and there are lots of places there to choose from."

Bettina tilted her head to give Pamela an approving smile. "How about the Café Venezia? My treat."

"Café Venezia it is." Pamela reached out a hand to help Bettina rise from the bench.

In addition to its restaurants, Haversack offered other interesting venues. By the time they returned to the Wendelstaff campus at two p.m., they'd eaten a sumptuous meal at the Café Venezia, featuring eggplant parmigiana and tiramisu. They'd browsed in Pamela's favorite thrift store, where she found an old print showing a child in a pinafore watching her mother cook. And since Bettina was always eager to help the animal shelter publicize its adoption drives and fundraising activities, they had stopped by the shelter. A kitty and doggie fashion show was in the offing, and Bettina promised to cover it for the *Advocate*.

Bettina had insisted Pamela park in the lot near the student union, refusing to hike all the way across the campus—though she insisted her shoes were very comfortable. The walk to the older dorms took only a few minutes, and Unit 3, where Dermott's room was located, soon came into view.

"What are we going to say?" Pamela asked suddenly. She had to wait for a few seconds while Bettina caught up with her.

"What do we want to know?" Bettina inquired when she reached Pamela's side.

"Whether he has an alibi for the hour or so when Dr. Critter was at Sufficiency House being poisoned, of course."

"I'll think of something," Bettina responded as she took the lead.

The buildings, eight of them, were arranged in pairs, each pair sharing a concrete courtyard. Concrete paths connected the courtyards with each other and with other paths leading to the main part of the campus, to the parking lot, and to the sidewalk that ran along the street. The side of Unit 3 that faced them had no doors, so they followed a path that led around to its courtyard. There they could see that each room had a numbered door opening to the outside, like garden apartments or old-time motels.

"Room 4?" Bettina asked, scanning the row of doors.

"Room 4," Pamela responded, and Bettina took a few quick steps and tapped on the door.

Dermott answered on the first tap, flinging the door open wide. "Hello," he said pleasantly. His fair hair, unruly as it was, gave him an angelic air, though belied by his tattered jeans and a black tee-shirt with a skull on it.

"Oh!" Bettina raised a hand to her mouth and stepped back. "Am I in the wrong place? Isn't this Unit 4?"

"Unit 3," Dermott said. "Unit 4 is just across the way. He stooped forward to get a closer look at her, then his gaze shifted to Pamela. "Weren't you guys at that reception for Critter? Friends of Professor Delano?"

"Why, yes," Bettina exclaimed. "Yes, we were. And here I am knocking on your door by mistake. Such a co-incidence."

Standing behind Bettina, Pamela had been trying not to stare—but the room hardly looked like that of a typical college student.

He noticed her interest and laughed. "You're right," he said. "My room's a mess. But I'm the only one who lives here—RAs get private rooms."

Taking his acknowledgment of Pamela's curiosity as permission to be nosy, Bettina stepped closer. "Are those noodles?" she cried. "Homemade noodles?"

Looking pleased, Dermott nodded and the unruly strands of hair that had eluded his ponytail bounced. "They turned out quite well, if I do say so myself. It's a lost art." He backed out of the doorway and invited them in with a wave of his arm.

"Oh, my goodness," Bettina breathed as they surveyed the room they had just entered.

A network of heavy string had been created at the far end of the room, strung between nails driven into opposing walls. Dangling from it were long strands of what Pamela now knew was pasta, though she wasn't sure she would have identified it on her own. Some strands were so long that they nearly reached the top of the desk beneath the installation.

"I can't buy pasta that's as long as what I need," Dermott said matter-of-factly, "so I figured out how to make my own. It's not that hard actually, but you have to roll the dough out really thin or what you end up with is too thick to work with once it's dried and cooked."

"Where do you . . . ?" Bettina looked around as if searching for a kitchen.

"I've got a buddy who works for the campus food service. He lets me into the kitchen when nobody's around. They have one of those dough mixers. And I borrow a few of their supplies. But it's mostly just flour and that's cheap. I do most of the work here. I roll it out on that desk."

"And then what do you . . . ?"

"Do with it?" He grinned. "Weave it, of course. That's why it has to be long." He strode across the room and delicately lifted one of the longer strands from its drying line. Returning to where they stood, he held it out. "It's nice and dry now. I just haven't taken it down yet. Feel it." Pamela and Bettina each fingered the strand, which Pamela thought felt—and looked—quite authentic. "It gets boiled," he went on. "Just like making spaghetti."

He strode back across the room and returned the strand gently to its place. Remaining where he was, fondling the strands almost reverently, he said, "I made these for the conference workshop I proposed, the one Critter shot down. It would have been terrific, but that—" He paused and seemed to censor himself, then went on. "No imagination at all! And the things he said about me last spring at my critique! But luckily I have a lot of self-confidence. Anyone else would have been crushed."

"It's . . . it's a good project," Bettina ventured. "But why would a person want to weave pasta?"

"Why?" Dermott extended his arms. "Because it's

there. And think of the other foods we weave—lattice pie crust, for example. Or that we could weave, if we wanted. Long beans. Scallions. People's thinking is so pigeon-holed, and art is about freeing the mind. What is food? What is art? What is architecture? Gingerbread houses! What is literature? What tale would a squid write with its own ink?

"And then there's hemp!" he went on, warming to his subject. "It can be woven into fabric. Or knitted. But you can eat it. Haha! Stinging nettles—soup or tea, but you can weave them. They sting of course, but not when they're woven. Clothing can be dangerous though. Don't forget the Greek myth where Hercules dies when he puts on a poisoned shirt."

He had become so excited that Pamela and Bettina turned to each other in alarm, Bettina's eyes wide.

"It all comes together." As if drawing his ideas into an embrace, Dermott retracted his arms and folded them tightly across his chest.

"Was the poisoned shirt poison because it had been dyed?" Pamela inquired. She vaguely recalled the myth from art history. Paintings of Hercules writhing in agony had been a popular theme in the Renaissance and beyond.

"Centaur blood," Dermott said. "But that's a good point. The poisoned dress—garment, whatever—is all over the place in folklore, and sometimes the poison comes from a plant."

"Bloodroot?" Pamela suggested.

"No." Dermott shook his head. "The poison has to be absorbed through the skin for the poison dress thing to work. With bloodroot, the person has to drink it."

Pamela tried to keep her expression neutral, lest it give

away how relevant this conversation was becoming—
though she was wondering how to work around to the
question of where he was during the Sufficiency House
coffee break.

"Bloodroot is much more useful as a dye," Dermott
went on. "*I* certainly wouldn't use it to poison someone.
It tastes awful—*dead* giveaway! LOL."

At that moment they were distracted, not by a knock
on the door, because the door was already ajar, but by the
entrance of a very tall, very young man.

"Derm?" he said in a meek voice.

Dermott shifted his attention to the new arrival with a
genial, "Hey, buddy! What's up?"

The young man eyed Pamela and Bettina and then directed his gaze at the floor. Bettina had raised sons and
perhaps knew better than Pamela just how miserably
awkward they could feel. "We'll be going," she said,
reaching for Pamela's arm. "Good luck with your projects."

As Pamela, following Bettina, stepped over the threshold, she heard a mournful voice lamenting, "You said to
give it a week and I did, but my roommate still doesn't
like me."

"He certainly has interesting ideas," Bettina commented as they walked back to the parking lot.

"He knows about bloodroot too."

"But maybe he's right—about how it tastes. You said
Critter drank his whole cup of coffee."

"I did." Pamela nodded. "Dermott has a strong motive
though, and it sounds like he knows a lot about poison.
He could have used something else. And he has a buddy
in food service too."

They had reached the car, and Pamela unlocked the passenger-side door for Bettina. "I liked him though," she added as Bettina slid into her seat.

"I did too," Bettina said, looking up at Pamela. "He wouldn't have that job if he wasn't gentle with those poor young kids—away from home for the first time and trying to adjust to living with strangers. But we still don't know if he has an alibi."

Pamela dropped Bettina off in front of the Frasers' house and then parked her serviceable compact in her own driveway. It was only a bit after three and the day was lovely, too lovely to spend the rest of it indoors. Besides, she'd eaten nearly everything she'd bought at the Co-Op the previous week. There were two more articles to evaluate, about the Bayeux Tapestry and pueblo textiles, but the evaluations weren't due back until Thursday and today was only Monday.

She collected her mail from the mailbox and let herself into her house, where she was greeted by Catrina and Ginger, while Precious merely glanced over from her perch on the arm of the sofa. Most of the mail went immediately into the recycling basket, all but the bill from the water company.

In the kitchen, she took out one of the notepads that charities kept her well supplied with—this one reflecting the season, though a bit prematurely, with a border of acorns and varicolored maple leaves. She jotted a quick list, making sure to include celery, carrots, onions, and egg noodles to aid in transforming the carcass from last week's chicken into a sustaining batch of chicken soup.

Tonight, though, would be fish, chosen after inspecting the fish counter's offerings.

Writing the word "fish" made her think of Shane Bennett's quip that a woman without a man was like a fish without a bicycle. Meaning, Pamela supposed, why want something you have no use for? But everything didn't need to have a use. Her house was full of useless things—all those tag sale and thrift shop treasures . . .

Where was this train of thought leading? She shook her head, added cucumbers to her list, and a few minutes later was on her way.

CHAPTER 19

Bettina had suggested they get an early start for the drive to Newfield, which was a considerable distance to the west, and she had offered to drive. So the next morning, instead of dawdling over coffee and newspaper—not that the *Register* had featured any updates on the Critter case since the first few days after his demise—Pamela ate her toast and drank her coffee with dispatch. Breakfast over, she rinsed her cup and plate at the sink and hurried upstairs to dress.

She was back downstairs and waiting in the entry by the time Bettina appeared on the porch. Even through the lace that curtained the front door's oval window, Bettina cut a striking figure in her bright chartreuse ensemble. As she stepped over the threshold, the outfit was revealed to be cropped pants and a peplum jacket, accented with a necklace and earrings fashioned from spiky chunks of natural coral. Coral-colored espadrilles completed the look. Pamela herself was wearing sandals, jeans, and a nondescript blouse, but she never minded being eclipsed fashion-wise by her stylish friend.

The drive to Newfield was lovely. Heading west, they soon left the compact suburbs behind and cruised past rolling fields, some under cultivation, and stands of forest. Newfield itself was an old town, founded in 1767, according to a wooden sign whose flowing script imitated the effect of a quill pen. The main street featured one charming storefront after another, shops and restaurants catering to people who might as well have been the landed gentry of yore.

"Watch for Armory Street," Bettina advised as they neared the end of the commercial district. "It goes off to the left. Wilfred always drives when we come out here together, but I think we're getting close."

Ten minutes later they had left downtown Newfield behind and were turning into a large parking lot that served a complex composed of barn, sheds, and a farmhouse. Beyond the complex, grassy fields sloped down to a meandering stream. Vehicles in the lot ranged from luxury SUVs to more humble modes of transportation, and a section of the lot closest to the barn seemed set aside for the vans and trucks of the market vendors.

People carrying bags and boxes were emerging from the large open doorway at the end of the barn and heading toward their cars, while empty-handed people were making their way from their cars toward the barn. Bettina pulled into an empty spot between a Volvo and a Volkswagen, and she and Pamela joined the procession of shoppers.

Inside, the barn was cavernous, echoing with talk and

laughter. Bright lights suspended from the rafters illuminated a lively scene, with stalls arranged on a busy grid of crisscrossing aisles and offering wares both edible and inedible. The aromas—of fresh fruit, ripe cheese, freshly baked bread—gave a preview of the variety to be found within.

Pamela and Bettina set out down the aisle leading straight back from the entrance, passing counters piled with cauliflower, zucchini, jars of honey, heirloom tomatoes, and apples. They turned left when Bettina said she spied a few stalls offering craft items. Just after they passed a display of squat handmade candles, they recognized Yvonne Graves presiding over a counter covered with rustic textiles in deep, rich shades. Hanging from a screen at the back of the stall were long scarves in the same colors, and Yvonne was wearing a simple dress fashioned from similar cloth.

"Oh, here you are," Bettina exclaimed.

Yvonne managed to look pleasant, confused, and interested all at the same time. As Pamela had observed when meeting her at the reception, her face was lined, but the lines had been carved more by cheer than gloom.

"You're wondering who we are," Bettina said. Pointing to Pamela and then to herself, she said, "Pamela Paterson and Bettina Fraser. We met you at Wendelstaff, at the reception for . . . your . . . uh . . ."

"Ex-husband," Yvonne said unperturbedly.

"Yes, ex-husband." Bettina nodded.

"And now you're here?" Yvonne paused, as if awaiting an explanation of their presence.

But Bettina had an explanation, and a plausible one at that. "I come here all the time with my husband, Wilfred," she said. "It's quite a drive from Arborville, where we live, though it's worth it for the fresh produce and the hams and the cheese and . . . just everything. Wilfred was busy today, but Pamela has heard us talk about the New-field farmers market endlessly and she'd never been here, and with this being maybe the last chance to get Jersey peaches this season, and they've been so good . . ." Her voice trailed off in response to Yvonne's murmured agreement.

"And then," she resumed, "while we were on our way, we remembered that someone else we met at the reception—maybe Dean Tate, or at Wendelstaff somewhere—mentioned that you had a stall here. So we thought we'd say hello."

"Hello, then." Yvonne offered her hand, first to Bettina and then to Pamela.

Bettina had been eyeing Yvonne's wares from the moment they halted before her stall. Now she picked up a napkin, woven from smooth cotton fiber in a rich brown, with occasional stripes of gold, green, and red. "From Guatemala, I believe we heard?"

"A women's collective. They do beautiful work, and I go down there once a year and ship back as much as I can to sell for them. The stall isn't always just Guatemalan textiles—I handle things for local weavers too—but I was in Guatemala at the end of summer and the collective had been very busy."

"This is certainly lovely." Bettina stroked the cloth. "Do you think you have eight like this? And how about a matching tablecloth?"

Yvonne was occupied for a bit then, as she turned away to rummage for more napkins and retrieved the matching tablecloth from a tall pile on the counter. Bettina was just getting started, however, and noting that

Christmas would be upon them before they knew it, selected napkins, placemats, tablecloths, and scarves with abandon, declaring that her Boston daughter-in-law, who loved all things natural, would be especially delighted with the gifts destined for her.

Pamela, too, was tempted by the lovely offerings and bought a scarf in an interesting aquamarine and brown check for Penny.

As Yvonne was packing their selections into bags, Bettina commented, "I'll bet this place really gets crowded on Saturdays, especially this time of year, when a drive in the country is so appealing."

"It does," Yvonne agreed. "Frantic sometimes. Luckily I have a lot of stock, and I love being able to help those talented Guatemalan women find a market for their work."

"I guess you had to lose a day of sales for the fiber arts and crafts conference though . . ." Bettina's sympathetic expression did a good job of concealing the real motive for her comment.

"Half a day." Yvonne looked up from wrapping a set of napkins in tissue. "I drove right out to Newfield after the luncheon." Her lips widened into a smile and the skin around her eyes crinkled. "People keep asking me if I killed him—and not just the police either—especially after that scene I made at the luncheon. I'm really not sorry I spoke up though."

The proprietor of the stall next door, which sold handmade doll clothes, had begun listening intently when the conversation shifted away from the gifting possibilities of Guatemalan textiles. Now she joined the conversation.

"She *was* here that Saturday," she said, with an emphatic nod of the head. "From about two p.m. on. And I told the police that too."

"I didn't want him to be dead," Yvonne said. "Especially not *now,* with his book just out. I wanted him to be alive to read the reviews that are going to tear his ideas (the ones that weren't mine) to shreds." Her voice rose and she thrust the tissue-wrapped napkins into a shopping bag with a gesture that was less than gentle.

"He must have been a hard man to be married to."

"Stealing my ideas—and acting like he had a right to them because I was his wife!" Yvonne's face seemed unaccustomed to frowning, but she was frowning now. "That was the worst. I almost didn't mind the philandering. If those women wanted to fawn over him and flatter him, God bless them. It meant I didn't have to." She stooped, reached beneath the counter, and came up with another batch of tissue paper, which she slapped down on the counter with a thud.

"Philandering? Really?" Pamela turned away to hide her smile at Bettina's feigned amazement—and her overacting. The woman was shameless, but all in the service of finding out what they wanted to find out.

"Argh . . ." Yvonne flung out her hands in a gesture that implied no words could do justice to the tale that needed to be told.

"There was more than one . . . ?" Bettina probed delicately.

"Joan was the latest," Yvonne said. "He used to go after students, the attractive young ones, then attitudes changed and he realized getting caught would mean trouble. Joan was a student too, but I think she was older, so I guess he thought that was okay. I overheard him sometimes on the phone when he didn't know I was around."

"My, my goodness." Bettina laid a carefully manicured hand atop one of Yvonne's. "You're well rid of him." With a sharp intake of breath, she raised the same hand to her mouth. "I meant, the divorce of course, not . . ."

"I know what you meant." Yvonne chuckled. Then her gaze traveled past Bettina and she greeted a new arrival.

"Beautiful things," an elderly woman exclaimed. "Have you always been here?"

"Just about," Yvonne said, "but I don't always have these particular textiles."

The woman edged past Pamela and picked up the top-most tablecloth from the tablecloth pile, deep green with a brown and red border. Pamela stepped aside to give the woman more space and Bettina, sensing that another customer had arrived, stepped aside too.

"Help yourself," Yvonne urged the newcomer. "I'll just finish packing these things up for these ladies and then I'll be right with you."

Ten minutes later, Pamela and Bettina had stowed their purchases in the trunk of Bettina's car and returned to the barn in quest of peaches. Following Wilfred's directions, Bettina located the stall responsible for the orchard bounty that had been transformed into three peach pies. But—

"No, I'm sorry ma'am," the genial proprietor said when Bettina asked about peaches, none being in evidence. "I had a bumper crop, but they're over for the season—the good ones anyway, and I don't like to bring the so-so ones to market. I've got to consider my orchard's reputation."

He waved his hand over the pyramids of plums ranged along his counter. "Plums I've got—Santa Rosa, Red Ace, Ruby Queen, Fortune. Take your pick."

With a flirtatious tilt of the head, Bettina said, "I'll take some of each."

"Some of each" filled two small shopping bags, and Pamela and Bettina went on their way each carrying a bag. They were in the produce section of the market now, admiring crates filled with pears and apples while inhaling their fruity scent, strolling past counters barely visible beneath bundles of carrots with their feathery leaves still attached.

Pamela hesitated before a stall offering heirloom tomatoes. The display featured tomatoes in every size, shape, and color. Tiny ones were bright red and shaped like cherries, or yellow and resembling miniature pears. Others, medium sized and round, ranged from yellow to orange to classic tomato-red to dark brown. Still others were huge, ruby red, and curiously shaped, as if by a potter smoothing several lumps of clay into a knobby whole.

"I'm so tempted," she said, "but my vines are still bearing and I have more than enough—and for you and Wilfred too."

A few more steps brought them to a stall with an arresting display of eggplant and zucchini. Pamela *did* make a purchase there, coming away with several small eggplants, the kind with the purple and white streaks, and several large zucchini. Now they each had two bags to carry.

They had made a circuit of the produce section and were approaching the barn's entrance. Just within the wide doorway were a few stalls offering soup and chili, made-to-order sandwiches, ice cream, and cookies. The aromas of soup and chili reminded them that lunchtime had come and gone while they had been occupied with their sleuthing and shopping.

"How about we put our plums and vegetables in the car and come back for soup . . . or chili . . . or sandwiches?" Bettina suggested. "I noticed some tables and benches on the grass at the edge of the parking lot."

The shopping bags were stowed in the car and lunch was purchased: pastrami sandwiches on rye, judged more exciting than soup or chili—especially given that the pastrami was locally made and the rye bread came fresh from a neighboring stall.

As they ate, looking out over the green field that sloped down to the meandering stream and with a clear blue September sky overhead, they discussed what they had learned from their conversation with Yvonne.

"That's one less suspect," Pamela said after half of her sandwich was gone and her hunger had ceased to gnaw. The pastrami was deliciously moist and peppery, with a hint of more exotic spices too, and the rye bread was so fresh and fragrant it had to have been baked that morning.

"I agree." Bettina lowered her soda can, leaving a bit of lipstick on her straw. "That woman in the doll-clothes stall who said Yvonne was there from two p.m. on the day of the conference looked pretty honest. And her things were so cute!"

Pamela nodded. "Whoever put the poison in the coffee dispenser did it after three, because it had to be done after the knitters had all been served."

Bettina mirrored the nod. "I was happy to hear that Clayborn had the sense to follow up with the idea of Critter's ex-wife as a suspect. I'm sure more than one person told him about how she attacked him—or at least his book—at the luncheon."

"We have a name for seduced and abandoned now too," Pamela said. "Joan."

"No last name," Bettina observed, "but it's a start." She took a bite of sandwich and stared out at the lovely view, chewing meditatively. They were both silent for some minutes. "I just wish," Bettina said at last, "that the Boston children would let me buy girly things for that adorable little Morgan."

Pamela commanded herself not to laugh, especially since she had just taken a large sip of soda. Bettina and Wilfred's younger son and his wife lived in Boston, where they were both professors. A few years earlier they had presented Bettina and Wilfred with their first grand-daughter—the Arborville son and his wife had only the two boys. But the Boston children, as Bettina called them, had declared they were raising an ungendered *child*, not a *girl*, and to Bettina's unending sorrow, had forbidden her to indulge her only granddaughter with the frilly dresses and girly toys she longed to provide.

Before they set out on the drive back to Arborville, they returned to the barn and came away with a pound of sliced pastrami, a loaf of fresh-baked rye bread, and a big jar of pickles. The pickles had been made from pickling cucumbers the pickle-maker herself grew.

"I don't have anything on my schedule for the after-noon," Bettina said as they returned to her car. "Do you?"

"No." Pamela settled the bag containing pastrami and rye bread onto the backseat next to the bags of plums and vegetables. Leaning in through the opposite door, Bettina added the jar of pickles. "Are you thinking we could stop by the Wendelstaff campus to see if we can learn more about Joan?"

"That's exactly what I'm thinking." Bettina slid in be-hind the steering wheel and Pamela took her place in the passenger seat.

CHAPTER 20

Their journey east was uneventful until they neared the intersection where County Road crossed the curving road that led past the Wendelstaff campus. The line of cars ahead of them suddenly stopped moving, and Bettina hit the brakes. When a siren whooped and drew closer, they realized that the backup was not the result of a red light but something untoward. Pamela twisted in her seat, scanning the scene behind them and blinking at the rapid-fire lights flashing across the roof of an oncoming police car. The police car was straddling the white line that divided the lane they were in from oncoming traffic, and the cars in that lane were edging to the side as best they could.

"An accident up ahead, I suppose," Bettina commented.

That the police car was followed by another police car

and then by an ambulance, adding its wail to the whoops of the police cars, made that seem likely.

Minutes passed and it appeared they would be waiting there, unmoving, for quite some time. Bettina turned off her engine and they both rolled their windows down. Car doors began opening and soon people were milling about, striking up conversations and wandering toward the intersection to see what was happening. Word filtered back. A truck had hit the pole that supported the traffic light and then been rear-ended by a sports car, with serious injuries to the driver of the sports car. The intersection was impassable because the pole, with traffic light still attached, had fallen across it, taking out power wires in the process.

"Well, this is ridiculous," Bettina said. "I don't want to sit here all afternoon."

The lane headed the other direction had no traffic at all, since cars heading south were backed up on the other side of the problem intersection. A few cars ahead of them had begun making U-turns and heading back the way they had come. With those cars out of the way, a space had opened up ahead and Pamela noticed that they were very near a cross street. It was the cross street with the large apartment building on the corner and the derelict houses whose lots backed up to the Sufficiency House land.

"Why don't you turn left up there?" she suggested. "Maybe we can find a back route to the campus. We're pretty close right now."

Bettina turned the key in the ignition. The Toyota's engine growled a few times and then caught. She pulled ahead and obediently made the turn Pamela had suggested. They cruised past the side of the apartment building, the shabby little wood-frame houses, and the scruffy park with the pond and the wild ducks. Up ahead was the nature preserve, separated from the park by the gravel road. Other than the gravel road—and who knew where that went?—the street they had turned onto was a dead end.

"I guess that wasn't a very good idea," Pamela said, "unless you want to see if this gravel road leads anywhere."

"I don't, actually." Bettina brought the car to a halt and turned off the engine. "I hope those cars heading into the blocked intersection haven't gotten all bunched up again so we can't get across into the southbound lane."

"I do too," Pamela said. "But I'm sure people's GPSs have started directing them away from this stretch of County Road."

They were facing the edge of the nature preserve, which offered a soothing vista. Pamela was enjoying the shifting patterns of light and shade created by the movement of leaves in the breeze when she noticed a human moving about among the trees. It was a young man, meandering here and there and bobbing up and down, as if looking for something. He was carrying a plastic bin.

Bettina noticed him too and she was the first to make the identification. "Isn't that Dermott?" she said. "The weird food guy?"

It was. And he had stopped bobbing up and down and was walking straight toward them. He was wearing a white tee-shirt today, but otherwise looked the same, in tattered jeans and with his blond hair escaping from a careless ponytail. He emerged from the woods and headed for Bettina's side of the car, calling, "Car trouble?"

Then he recognized them. He stopped walking and

studied them for a moment through the windshield, glancing from Bettina's side to Pamela's.

"Oh, it's you!" Smiling, he continued his advance. "What brings you here?"

Pamela pushed her door open and stepped out onto the ragged asphalt where the road met the gravel. She explained that they'd been on their way to the campus and described the backup at the intersection, along with what they had learned of its cause.

"I heard the sirens." Dermott nodded. "Sounds like a mess."

Bettina had climbed out of the car at this point too. "What brings you here?" she inquired, echoing his question.

"Mushrooms." He extended the plastic bin, which held a few earthen-colored nubs and paler disks with fibrous stems attached. "It's a little early for them, but they're starting to come out. It's very moist back in these woods—that's what mushrooms like. Would you like to see some growing?"

Bettina displayed a foot shod in a coral-colored espadrille. "I don't think my shoes are suited for a walk in the woods." Her bright lips shaped an apologetic smile.

"Too bad," he said. "There's a shortcut to the campus right through there." He turned and pointed back in the direction he had come from. "It's just a footpath. But it's much faster and easier than the roundabout route you have to take if you're driving."

"We don't have to do the campus errand right now." Pamela addressed Bettina—though she herself wouldn't have minded a walk through the woods. Looking past Dermott, she could see a hint of a path, though in most places the ground beneath the trees was covered with dead leaves from the previous fall interspersed with tufts of feeble shade-grown grass.

Turning back to Dermott, she said, "Do you by any chance know a student in your department named Joan? Somebody older, returning to school?"

"Hmmm." He fingered his chin and drew his brows together. "Yes!" he exclaimed suddenly, replacing the contemplative pose with a grin. "There is a Joan. Joan Robbins. She was in my design class last term, but I haven't seen her lately. Maybe she didn't re-enroll. Or maybe she did. You could ask in the office." He took a few steps backwards and gestured toward the woods. "Are you sure you don't want me to show you the path?"

Bettina looked down at her feet and made a whimpering sound. "We can call the office," she said. "We don't have to go there in person."

"Good point!" Dermott turned to go, saying, "Mushrooms await." But he swung back around and added, "You were interested in my food ideas the other day. I'm having a demonstration picnic Friday at lunch time, showing off some of the recipes I've been working on. It will be on those tables by the river behind the dorms and everybody's invited. Come on by if you're free." And he was off, humming to himself.

The traffic had eased by the time they retraced their route to the corner. Bettina was able to make her right turn and soon they were on their way back to Orchard Street.

"Joan Robbins," Pamela murmured. "Our Wendelstaff errand wasn't wasted after all."

"Make that call," Bettina said. "Fine and Professional Arts. You've got your phone and I'm curious. Say we understand she is or was a student in that department and we need to get in touch with her. This could be a break-through."

But it wasn't. The woman who answered the call with a crisp "Fine and Professional Arts. How may I help you?" was not helpful at all. "We do not give out information about students," Pamela was advised in even crisper tones.

As Bettina steered the Toyota through the big intersection where County Road crossed Arborville's main east-west street, Pamela continued to finger her phone, searching the internet for people named Joan Robbins. There were a lot and some were no longer alive, having died at age 97 in Topeka, Kansas, where they were mourned by family and friends. Others were alive, but lived in similarly remote locations, or held important positions at Fortune 500 companies, or had chaired the Nantucket Lobster Festival five years running.

She reported her lack of results to Bettina, adding, "Too bad she doesn't have a more unusual name."

"We'll find her." They had reached Orchard Street, and Bettina paused for a break in the traffic to make her turn.

Knit and Nibble was meeting that night, but not till seven, and just across the street at Bettina's. It was only a bit past three. After greeting the cats, Pamela sorted the mail that she had plucked from her mailbox, stored her eggplant and zucchini in the refrigerator, and climbed the stairs.

In her bedroom, she tucked the Guatemalan scarf away on the closet shelf where she stockpiled gifts collected throughout the year. In her office, she pushed the buttons that would bring her computer to life, waited through the chirps and whirs that accompanied that process, and waited again as three new messages appeared in her inbox.

Only one was of interest, from delanob@wendelstaff.edu. It read,

> *Hi, Pamela,*
> *Thinking of you today, and every day. I hope*
> *you're free at least one night this weekend. No*
> *gallery openings on the horizon, but I have a few*
> *ideas.*
> *Brian.*

Pamela smiled to herself. She wasn't sure she was thinking of him *every* day. But it was enjoyable to spend time with a pleasant man, and maybe . . . slowly . . . realize that he was more than simply pleasant.

"Hi, Brian," she responded. "I'm free."

The articles she was to evaluate were due back Thursday morning, and so far she had read only one. There was plenty of time to do some work for the magazine before that evening's Knit and Nibble, but first she descended to the kitchen.

A carcass with plenty of meat attached remained from the roasted chicken that had provided several satisfying meals. Now it was time to transform the carcass into the chicken soup that would provide yet more satisfying meals. Pamela took the carcass from the refrigerator, lowered it into her largest pot, and covered it with water.

It would simmer and simmer until the meat fell from the bones and the water was transformed into a rich broth. Once that step was complete, she would simmer carrots, celery, and onion in the strained broth, season it with salt and pepper and sprigs of thyme from the pot on the back porch, and add egg noodles.

But until the first step was complete, she immersed herself in "The Bayeux Tapestry and the Battle of Hastings: Embroidering History, 1066."

Pamela rang Bettina's doorbell at a quarter to seven, fifteen minutes early for the evening's Knit and Nibble meeting, but by design. The article on the Bayeux Tapestry had talked more about the Norman Conquest and its implications for English culture and the English language than about the creators' fascinating achievement of embroidering the lead-up to the battle and the battle itself on a 230-foot-long strip of linen.

Her mind had wandered, and in its wanderings had revisited that afternoon's encounter with Dermott Sparr. He'd revealed Joan's last name, which was an important contribution to their sleuthing. But he'd revealed something else too, and the import of that something else had occurred to her only a few hours ago. Now she was about to reveal that to Bettina.

But Bettina had other ideas.

"I know I'm early, but . . ." Pamela began.

"I don't mind," Bettina cut in. "I can use a hand. Wilfred is upstairs on the phone with his cousin. They're planning a fishing trip."

She led Pamela to the kitchen and began opening cupboards and drawers. The idea Pamela wanted to discuss would require Bettina's full attention, so instead of talking, she joined in, collecting mugs and dessert plates from Bettina's sage-green pottery set and forks and spoons from her Danish stainless steel. She arranged them on the scrubbed pine table while Bettina set out the sugar bowl and cream pitcher from the sage-green set and disappeared into the dining room. Pamela heard a drawer open and close, and Bettina returned with the napkins she had bought for herself that morning.

"The brown with the colored stripes goes nicely with my pottery, don't you think?" Bettina stepped back to admire the effect. She was still wearing her outfit from earlier in the day, the chartreuse pants and jacket, and the coral jewelry that matched her espadrilles.

"Are we through?" Pamela inquired, looking around.

Preparations for the refreshments were now complete, with plates staged for the main attraction. But what was that to be? Usually when Bettina hosted Knit and Nibble, Wilfred had been hard at work in the kitchen all afternoon and the results of that labor waited on the high counter that separated to cooking area from the eating area—a cake or a pie or a cobbler, tempting the appetite with its sugary aroma.

"Yes." Bettina nodded, despite the empty spot where the evening's treat usually waited. "Except for coffee and tea, of course, but we won't do those until Roland reminds us that it's eight p.m."

"Sit down for a minute then." Pamela herself slipped into one of the chairs that surrounded the pine table.

Bettina's expression modulated from satisfied pleasure to apprehension. "What is it?" she asked.

"The path," Pamela said. "Dermott told us that there's a path, a shortcut through the woods from the Wendelstaff campus to where we were in the car this afternoon."

"Yes . . . ?" Now Bettina just looked puzzled.

"It's only about a five-minute walk to the Sufficiency House gardens from there, by cutting through the back-yard of one of those old houses like I did that day. And a path through the gardens leads right up to the back door of Sufficiency House."

Bettina let out a yelp of surprise. "So somebody from the campus, maybe even Dermott, could sneak into the Sufficiency House kitchen without being seen by any-body—no car to call attention to an unexpected visitor . . ."

At that point they were interrupted by the doorbell and both rose.

CHAPTER 21

The first to arrive was Nell, the tousled state of her white hair testifying to her brisk walk down the hill from her own house. She stepped into the Frasers' welcoming living room with a cheery greeting and, at Bettina's urging, took a seat in one of the comfy armchairs.

Voices were calling hello through the dusk, and Pamela remained at the open door, stepping back after a few moments to admit Holly and Karen.

"Roland is just coming," Holly said with a giggle. "He's double-checking the alternate-side parking signs."

"Honestly!" Bettina sighed. "How many times has he parked on my side of the street, always on Tuesday night? The regulations never change."

"Better safe than sorry." Wilfred had appeared at the bottom of the stairs. He advanced to the front door as Roland entered and welcomed him with a hearty handshake. Next he circled the room, paying his respects to the other knitters as they were getting settled. Then, followed by Woofus, who had been lingering diffidently at the edge of the room, he made his way toward the kitchen.

Roland, perched on a cushion on the hearth, set to work immediately, drawing his lavender yarn with its silver lurex threads from his briefcase, along with a set of knitting needles, and beginning to cast on a new section of his project.

Holly was sitting at the end of the sofa nearest the fireplace, with Karen next to her and Pamela at the other end. Across the coffee table from Pamela was an armchair waiting for Bettina, who was in the kitchen with Wilfred. From the kitchen came the sound of an electric mixer.

Nell had joined Roland in his industry, casting on for a new project, judging by the change in color. Whereas last week's donkey had been a realistic shade of gray, this week's—assuming it was another donkey—was destined to be pale green. Holly had extracted her in-progress argyle sock from her knitting bag, with its dangling bobbins in shades of orange, yellow, brown, and dark green. But instead of tending to her own knitting, she was watching Roland. He had already finished casting on and was a few rows into the very narrow production hanging from his needles.

"I love the lavender with silver," Holly cooed, bending toward him.

Roland neither looked up nor responded.

"It's so small," she added. "And so cute. What is it?"

Roland cleared his throat and continued knitting.

At this point Bettina returned from the kitchen and took her seat in the armchair. She lifted her knitting bag onto her lap and drew out what Pamela recognized as the beginnings of a sleeve for the stylish tunic, in a dramatic shade of burnt orange, that her friend was knitting for herself.

Before launching into her project, however, Bettina surveyed the group. "It's so nice to get together like this," she said, "and catch up with everybody." Her gaze landed on Roland. "Roland!" she exclaimed.

Now he actually did look up, but not in pleased anticipation.

"How was Cape May?"

"Yes!" Holly chimed in, aiming one of her dimply smiles at Bettina and then at Roland. "I'll bet you had a wonderful time! It's so pretty down there! And you really deserve to get away once in a while. You work so hard—"

"I *like* to work." Roland favored Holly with a scowl but, undeterred, she continued to smile. "At the moment I am knitting, because this is the Knit and Nibble group, not the knit and chatter group. And at eight p.m. I will be pleased to join you in a nibble, because this is the Knit and Nibble group, and then I will go back to my knitting, and it's no one's business what my project is."

Nell had stopped knitting while this exchange was going on, glancing from Holly to Roland as if she couldn't decide where her sympathies lay.

Finally she directed an encouraging smile at Holly and said, "Harold and I used to love going down to Cape May. We always stayed in the same Victorian B and B."

"We like the Victorian B and Bs too!" Holly's tone suggested she found the coincidence remarkable—never mind that Victorian B and Bs were the main drawing point for Cape May. "We usually stay at the Daffodil Cottage. It's just a block from the shore, and it's right next to the most wonderful restaurant—all vegetarian, though Desmond and I eat meat too. They do the most amazing things with mushrooms."

Nell was nodding encouragingly. "Mushrooms are an excellent substitute for meat. Very healthful—lots of minerals."

Bettina joined the conversation. "The Boston children grill those giant ones and serve them on buns. You'd think you were eating a hamburger."

"They're popping up all over the place in our yard now—not the giant ones but those little button ones, like they sell at the Co-Op. Sometimes I'm tempted—" Noticing Karen's frightened squeal, Holly interrupted herself.

"You have to grow up in a mushroom-gathering culture to really know which ones are safe to eat," Nell said. "The Nature Channel had a program on a town in Poland where people depend on the mushroom season for part of their income."

Bettina leaned forward. "Pamela and I talked to someone just this afternoon who was collecting mushrooms in that piece of the nature preserve over by Wendelstaff. He's a student there."

"I hope he knows what he's doing." Nell compressed her lips into a worried knot. "Some of the most dangerous ones look perfectly innocent."

"He seems to know a lot about food." Pamela had been following the conversation while keeping track of the knit two, purl two sequence that would create ribbing. She was starting the second sleeve of the sweater that was to be a Christmas gift for her father. Now she lowered her knitting into her lap. "Unusual food," she added. "Blue potatoes. Squid ink." At this point, Roland was the only one still at work.

Nell's expression brightened. "Could that have been Dermott you talked to?" she asked. "Dermott Sparr? Blond ponytail?"

"You know Dermott?" Pamela and Bettina spoke at once.

"He volunteers at the women's shelter in Haversack."

Pamela's "He does?" overlapped with Bettina's "Really?"

"Yes." Nell nodded, setting her halo of white hair in motion. "Dermott is a lovely young man—quite the junior version of Wilfred. He teaches a cooking class. Some of his cooking ideas are a bit unusual, but the women love him, and the kids think he's terrific. He's there every Saturday afternoon, without fail. So generous with his time."

"Always Saturday afternoon?" Pamela inquired.

"Always."

Pamela stole a glance at Bettina, whose expression made it clear that she understood the significance of what Nell had just revealed.

With a glance at Roland, whose busy-ness had not flagged, Nell took up her project again. She stared at it for a moment, smoothed out the work she had done so far, and launched a new stitch with a thrust of her right-hand needle.

Taking their cue from Nell, the other knitters bent to their tasks once more. Pamela resumed the knit two, purl two sequence she'd abandoned in mid-row, pleased again that she'd chosen red wool for the project rather than the sedate brown she had first considered. Her father, for whom the sweater was destined, was a vigorous man and barely seventy. Why not have a red sweater for Christmas?

Holly and Karen had begun chatting quietly. Occasional words reached Pamela, suggesting that the topic was a forthcoming visit from Karen's sister, who had moved to Vermont when she married a man she met on a ski trip there. Bettina, looking annoyed, was ripping out a row of knitting. The work hanging from Nell's needles was already coming to resemble a donkey.

Wilfred had not emerged from the kitchen, though there had been no more sounds connected with food preparation since the chugging whir of the electric mixer had ceased. Now though—Pamela lifted her head from her knitting and inhaled deeply—a hint of brewing coffee was beginning to scent the air. She glanced toward the hearth to see that Roland had evidently finished the piece of knitting he had started at the beginning of the evening.

With a flourish, he snipped the yarn that tethered it to the skein of lavender and silver yarn and set it on a neighboring cushion. That done, he pushed back his faultlessly starched shirt cuff, consulted his impressive watch, and intoned, "It's just eight p.m. Time to nibble."

Like an actor who had been waiting in the wings for his cue, Wilfred stepped into the arch that separated the living room from the dining room. "Coffee and tea will be served momentarily," he announced, "and I hope everyone likes banana cream pie."

Bettina's back was to him but she half-turned in her armchair when he began to speak, and she started to rise when he finished. But Wilfred bent toward her murmuring, "Sweet wife, do not disturb yourself."

Across the room, however, Holly had bobbed to her feet. "Someone has to help," she exclaimed. "And banana cream pie sounds scrumptious!"

Pamela followed Holly as she fell into step behind Wilfred, and the three of them proceeded through the dining room and into the kitchen. The banana cream pie sat on the pine table—a luxuriant expanse of whipped cream, decorated with banana slices and nearly overflowing a fluted pastry rim. The aroma of brewing coffee was much more intense in the kitchen, rich and dark and almost intoxicating.

"Ohhh!" Holly clapped and smiled the smile that displayed her perfect teeth and brought her dimple into play. "It's perfect! You are such a talented cook!" Her blouse was a deep ruby red that accented her dramatic beauty and made her skin glow. Wilfred couldn't help but be pleased, and his ruddy skin became even ruddier as he bowed in acknowledgment of her praise.

Serving the pie was delicate work, since beneath the whipped cream was a layer of vanilla pudding intermingled with more banana slices, and one could scarcely be said to *cut* whipped cream or pudding. Despite Wilfred's care and skill, the portions that made their way onto the plates were more amorphous than wedge-shaped, as gobbets of pudding and whipped cream spilled from the cut edges onto the sage-green plates.

Pamela filled five of the sage-green mugs with coffee while Holly arranged forks, spoons, cream and sugar, and napkins on a tray and carried it to the living room. After several trips, every knitter had been served pie and a mug of coffee or tea. Wilfred made one last trip to the kitchen for his own refreshments and joined them on a chair imported from the dining room.

In movements so synchronized as to seem choreographed, seven hands raised forks bearing tidbits of flaky crust topped with banana, swathed in pudding, and garnished with whipped cream. Reactions ranged from variations on "mmmm" through "heavenly" to "Wilfred, you have outdone yourself"—this latter from, of all people, Roland.

Wilfred's banana cream pie really was excellent. Pamela herself had never tried making a banana cream pie. She enjoyed the process of making traditional two-crust fruit pies: the tempting aromas as they baked and the satisfying result as the raw fruit created its own sugary, bubbly syrup and the pale crust emerged from the oven a flaky golden-brown.

But as she savored Wilfred's creation, she reflected that banana cream pie made perfect sense. There was something vanilla-pudding-like about bananas themselves, the mild flavor and the undemanding texture. The whipped cream didn't contrast with the other components so much as add yet another soothing flavor and texture.

When plates were nearly empty and people began to speak again, it was to repeat their congratulations to the chef, which Wilfred acknowledged with pleased nods all around. People addressed themselves to their coffee and tea, sugaring and creaming, and alternating sips with nibbling up the last bits of pie left on their plates.

"This is a perfect dessert for a summery day," Holly observed, setting down her fork. "I can see how it would be popular in hot climates—though a person would have to turn on the oven to bake the crust."

"Banana pudding solves that problem," Nell said. "Mostly the same ingredients, but with vanilla wafers instead of a pie crust."

"Do people ever bake bananas?" Karen inquired.

Puzzled looks all around, until Wilfred's widening eyes and intake of breath suggested sudden enlightenment. "Bananas Foster," he said. "Sautéed though, I think, and then flambéed with brandy."

After the culinary possibilities of bananas had been thoroughly explored, the conversation moved on to the end-of-summer sale at the garden center and from thence to the question of when to plant tulip bulbs.

Soon Roland set down his coffee mug and picked up one of his knitting needles, signaling that, for him at least, the nibble portion of the evening had come to an end. He pulled the skein of lavender and silver yarn closer and began to cast on—for what, no one inquired this time. Pamela rose to help Wilfred clear away and then resumed her knitting with renewed energy.

An hour later, Bettina had seen most of the knitters on their way, but Pamela lingered on the threshold.

"Three steps forward, two steps back," she said. "The more I thought about the footpath from the campus to Sufficiency House, the more excited I got about Dermott as a suspect."

Bettina seemed ready to interrupt but Pamela hurried on.

"The only problem is that Dermott isn't a suspect anymore. If he spends every Saturday afternoon at the Haversack women's shelter, he can't have been putting poison in the coffee dispenser during the knitting bee coffee break."

"I want to go to his picnic," Bettina said, "especially now that we know more about him. He seems like a very nice young man."

As Pamela stepped out onto the porch, Bettina added. "The footpath is still exciting. Someone else could have used it. We just have to figure out who."

CHAPTER 22

The corridors were endlessly long and confusing, and then the room she was looking for wasn't even in that building. She was already late for the exam and time was passing and now she was outdoors, searching for another building. The semester was drawing to an end, papers were due, and she had checked her schedule of classes that morning only to discover an extra class she had forgotten all about. She hadn't even attended once! And she'd struggled so hard to get into the college in the first place. Now she had squandered her chance. Surely she would fail that course and worse . . .

She dashed on, in a state approaching panic. She was in another building now, opening doors to peer inside rooms, not sure exactly what she was looking for. The exam that she was late for? All the rooms were dark and empty, except for . . . cats! At least the *sound* of cats—

mewing. And she opened her eyes to see cats, two of them, perched on her chest and staring at her.

It had been one of those dreams from which it was a relief to awake, a rerun of a frequent dream. Pamela had been a good student, and highly conscientious, but in the dream she became forgetful and disorganized. She hadn't had the dream lately, but perhaps it was newly interesting to her unconscious mind because she'd been spending so much time on the Wendelstaff campus. And searching for the answer to the puzzle of who killed Dr. Critter, and how.

Catrina and Ginger had already leapt to the floor. Once they saw her on her feet and reaching for her robe, they trotted out the door and led the way down the stairs. En route to the kitchen, Precious joined the parade. Once portions of seafood medley had been scooped into bowls and water refreshed, Pamela headed out to collect the *Register*.

She didn't expect any dramatic news on the Critter murder case, so she didn't even remove the paper from its plastic sleeve until she had finished her toast and taken a few sips of coffee. Then she worked her way through Part 1, lingering over an editorial calling for more arts funding in New Jersey. The front page of the "Local" section offered nothing that piqued her interest. She was skimming subsequent pages preparatory to setting the section aside in favor of "Lifestyle" and its Wednesday food feature, when a headline caught her eye.

"Police Admit No Progress in Critter Murder," it read, with Marcy Brewer's byline. She skimmed the article, which quoted Detective Lucas Clayborn of the Arborville police, but added nothing to the information communicated by the headline

The food feature, on the other hand, made for rewarding reading. The *Register*'s food editor had been thinking about bananas too, it seemed, as well as their more versatile cousins, plantains. She offered several recipe ideas, including the very simple suggestion of slicing ripe plantains on the diagonal and frying them until the sugar caramelized.

Pamela was running through her repertoire of recipes in her mind, wondering what fried plantains would complement, when the doorbell chimed. Precious skittered away but Catrina and Ginger followed Pamela to the door, which she opened to admit Bettina. Bettina had dressed for the day, but hastily, and her face was free of makeup. She was carrying her own copy of the *Register*, which she flourished in a way that made Catrina and Ginger scatter.

"Did you see Marcy Brewer's article?" she demanded.

"I did," Pamela said.

"No progress?"

Pamela nodded.

"Well, he may have admitted it to Marcy Brewer, but he didn't admit it to me, and I called him yesterday to ask if there was anything new for the *Advocate*." Bettina tipped her head in the direction of the kitchen door and made a show of sniffing. "Is there any more coffee?"

"A bit." Pamela stepped aside and waved Bettina through the doorway.

When they were both seated at the table and Bettina had a cup of coffee in front of her, with sugar and cream pitcher at hand, and Pamela had refreshed her own coffee, she said, "Does Detective Clayborn know about Joan Robbins? If so, I'd think the Fine and Professional Arts department would have to give the police her contact information even if they wouldn't give it to us."

Bettina added a spoonful of sugar to her coffee and stirred vigorously. "Clayborn would likely only know about Joan if Yvonne told him," she responded. "Maybe she didn't. Maybe she feels sorry for Joan."

"Do we?" Pamela asked. She thought of the dream. Maybe her unconscious mind had integrated Joan's story into her old college anxiety dream. In last night's version of the dream, perhaps she'd been Joan, eager to improve herself but lost and confused in an unfamiliar world.

"Of course." Bettina added more sugar and continued stirring.

"Then why are we looking for her?" Pamela asked.

Bettina looked up. "Because *Fiber Craft*? Hello? Your employer? The conference? Somebody has to figure out who killed Critter. Obviously Clayborn isn't doing it."

She tipped the cut-glass cream pitcher over her cup to add a significant dollop of cream to her coffee, stirred, and took a sip. "Just right," she said, "but . . ." She looked pointedly at the toast crumbs remaining on the plate in front of Pamela. "Do you think I could have a piece of toast to go with it?"

"Of course." Pamela rose and stepped toward the counter.

"And with some of that Tupelo honey Wilfred and I gave you? I know you never eat it."

As Pamela slipped a slice of whole-grain bread into the toaster, Bettina continued to speak, but returning to the topic that had occupied them earlier.

"Joan could have used the footpath," she said.

"Joan is the only suspect we have left." Pamela spoke

over her shoulder. She was exploring a cupboard in search of the Tupelo honey.

"Unless . . . Flo?"

"No motive that we can think of." Honey in hand, Pamela turned her attention to the toast, which had just popped up.

"And if Derm is right about bloodroot tasting bad, the fact that Flo grows it and uses it for dye doesn't mean anything. The killer likely used something else." As Pamela buttered the toast and spread a thick layer of the amber honey on it, Bettina stood up.

"It's almost ready," Pamela said. "Where are you going?"

"I want to look up bloodroot and I didn't bring my phone. Is yours around?"

"Maybe in my purse in the entry?" Pamela settled the toast, with honey already dripping off its edges, on a small wedding-china plate and set it at Bettina's place.

In a few moments, Bettina was back with the phone, and a few moments later she looked up from the screen to announce, "Bloodroot, containing the alkaloid sanguinarine, has a strong bitter taste. It is poisonous in large amounts."

Pamela had returned to her chair. "The taste would really be obvious in coffee then, even black coffee, especially because just a little bit wouldn't do the job." She sipped her own coffee, trying to remember whether Critter had added sugar and cream to his cup. But a person who liked coffee sweet would especially notice bitterness, one would think.

"Dermott did say it tastes awful, but maybe Flo knows about other plants that are poisonous, but tasteless." Bettina set the phone down and focused on her toast and coffee.

"Detective Clayborn must have interviewed her extensively," Pamela said. "And asked other people about her. If she had a motive, he'd have found it, wouldn't he?"

Bettina shrugged and licked a bit of honey from her fingers. They were both silent for a bit. When both coffee cups were empty and all that was left on Bettina's plate was a smear of honey and a few crumbs, Bettina rose.

"I have to go," she explained. "I have to put some makeup on and get over to the senior center. One of the members won a big jackpot on last week's Atlantic City outing and I'm meeting the *Advocate* photographer there for a photo op and an interview."

Pamela accompanied her to the door, but Bettina hesitated in the open doorway and turned to Pamela. "Why don't you and Brian come to dinner Saturday?" she suggested. "I know Wilfred would like to meet him."

"Umm." Pamela closed her eyes.

"Is the 'umm' about coming to dinner or inviting Brian?"

Pamela opened her eyes to find Bettina looking inquisitorial. "I'll cook," she said suddenly. "You and Wilfred cook for me all the time."

"Will Brian be here?"

"Wait and see."

Bettina stepped out onto the porch and Pamela closed the door. But before she was halfway to the kitchen, she heard a tapping and returned to the door. Bettina was still out there, visible through the lace that curtained the oval window.

Preparing to explain that she had to think a bit before including Brian in the . . . well, the *family* she had created with her best friends, Pamela opened the door. Without speaking, Bettina extended a box, a cardboard box about the size of a shoebox, taped closed with wide package tape. The words "For Pamela Paterson" had been written on the top with a Sharpie.

"It was at the bottom of the steps," Bettina explained. "Were you expecting something?"

"Not really." Pamela took the box and, knowing how curious Bettina could be, ushered her into the entry. "I need a knife for this tape," Pamela said, and headed for the kitchen with Bettina following.

She cut the tape and folded the box's flaps back to discover a note, which read, "You might have a use for these. I don't, anymore. I loved not wisely but too well. No more red socks." Beneath the note were what looked like small sweet potatoes with a sparse growth of long hairs. Bettina and Pamela nearly bumped heads as both peered more closely.

"Bloodroot rhizomes, I'm sure," Pamela said. "The box must be from Flo."

Bettina raised her head. "Why would she send them to you?"

"I suppose because I was chatting with her at the bee about the yarn she had dyed with them," Pamela said. "They produce a beautiful shade of red."

"And the red socks?" Bettina's lips formed a puzzled zigzag.

"She was knitting socks at the bee. Well, one sock. But I guess they broke up."

"What . . . ?" No sooner had Bettina uttered the word than she followed it up with widened eyes and a smile. "Ahh," she breathed. "The man in the Sufficiency House garden shed."

Pamela nodded. "Everyone deserves to find love, but apparently this particular love didn't work out."

Bettina went on her way then. After getting dressed and making her bed, Pamela sat down at her computer, happy to immerse herself in "Ceremonial Textiles in Traditional Pueblo Life." Around noon, she took a break for a bowl of the chicken soup she'd made Tuesday night. After lunch, she wrote up her evaluation for the pueblo textiles article (a definite yes) and checked over what she'd said about "Seeing Red" and "The Bayeux Tapestry and the Battle of Hastings: Embroidering History, 1066."

Feeling pleased about finishing ahead of time, she attached the evaluations to an email and sent them off to her boss. Before she had even risen from her chair, a reply popped up in her inbox, bringing with it attachments.

"Since you're finished early," the message read, "you might as well get started copyediting these because I need them asap. They're for the upcoming issue on quilts. Can you get them back by Friday morning?"

"Yes," Pamela responded, and she opened the first attachment, "The Tumbling Blocks Quilt Motif as Op Art."

Two hours later, she rolled her chair back from her desk, shut her eyes, and raised her arms over her head in a luxurious stretch. Sensing that change was afoot, Catrina, who had joined her a bit after lunch, jumped from her lap.

Pamela saved her work, closed the file and Word, and told the computer to shut down. She'd worked hard, she'd been in the house all day, and a break and some fresh air before dinner would be welcome. Why not drive over to Sufficiency House to thank Flo in person and get some pointers on extracting the dye from the rhizomes?

The "Sheep to Shawl" article, disappointing as it was, had mentioned that undyed wool was readily available. It could be fun to make a knitted garment with yarn one had dyed—and maybe even spun—by oneself.

The turnoff for Sufficiency House was a few blocks before the intersection where the truck had knocked over the traffic light pole, but traffic was flowing perfectly fine on County Road, suggesting that the effects of that accident had been remedied. Pamela eased her serviceable compact to the curb across from Sufficiency House and crossed the street carrying a bakery box containing a generous portion of crumb cake. A gift in return for a gift seemed appropriate, and she had made a stop at the Co-Op.

There was no response when she rang at the front door. But it was a lovely September afternoon, a perfect time to be working outdoors, and so she made her way along the side of the house to the gardens in the back. No figures were moving among the rampant vines bearing squash, pumpkins, and melons, or harvesting greens from the tidy beds, and nobody answered when she called Flo's name.

She crossed to where the gravel path led from the back of the house to the far edge of the lot and prowled along it, glancing right and left at each of the narrower paths that marked off the garden's grid. Returning to the house, she climbed the steps to the back porch, advanced to the back door, and—without exactly planning to—reached for the doorknob and gave it a twist.

The door opened. It was odd to have the door unlocked and no one home, she reflected, and stepped inside, calling Flo's name. The kitchen was empty, as was the dining room, but she found Flo in the living room, lying motionless on the floor in one of her much-washed housedresses.

Pamela had been carrying the bakery box all this time.

Hardly aware of what she was doing, she set it on the coffee table and knelt down next to Flo, or Flo's body, as she quickly realized. Flo's eyes were open but unblinking, the air was unstirred by her breath, and the handle of a knife protruded from her chest.

A voice was saying "Oh, no" and she realized it was her own. She closed her eyes, opened them, and shakily climbed to her feet. Her purse was still over her shoulder and she fumbled in it for her phone as she backed up toward the hassock that matched the roomy upholstered chair. Feeling curiously removed from the scene around her, as if watching it unfold in one of the BBC mysteries she enjoyed so much, she tapped 9-1-1 into her phone's screen.

She remained sitting on the hassock, as unmoving as the corpse on the floor at her feet, for how long she wasn't sure, though she was dimly aware of sirens rising and falling. She only stirred when voices on the front porch and the doorbell's ring aroused her.

She opened the door to two uniformed officers, the boyish faced Officer Anders and an older officer she didn't recognize.

"She's . . . in here." Pamela edged away from the doorway, looking at the floor rather than at Flo.

"Was it you who called?" the older officer inquired after he had knelt by Flo's body and apparently satisfied himself that she was really dead.

Pamela nodded.

"Can you identify the deceased?"

Pamela nodded and said, "Flo—Flower, actually—Ransom."

"And your name?"

Pamela gave her name and added, "I came to thank her

for something she dropped off at my house, and when no one answered the doorbell I went around to the back. The back door was unlocked so I came in and . . ."

Tiny spots had begun to appear before her eyes and her head felt wobbly on her neck. She swayed and closed her eyes. The next thing she knew, she was sitting on the nubbly sofa, holding a glass of water. The older officer had retreated to a far corner of the room and was speaking on his phone, and Officer Anders, sitting on the hassock, was facing her and holding a small notepad and a pen.

"Once more again, please," Officer Anders said. "You came to thank her and . . ."

Pamela had no sooner finished repeating her simple narrative than the doorbell rang. The older officer opened the door to admit Detective Clayborn.

He surveyed the room, his gaze landing on Pamela. With his homely features betraying no hint of surprise, he remarked, "You're here." Then he added, "Why?"

Pamela returned his gaze, as her heart's heavy thumps sped up to a rapid tick-tick. She described once again how she had come to pay a thank-you visit and discovered that Flo was dead.

"Was the box here when you got here?" Detective Clayborn inquired, tipping his head toward the bakery box on the coffee table.

"I brought it," Pamela said. "It's crumb cake from the Co-Op."

Officer Anders yielded the hassock to Detective Clayborn, who took a seat and removed a small notepad and a pen from the pocket of his nondescript sports jacket. Looking up at Officer Anders, he said. "Get the county here." Then he leaned toward Pamela. "Let's just go over this in detail."

Ten minutes later, he tucked the notepad and pen away and began to rise, but Pamela remained where she was on the sofa.

"Was there something else you wanted to say?" he asked without sitting back down.

"Flo had just broken up with someone," Pamela said. "Sometimes people who have been rejected can do . . ."

Her voice trailed off. Without saying a word, Detective Clayborn made it clear—something about the way the skin around his eyes tightened—that the inquiry into Flo's death was police business, not hers. He waited as Pamela rose and, with a chivalrous hand at her back, escorted her to the door. "We'll need to keep the crumb cake," he said.

As Pamela climbed into her car, a silver van with the logo of the sheriff's department pulled up in front of Sufficiency House.

CHAPTER 23

Bettina must have been watching from a window, because no sooner had Pamela parked in her own driveway than her friend launched herself across the street. "It's already on the internet!" she exclaimed when she reached Pamela's car. "Are you all right?" She peered through the car's window.

Pamela pushed the door open and stepped onto the asphalt. "Yes," she sighed.

Wilfred joined them on the driveway then, the apron tied around his ample waistline indicating he'd come directly from the Frasers' kitchen. "It never rains but it pours," he said with a sad headshake. Bettina, meanwhile, had gathered Pamela into a hug.

The three of them stood there without speaking for a few moments. The next voice Pamela heard belonged to Marcy Brewer. She was hurrying along the sidewalk, leaving a young man with a camera and a tripod struggling to keep up, though he was easily a foot and half taller than she was and had correspondingly longer legs.

"Ms. Paterson, Ms. Paterson," she called. "Marcy Brewer from the *County Register*. May I have a moment of your time?"

Bettina relinquished her hold on Pamela and darted around the back of Pamela's car. Marcy Brewer had reached the edge of the driveway and Bettina met her there.

"Ms. Paterson is not speaking to reporters," Bettina announced in her most authoritative voice. "None at all. No! So go back where you came from." She made shooing motions with her hands.

Meanwhile, Wilfred put his arm around Pamela and guided her along the side of the driveway and up onto the porch. She probed in her purse for her keys and handed them to Wilfred.

Bettina caught up as Wilfred was unlocking the door. Once they were all safely inside and the door was closed, they crowded together behind the lace curtain to watch Marcy Brewer and the photographer return to their van.

"They're really gone," Bettina declared after a few minutes. "Quick, while we can escape! Across the street, before more of them come! Then let the reporters ring your doorbell all night if they want."

Bettina's strategy seemed a good one, so they decamped for the Frasers' house, the kitchen specifically. Wilfred had been peeling steamed potatoes when Bettina dashed from the house to greet Pamela and offer comfort, and he had set down his paring knife to follow her on her errand.

"Dinner in less than an hour," he said as Pamela and Bettina took seats at the scrubbed pine table. "Fried chicken, potato salad, and coleslaw. And how about some wine to sip while you're waiting?"

Glasses of Chardonnay appeared before them on the table, along with a basket of crackers and a small bowl of Bettina's favorite pimento cheese. Wilfred returned to the cooking area of the kitchen and his potato-peeling task.

"I guess that means Flo isn't a suspect." Bettina spoke hesitantly, as if testing whether Pamela wanted to discuss the implications of the scene she had happened upon that afternoon.

Pamela set down her wineglass and raised a hand to finger the crease she felt forming between her brows.

"Have some pimento cheese," Bettina suggested hastily. "I'll fix a cracker for you."

Watching her friend busy with the cheese spreader, Pamela laughed. "It's okay," she said. "I don't mind talking about it. I *want* to talk about it. Flo's death does make things more complicated . . . or maybe simpler."

She accepted the cracker, with its colorful topping of bright orange cheese flecked with bright red pimento bits. "It wasn't poison," she said. "Flo was stabbed."

"How does that make things more complicated?" Bettina looked up from preparing a cracker for herself.

"Maybe Flo killed Dr. Critter, and someone who liked, or even loved, Dr. Critter killed her in revenge."

"But we never figured out a motive for Flo to kill Critter," Bettina pointed out. She took a bite of the cheese cracker.

"No, we didn't." Pamela nodded. She sipped her wine, enjoying the refreshing chill and the slight hint of vanilla.

From the stove, where he was heating oil in a wide skillet, came Wilfred's voice. "How does Flo's death maybe make things simpler?"

"Yes, how?" Bettina paused with a cracker in her hand.

"It disqualifies Joan," Pamela said. "If she killed Dr. Critter because he seduced and then abandoned her, why would she also kill Flo?"

"If the murder technique was the same . . . that would make it almost certain the same person killed them both." Bettina pondered the rest of her thought while applying pimento cheese to the cracker. "But the murder technique wasn't the same . . ."

Wilfred answered from the stove. "Brad Scott might have wanted to pave the way for his buying Sufficiency House and its land." The sharp sizzle of chicken meeting hot oil added drama to his statement. "But I doubt he'd go to the extreme of stabbing someone."

"Two different killers then . . . ?" Bettina sighed. "So, as far as Critter's murder is concerned, Joan isn't disqualified after all—or Brad Scott. Clayborn doesn't appear to know about Joan—but why hasn't he gone after Brad Scott?"

"Money is the root of all evil." Wilfred spoke over the crackling sound of frying chicken. Pamela looked over to see him prodding the contents of the skillet with a long fork. Apparently satisfied with his rearrangement, he resumed speaking. "Maybe Brad Scott bribed Clayborn to let that investigation wither away?"

"Clayborn certainly hasn't made any progress." Bettina's disgusted expression involved a furrowed brow and lips pressed tight together. "And now he has another problem."

She occupied herself with the crackers and pimento cheese, and for a while the only sounds were those of food preparation. The aroma of frying chicken, notably the effect of the floury coating being crisped by the bubbling oil, was becoming intense.

"Ten minutes," Wilfred called from the stove.

Bettina hopped to her feet. "Shall we eat in here?" she inquired.

"Of course, of course." Pamela rose too. "You don't need to make things fancy just for me," she said, though she knew Bettina welcomed any chance to use her pretty things.

Bettina fetched placemats and napkins from the dining room sideboard while Pamela gathered plates and flatware. Once the crackers and pimento cheese were cleared away and the table was set, Wilfred stepped around the high counter with a bowl of coleslaw. He followed with a larger bowl containing potato salad, dotted with bits of celery and red onion and garnished with slices of hard-boiled egg.

Bettina added a bit more wine to their glasses and to the glass Wilfred had been sipping from as he worked, which she set near the plate that was to be his.

"Please be seated, dear ladies," Wilfred urged. He returned to the stove and a few minutes later made a triumphant entrance bearing one of Bettina's sage-green pottery platters laden with chicken pieces fried to a perfect golden brown.

An hour later, Pamela and Bettina were relaxing on the sofa in the living room. Wilfred, after a trip across the street to feed Pamela's cats, had brewed and served coffee and settled into one of the comfy armchairs, where he was soon joined by the Frasers' cat, Punkin.

The conversation had been desultory, and Pamela had found her responses dwindling away to monosyllables and then merely the occasional *hmmm*. The sofa was comfortable and she let her head loll back and her eyes close. Eventually she lost track of the topic completely.

"Pamela! Pamela!" Bettina's voice was low but urgent.

"What?" Pamela opened her eyes. Bettina was on her feet and leaning toward her, holding out something in her hand.

"What!" Pamela raised her head and pulled herself upright.

"It's Penny," Bettina said. The something was a telephone handset. "She's frantic!"

"What's happened to her?" Pamela felt a movement in her chest, and the next thing she knew her heart had migrated to her throat.

"She's fine," Bettina said, "but she thinks you're not. She's been trying to call you all evening."

Pamela took the phone.

"*Mo-om!*" The pleading note was all the more wrenching in that Penny's voice seemed to be coming from a great distance. "I've been leaving messages on your voicemail," Penny said mournfully, "and calling the land-line . . ."

"I'm at the Frasers'."

"*Duh!* I figured that out." Pamela was about to speak when Penny added, "Bettina said you're okay."

"I guess you know about the . . . what happened today."

"We do have internet up here, Mom." Penny's tone was dry.

"I know that."

"You're going to let the police handle this, aren't you." It wasn't a question.

"Of course," Pamela said. "Why wouldn't I?"

Bettina had lowered herself onto the sofa when Pamela began to speak. Now she whispered, "Let me talk to her," and held out her hand for the phone.

Pamela handed it over, let her head loll back, closed her eyes, and listened as Bettina's comforting voice assured Penny that Pamela was fine and would be fine and she, Bettina, would make certain of that.

"You are sleeping in the guest room," Bettina announced when the phone call had ended. "Don't even try to resist."

So a very short time later, much before her usual bedtime, Pamela exchanged her clothes for one of Bettina's frilly nightgowns and brushed her teeth with a brand-new toothbrush Bettina produced from the bathroom cupboard. Bettina had put fresh sheets on the bed that had been Wilfred Jr.'s and Pamela slipped gratefully between them.

On the edge of sleep her mind returned to the puzzle of Critter's death, made more puzzling by the day's events. Brad Scott, she thought, actually had nothing to do with it. Dr. Critter was the target, not Sufficiency House, and Flo could have been killed because she knew who the killer was.

Bettina looked up from the *Register* as Pamela entered the Frasers' kitchen the next morning.

"Nothing about Flo in here that you don't already know," she said, folding the paper and setting it aside.

Wilfred, with an apron tied over his robe, was busy at

the counter, but no sooner had Bettina gestured for Pamela to join her at the pine table than he appeared at her side with a steaming cup of coffee. A hearty breakfast of pancakes and sausages followed, and then both Frasers escorted Pamela across the street to her house.

The cats seemed blasé about her overnight absence and not unduly stressed by the fact that their breakfast was being served a bit later than usual. That chore taken care of, Pamela sat down at her own kitchen table, pulled her own copy of the *Register* from its flimsy plastic sleeve, and spread it out.

On the front page of Part 1 a bold headline screamed, "Caretaker Found Dead at Wendelstaff's Sufficiency House." Smaller print beneath it read, "Another Death Linked to Conference?" The article explained that Flower Ransom had been stabbed with a knife from the Sufficiency House kitchen and police were trying to match the fingerprints on the knife with fingerprints in the national database.

Pamela folded the paper back up and climbed the stairs to her office. She pushed the button to bring her computer to life and listened to the chirps and whirs that accompanied the process as the screen brightened. Five messages were waiting in her inbox and a sixth arrived as the chirps and whirs subsided. Only two were from actual people, one from delanob@wendelstaff.edu and the other from her boss.

She'd always been a "save the best for last" person, and Brian's message was likely to be pleasanter than that from her boss. She opened her boss's message first.

"I do not know what to say," her boss had written. "I know you could not have gone sneaking away and let someone else discover that poor woman's body later, but the magazine doesn't need the spotlight on one of its editors (you) added to the fact that Flower Ransom was involved in the knitting bee (that we hosted at that same venue) where Dr. Critter was poisoned."

Pamela sighed. But apparently no response was expected, so she clicked on the message from delanob@wendelstaff.edu. It read,

> *Dear Pamela,*
> *I phoned a few times but I think you're not check-*
> *ing for messages and I can understand you don't*
> *want people hounding you to retell the story. Any-*
> *way, I'm here and I can be there (with you) if it*
> *would help. Here's my cell # in case you don't have*
> *it handy.*
> *Brian*

It would help, she thought. But not quite yet. Meanwhile, thankfully, there was work. "Victorian Crazy Quilts: No Scrap Wasted" sounded somehow more soothing than "Quilts as Transgression: Outsider Artists Make a Statement," so she opened the crazy quilt file and was soon marveling over the colorful photographs of quilts the author had included.

The quilts had an offhand elegance that juxtaposed luxury and frugality. The fabrics were rich silks, satins, and velvets in deep glowing tones. But the point of the quilts was, as the article's title made clear, no scrap wasted. So the patchwork pieces were random shapes, like fragments left after pattern pieces for a fancy garment had been cut. And the pieces were assembled as if for a puzzle, tucking a small triangle in one spot, grafting on a narrow strip elsewhere. A simple embroidery stitch joined the pieces to each other, the embroidery floss changing color at random as if the goal even there was to use up odds and ends.

When the first go-through of the article was finished, Pamela leaned back, closed her eyes, and took several deep breaths. Opening her eyes again, she clicked on her computer's email icon and reread the message from Brian.

It was a bit after noon. Where was he now? she wondered. Not in class perhaps, given that it was lunchtime—though the pancakes and sausage had been so satisfying that she wasn't sure when she would want to eat again. She swiveled her desk chair to the side and picked up the phone.

She waited through a few rings, wondering what message she would leave if she reached his voicemail. But then a familiar voice, deep but genial, said, "Hi, Pamela. How are you?"

"I'm okay, really," she said. "I got your email, just this morning and . . . thanks."

"The campus is buzzing, of course. I haven't seen any police—though I guess the detective ones blend in."

"They wear normal clothes," Pamela said, picturing Detective Clayborn.

"Can I do anything for you?" Brian asked. "Grocery shopping? Laundry? Dining and dancing this weekend?"

Pamela laughed. "Come to dinner Saturday. My neighbors from across the street will be here—you've met Bettina, and I think you'll like her husband, Wilfred."

When he accepted the invitation, Brian's voice had the lilt of a person who was smiling.

Pamela wandered down to the kitchen and pulled a

cookbook from the shelf. The eggplant and zucchini, along with some of her own tomatoes, would become ratatouille, but what to serve with it? She would have to think. With a meal to plan and another article to copyedit, she was feeling a bit more like herself. She climbed the stairs to her office and set to work again.

The outsider art quilts weren't actually all that transgressive—no alarming images or appliquéd manifestos. In fact they looked like quite normal quilts. Pamela was contentedly adding and removing commas, and in general making the punctuation conform to *Fiber Craft* style, when the doorbell chimed.

She stepped across the hall to look out her bedroom window at the street. No media vans were in evidence, so she descended the stairs. Even from the landing it was clear that her visitor was Bettina, visible through the lace that curtained the oval window in the front door.

Bettina sailed in carrying a tray covered with foil. "I can't stay," Bettina announced, "but this is your dinner. Or maybe lunch. Have you eaten since breakfast?" She scanned Pamela up and down as if the answer would be evident. "I hope you haven't been just sitting around fretting," she added.

"No," Pamela said. "I have a lot of work for the magazine. It's due tomorrow morning." She accepted the tray and carried it toward the kitchen, Bettina following.

As Bettina stepped through the doorway, she noticed the cookbook Pamela had left out on the table. "*The Cooking of Southern France!*" she exclaimed. "What's the occasion?"

"My best friends are coming to dinner Saturday night," Pamela said with a smile.

"Will ratatouille be on the menu?" Bettina returned the smile. "I recall that you brought some eggplant and zuc-chini home from Newfield."

"Absolutely!"

"How would homemade plum ice cream be for dessert?" Bettina asked.

"It would be perfect!" Pamela set the tray of food on the counter, hugged Bettina, and they started toward the door. Once it was open, however, Bettina paused on the threshold.

"Will anyone else be here," she inquired with a sly glance from beneath a shadowed eyelid. "Besides the three of us?"

"I hope you don't mind," Pamela said with a teasing laugh. "But I invited Brian Delano."

CHAPTER 24

The next morning Bettina was back. Pamela was dawdling over coffee and an article in the *Register* about a local couple's adventures with their fixer-upper house when the doorbell chimed. She stepped around Catrina, who was already luxuriating in the patch of sun in the entry, and opened the door to admit her friend.

Bettina studied Pamela's face. "You look like you got a decent night's sleep," she said. "No nightmares I hope." Bettina herself was looking bright and cheerful in a crisp shirtdress, magenta and white checked cotton, accessorized with a necklace and earrings of oversize pearls. On her feet were magenta kitten heels.

Pamela shook her head no.

"I can't stay," Bettina went on. "I'm covering an event at the animal shelter this morning. I was hoping for a meeting with Clayborn today too, but no luck."

"There's nothing new in the paper," Pamela said. "I'm sure you saw that."

"You finished your work for the magazine?" Catrina had become aware of the visitor and Bettina leaned over to give her a head-scratch.

"It's done." Pamela nodded. "I just need to send it back."

"So what will you do all day?"

Pamela shrugged. "Knit?"

Bettina's lips, magenta today, parted in a laugh. "You can't stay inside. It's beautiful out."

"I could knit on the porch?" Pamela suggested.

Bettina laughed again. "I'll be through at the shelter by lunchtime. Let's go to Dermott Sparr's picnic."

Pamela's first reaction was to blurt out, "Why?"

Bettina looked so taken aback that Pamela laid a gentle hand on her friend's shoulder. She hadn't meant to sound dismissive, especially given Bettina's care and concern over the past few days. "I'm curious about the food," Bettina said. "I'll be back to pick you up a little before noon."

Bettina had been right. The day was too perfect to stay indoors, and the patch of grass behind the Wendelstaff dorms, with its view of the Haversack River, proved an ideal spot to savor the day's mid-September beauty. The tide was in and the river was high, the broad expanse of sky-reflecting water hiding the mossy rocks and litter that low tide revealed.

Dermott had greeted Pamela and Bettina warmly, seemingly unsurprised that they had taken him up on his invitation. "Help yourselves," he said with a sweeping gesture that took in two picnic tables draped with colorful cloths and laden with platters, bowls, and baskets of food. He handed them each a plate and a fork, saying, "Borrowed from the campus food service, so please don't walk off with them." In keeping with the occasion, the tee-shirt he wore today depicted a turnip with a human face. The greenery sprouting from its top resembled a leafy ponytail.

"Try some of the corn and tomato salad," a young woman hovering over the nearest table suggested.

Pamela stared at the selections. Nothing actually looked like corn and tomato salad.

"It's that one." The young woman pointed to a shallow bowl in which kernels of blue corn intermingled with chunks of deep brown tomatoes and petite rounds of something yellow.

"Carrots." The young woman smiled. "Not all carrots are orange. Some are yellow, and even purple."

"Close your eyes while you take a bite," said a voice at Pamela's elbow. "How much is taste? How much is looks?"

The salad was good, Pamela and Bettina agreed as they sampled it. So were the fried black rice, the tossed salad composed of radicchio, red tomatoes, and red bell pepper, and the ratatouille-like dish made with white eggplant.

People came and went—young people who were obviously students, various faculty members, a few men from the campus landscaping crew. Dermott was in his element, accepting congratulations, explaining the purpose of the picnic, posing for selfies with attendees documenting their attendance for social media.

Pamela found herself chatting with an older man who identified himself as Joe, the head of campus housing.

"Blue cornbread," he commented. "Derm's got quite the imagination."

They were joined by one of the men from the landscaping crew, Walt. For a bit the conversation focused on the menu. Then, as if they'd forgotten Pamela was there, it segued into campus gossip.

"I heard Bob's leaving," Walt said. "Is that true?"

"I hope so," Joe commented with a laugh. "The guy's everywhere, but he doesn't do much work that I can see."

"His brother got him the job, so . . ." Walt picked up his fork. "Did you try any of the white eggplant thing yet?"

"The ratatouille?"

"It looks weird but it's good," Walt said. "Nothing can beat my wife's though. She makes more things with eggplant than you can believe. Has to—it grows like a weed in our yard."

Dermott approached then. "So, what do you think?" he asked. From his beaming expression, it was clear that he was pleased with the success of his event.

"Everything is delicious," Pamela said. "And very artistic."

"Good work, Derm!" Joe slapped him on the back. "And it's a nice chance for the new dorm kids to get acquainted."

Bettina joined the group, congratulating Dermott and introducing herself to Joe and Walt. A slight breeze was rustling the leaves overhead and creating sunlit ripples on the river's surface, and Pamela was happy to let conversation flow around her as she nibbled on black fried rice, pickled squash blossoms, and deep purple bell pepper.

"Hey, Derm!" called a voice from behind Pamela. She

turned to see Bob drawing near. Dermott greeted him genially, as did Walt and Joe, despite what Pamela now knew to be their private view of him.

"So, Bob, my man, you're bailing out?" Joe commented after a bit of back and forth about Dermott's food and the new semester getting underway.

Bob's grin and a deep nod that involved not only his head but also his neck and shoulders made his answer superfluous, but nonetheless he replied, "Yep! I'm outta here."

For most of the journey home, conversation focused on Dermott Sparr and his creative food ideas. That topic exhausted, they were silent for some minutes as the nature preserve sped by on the right. But when Orchard Street drew near, Pamela recalled the errand Bettina had devoted her morning to.

"How did the animal shelter event go?" she asked.

"Oh, they're doing the cutest thing!" Bettina exclaimed, and the car lurched as she inadvertently stepped harder on the gas.

"I'll wait till you make the turn," Pamela said, "then I'd love to hear about it."

"It's the kitty and doggie fashion show, Cat Walk and Putting on the Dog," Bettina explained when they were safely around the corner. "Not in person, of course. The animals would be terrified. It will just be photos on the shelter's website. People can submit photos of their own pets wearing original creations, or donate kitty and doggie clothes for the shelter animals to model. It goes live Sunday, then people can vote for their favorites. Each vote costs five dollars, donated to the shelter, and some of the clothes will be auctioned off too. People have already submitted a lot of photos and I got a few for the *Advocate*."

"Wilfred is coming with the ice cream," Bettina announced as she stepped over Pamela's threshold several hours later, "but I wanted to see if you needed help. This is so exciting!"

To look at Bettina—eyes bright with anticipation and skin fairly glowing—one would have thought it was *she* who had been dating Brian Delano and that tonight's dinner was an opportunity to capture his heart once and for all. She had dressed for the occasion in a ruby-red sheath and matching suede pumps.

Pamela looked down at her own outfit, her nice black pants and a blouse Penny had found for her at a fancy charity shop, gauzy fabric with a streaky print in shades of green and indigo.

"I'm glad you got that blouse out again," Bettina said. "It suits you." She proceeded into the living room and from there through the arch to the dining room.

Pamela had already set the table, arranging her rose-garlanded wedding china on a lace tablecloth. She had added white linen napkins, tag-sale wineglasses with an etched filigree design, and silver candleholders holding tall white candles.

"I don't think you need any help here," Bettina commented.

"Everything is under control," Pamela assured her and led her into the kitchen.

On the stove top, a large skillet held ratatouille, fragrant with garlic and onion and—with its blend of purple eggplant, green zucchini, and red tomatoes—more colorful than Dermott's had been. A jar of rice stood at the ready on the counter, and a substantial flank steak lay in a shallow pan, sprinkled with salt and pepper and waiting to go under the broiler.

"There's to be Caesar salad too." Pamela pointed to a tin of anchovies and a chunk of Parmesan sitting near her favorite wooden salad bowl. "But my version, without the egg."

The doorbell chimed then, and Bettina darted to the entry with Pamela following. Jovial voices reached them even before the door was open, and once it was open, they found Brian and Wilfred engaged in genial conversation.

"We've met," Brian said, gesturing for Wilfred to enter first.

"Woofus and I were chatting with Rick," Wilfred explained, "and Brian pulled up and got out of his car. "Woofus took to him first thing, which is odd for Woofus. We'd finished our walk so I took him back home and picked up these."

He held out two shopping bags.

"I like dogs." Brian shrugged and his wolfish features softened as he smiled. "What can I say? And Rick is sure a friendly guy. He recognized me right off."

Pamela felt her heart lurch and she closed her eyes. Why the idea of Brian and Rick encountering each other on the sidewalk outside her house bothered her she wasn't sure, but she couldn't think about it now. Her guests were here and there was a dinner to serve. She smiled, belatedly, and accepted the shopping bags from Wilfred.

The casual dinners when Pamela hosted the Frasers

usually began with wine and conversation in the kitchen, as Pamela cooked and everyone chatted. Brian blended in easily, happy to stand near the refrigerator and join the others in sipping a glass of the Chablis he had brought. One of Wilfred's shopping bags had yielded up a plastic bin of homemade plum ice cream, which went into the freezer, as well as a Co-Op bakery box containing what Bettina described as "the best shortbread cookies you will ever eat." The box of cookies joined the open bottle of Chablis and a dish of mixed nuts on the table.

The other shopping bag was full of plums, lots and lots of plums, Wilfred explained, and they were now Pamela's, to do with what she wished.

Pamela measured rice and water into a saucepan and set it to boil, and then turned on the broiler as conversation ebbed and flowed around her. Wilfred discovered that Brian shared his interest in local history and the two compared notes on visits to sites unchanged since New Jersey was a colony. Bettina contributed the recollection of a trip she and Wilfred had made to a water-powered flour mill situated on a stream, coming away with a souvenir bag of flour.

By this time, Pamela had slid the flank steak under the broiler. After a few minutes of intense sizzling, the aroma of broiling steak became so distracting that conversation slowed and then stopped.

While Pamela kept an eye on the steak's progress, stooping periodically to peer through the window in her oven door and at one point turning the steak over, Bettina sprang into action. She spooned ratatouille and rice into a serving dishes from Pamela's wedding-china set and carried them to the dining room.

Wilfred had preceded her, and was lighting the can-

dles. He had drawn the cork from a bottle of red wine earlier and it sat at the ready in a silver wine coaster. Brian,
meanwhile, stood by as Pamela maneuvered the pan
holding the steak, now seared to a glistening deep brown
with a touch of char, onto a broad platter.

"It has to rest," Pamela said. "Then it gets cut into narrow slices."

The candles were a few inches shorter, the plates were
empty but for traces of the meal, and all that was left of
the wine in the tag-sale glasses was a hint of red in their
depths. Bettina was telling Brian how important it was
for Arborvillians to have a newspaper that covered local
events, even if it was only a weekly.

He was nodding sagely and interjecting an occasional
"Of course." From time to time, a hint of a smile under-
scored his support of the journalistic mission. Pamela
couldn't help noticing how the flickering candlelight flattered his dark good looks.

Wilfred had been chatting with Pamela. After compli-
menting her, for the third time, on the resounding success
of her meal, including the "inspired choice" of Caesar
salad, he rose, picked up his plate, and reached for
Pamela's.

"Wilfred, you don't have to," Pamela said, and she
rose too.

"No, no, dear lady." Wilfred gestured for her to sit
down. "Turnabout's fair play. You cooked a sumptuous
dinner. I shall clear away and serve dessert."

Brian was on his feet then too, observing that many
hands made light work as he gathered plates and silverware. The two men disappeared into the kitchen and Bet-

tina leaned toward Pamela. "He's so thoughtful," she breathed. "And so interesting." (Never mind that in her interactions with Brian that evening, she had done most of the talking.)

From the kitchen came the sound of china being rinsed and stacked, evidently Wilfred's chore, while Brian made a few additional trips to the dining room to collect serving dishes, the platter, and the wooden salad bowl. The freezer door opened and closed, Wilfred could be heard saying, "Bowls are up there," silverware rattled—and a few minutes later Brian appeared carrying a wedding-china plate heaped with the pale ovals that were the shortbread cookies. Wilfred followed with two bowls of ice cream and returned to the kitchen for two more.

"And you said you made this?" Brian held his spoon poised over the mound of rose-streaked creaminess in his bowl.

Bettina nodded. "You don't need one of those ice-cream makers that you crank. You just mix up a kind of custard and put it in the freezer. But you have to take it out every once in a while and stir and stir."

Everyone sampled their ice cream then.

"Mmm, wonderful," Pamela murmured after swallowing a chilly mouthful that unfolded in layers rich and sweet and tart.

"And you started with fresh plums?" Brian's appreciation was obvious from the heaping spoonful he had just scooped from his bowl.

"We—well really, Wilfred—peeled them and made a kind of plum compote," Bettina said, with a fond look at her husband.

It was time to pass the shortbread cookies then. Everyone agreed that they were the perfect choice, complementing the ice cream without competing.

"I make a mean cup of coffee," Brian volunteered when the last dribbles of ice cream had been scraped from the bowls.

"I just have beans," Pamela said. "I grind them fresh each time."

"No problem." He rose and Pamela followed him to the kitchen, where they worked in companionable silence, he on the coffee and she setting out cups and saucers and filling the cream pitcher.

An hour later Wilfred and Bettina exchanged a meaningful glance across the table, and Wilfred started to push his chair back. "It's getting on toward bedtime for us old folks," he said. "It's been a wonderful evening, Pamela." Once on his feet, he circled the table and offered Bettina a hand.

Brian stood up too, but Bettina motioned for him to sit back down. "No, no," she exclaimed. "You don't have to leave just because we're leaving. We'll be on our way and leave you young people to yourselves. The night is young!" She winked at Pamela, who was groaning inwardly but trying to remain expressionless.

Brian hadn't obeyed Bettina's gesture and was still on his feet. He stepped up to Wilfred, held out his hand, and said, "Great meeting you."

"Same here," Wilfred said, and clapped him on the shoulder.

"And Bettina"—he tipped his head in a slight bow—"so nice to see you again."

Together he and Pamela escorted the Frasers to the door and out into the balmy evening, waving them on their way. Once they were across the street, Brian turned to her, his expression hard to read.

Feeling bold, perhaps spurred on by the commotion that had arisen in her chest, she reached for his hands. "You really don't have to leave," she said. "We could go back inside and . . ." They were nearly the same height and she leaned forward, inviting a kiss.

Brian obliged, but he left his hands where they were, at his sides and gripped by hers. She loosened her grip and pulled him closer, pressing her palms against his back. After a moment, he edged away.

"There was someone else, Pamela," he said, "but it ended, and the end was painful." His expression, so tragic his handsomeness seemed erased, suggested he was reliving the breakup. "It's still painful," he said, "and I'm not ready . . ." He paused. "So I hope we can go on . . . as we've been. Maybe you're not looking for . . . a forever . . ." His hand fluttered as if searching for the right word.

She knew what he meant. "I thought I might be . . . looking . . ." she said, "but I'm . . ." *You're what?* asked a voice in her brain. Without answering the voice, she said, "Yes, let's go on . . . as we've been."

She enjoyed the goodnight kiss all the more knowing that it meant they would go on . . . as they'd been.

CHAPTER 25

Sunday had been uneventful, except for an email from Dean Tate with information about the memorial reception that the college was hosting for Flo Ransom the next day. Bettina had come by angling for details on what happened with Brian after she and Wilfred left the previous evening. She had gone away unsatisfied—though she had volunteered to accompany Pamela to the reception. Wilfred was leaving Monday morning for the fishing trip he and his cousin had been planning, she said, and so she figured she might as well do something useful with her time alone.

Accordingly, she showed up at Pamela's door Monday at one p.m., dressed in the navy-blue outfit accessorized with pearls that she had worn for Critter's obsequies. Pamela herself was wearing the black V-necked dress

Bettina had bought her, but with a scarf making the neckline less dramatic and with her hair hanging loose.

"Dean Tate said the first thought had been to honor Flo's work by hosting the reception at Sufficiency House," Pamela explained as they walked toward where her serviceable compact waited on the driveway. "But then she reflected that the house's associations were too grisly for people to feel comfortable there. So they're having it in the faculty club."

"Again with the faculty club," Bettina commented as she climbed into the passenger-side seat. "The food is good though. I'm glad I didn't eat lunch."

The room looked much the same as it had for the reception after Critter's funeral. The huge windows in the far wall gave a view of the river, which was at low tide today, revealing mossy rocks littered with detritus. Parallel to the windows, the buffet table held trays and platters and baskets and bowls, as well as two chafing dishes. The crowd, however, was sparser than it had been for Dr. Critter.

"We didn't issue a blanket invitation to the students this time," Dean Tate explained as she greeted them just inside the door. Like Bettina, she was wearing the same outfit she had worn the last time, the dark gray jersey knit. "It's just faculty and administration, if they wanted to come, and staff of course, and a few students who had particular connections with Sufficiency House."

"Flo didn't have relatives?" Bettina asked, her affection for her own family lending the question particular poignancy.

"A sister," Dean Tate said. "She took care of the funeral arrangements—actually Flo was cremated, but the sister didn't care to mix and mingle, and there are no other local relatives."

A gray-haired man with a professorial air claimed Dean Tate's attention then. Excusing herself, she encouraged Pamela and Bettina to help themselves to the buffet and stepped aside. Conversation buzzed around them, punctuated by occasional laughter, as they threaded their way through the small crowd. Younger faculty of both genders were in jeans and casual shirts, while older faculty and administrators wore dressier outfits. Pamela recognized Bitsy Daniels in a group of women whose manner, clothes, and grooming styles suggested that they, like Bitsy, were office staff.

"There are shrimp again," Bettina commented, speeding up as they drew closer to the table. Suddenly Pamela laid a hand on her arm.

"Wait," she whispered and stopped right where she was, anchoring Bettina at her side. "I think I hear that person," she added, still whispering.

"What person?" Bettina was gazing at the chafing dish containing shrimp.

"Joan Robbins. Seduced and abandoned." Pamela backed up, pulling Bettina with her. She turned in the direction from which the voice, with its nasal tone and distorted vowels, had come. Standing and sitting around one of the small tables against the wall, sipping wine and nibbling at plates of food, was a group of women various in age, shape, and size.

"I think it's a real shame," one of them said, the "I" coming out more like "Oi." The speaker was a meek-looking woman, slender but showing her age in the lines around her eyes and her tired complexion. Her hair, blonde dulled by a mixture of gray, was fastened back with a large barrette.

"That one," Pamela whispered.

Bettina stared. "That's not how I pictured her," she whispered back. "But let's see what she has to say."

Pamela followed Bettina across the floor, wondering what on earth her friend's approach would be—all the more when Bettina veered off to help herself to a glass of wine from the bar. She handed it to Pamela, fetched another for herself, and proceeded on toward the group around the table.

She paused when she got near and waited for Pamela to catch up with her, as if she'd been seeking an out-of-the-way spot for them to stand and sip their wine. But they were close enough to eavesdrop on the group's conversation. The topic seemed to be what effect Flo's death would have on the mission of Sufficiency House, though Joan's contribution was minimal.

Suddenly Bettina wheeled around to face the group. Fumbling at her purse with her free hand, she said, "Ladies, excuse me, but I have to put my wine down for a minute to take a phone call." She lowered her wineglass to the table, darted away, and pulled out her phone.

In a few minutes, after acting out one side of an imagined call, she was back. Joan, conveniently, was standing a bit away from the other women, as if she didn't know them as well as they knew each other. She fit the profile that Pamela had imagined for one of Critter's conquests—a woman likely swept off her feet, and amazed that the great Dr. Critter would notice her.

Bettina ducked toward the table to retrieve her wineglass, straightened up, and—as if she had just noticed Joan—said, "Terribly sad event, isn't it?"

Seeming relieved that she had a conversation partner, Joan brightened. "Yes," she said, "terribly sad."

"Did you know Flo Ransom?" Bettina inquired, her

mobile features primed to respond with appropriate grief if the answer was yes.

Joan nodded and explained that the previous spring she had done a project involving Sufficiency House. Warming to Bettina's interest, she described Flo's help with research into Depression-era cookbooks.

"Do you think the college will recruit a new caretaker," Bettina asked after a bit, "to continue the Sufficiency House programs? After the death of Dr. Critter, and now this . . . ?" She left the question unfinished.

Standing a few feet from Bettina, Pamela had been studying Joan as she talked. Now, at the mention of Dr. Critter, Joan stiffened slightly. All she said was, "I hope so," but she focused her gaze on the floor and seemed to lose interest in the conversation.

Pamela, feeling the effects of wine on an empty stomach, began to edge toward the buffet table. Bettina noticed the motion and, after a few pleasant words to Joan, caught up with her. Their wineglasses were empty and they handed them over at the bar. The noise level in the room had increased, suggesting that the bartender was having a busy afternoon.

"Shrimp, for sure," Bettina declared, after picking up a plate. "And meatballs, and some of the smoked salmon . . ."

They joined the ragged line of people working its way along the table, past a large tray of open-faced sandwiches, a cheese board accompanied by variously shaped crackers, meatballs in a chafing dish, shrimp in another chafing dish, a platter of miniature quiches, and a tray of raw vegetables with a bowl of dip.

One of the small tables against the nearest wall beckoned when they reached the end with full plates. Two empty chairs offered welcome perches, and soon they had lowered their plates to the table and lowered themselves into the chairs. They chatted as they ate, first about the food.

"I don't remember the crabmeat quiche from the last time," Bettina commented, half of a miniature quiche poised en route to her mouth. "Do you? They're delicious."

"I had one the last time," Pamela said. "It *was* delicious." She herself was nibbling on a sandwich featuring prosciutto topped with a dab of Dijon mustard on a thin slice of baguette.

But as their plates emptied, the conversation turned to Bettina's encounter with Joan.

"I'm glad we finally found her," Bettina said, "but she doesn't seem like the kind of person who would stab someone."

"We were thinking there could be two killers," Pamela reminded her.

"That was when we thought maybe Flo killed Critter and someone in love with Critter killed Flo in revenge," Bettina pointed out. "But we never figured out why Flo would kill Critter."

"True," Pamela agreed. "Joan has a motive—at least for murdering Dr. Critter—and she's the only suspect we have left."

"Why would she kill Flo though?" Bettina picked up the last meatball on her plate.

"Because Flo helped her arrange the murder, but then threatened to tip off the police? We know they knew each other—from the cookbook project."

"Oh my goodness!" Bettina set the meatball back down. "Flo served the coffee at the bee, so she could have timed things so the killer—Joan?—knew just when to add the poison to the dispenser." She paused and picked up the meatball again. "Why not just add it herself though?"

"She didn't personally want Dr. Critter dead," Pamela explained. "She was just doing a favor for a friend."

Bettina clapped her hands. "I think we've figured it out!" she exclaimed. "Now . . . how to steer Clayborn in the right direction?" She ate the meatball and swiveled around to study the buffet table. "They're clearing everything away," she murmured, climbing to her feet. "But there might be a few meatballs left."

The person doing the clearing away was Bob the maintenance man, pushing a rolling cart ahead of him and working his way along the table from the far end. Meanwhile, a young student server was setting out platters of brownies.

Bettina and Bob reached the chafing dish with the meatballs at exactly the same moment. Bettina peered inside. Looking up with a flirtatious smile, she said, "I'll just grab these last few."

"We meet again," Bob said cheerfully. "Help yourself." As Bettina speared the meatballs with the long toothpicks staged nearby, he added, "Two of these fancy dos in as many weeks. Think there'll be a third one soon?"

Bettina seemed a bit startled but she responded, "No, I don't think so."

Bob laughed. "Clairvoyant?"

"I cover crime for the *Arborville Advocate*." Bettina's tone reflected the seriousness with which she approached her profession.

"All the news that fits?" Bob laughed again. (Apparently even people outside Arborville knew of the *Advocate*'s reputation.)

"I'll have you know that I meet regularly with Arborville's chief detective, Lucas Clayborn. He's always interested in my insights." When provoked, Bettina could sound quite haughty.

Arborville's only detective, Pamela amended to herself.

"There will not be a third murder," Bettina said, "because the same person who killed Critter killed Flo and now it's all over. Flo was an accomplice and she and Critter's killer had a falling out and so Critter's killer killed her. Detective Clayborn and I will be discussing the case at our next meeting."

Back in Arborville, Pamela and Bettina chatted for a few minutes in Pamela's driveway and then Bettina crossed the street to her own house. Pamela climbed her porch steps, retrieved her mail, unlocked the door, and stepped over her threshold. All of the mail, including a flyer from a pest control company claiming, "They won't know what hit them," went into the recycling basket.

She had returned the three copyedited quilt articles that morning, and no new assignment had arrived from the magazine before she left for the reception. Nor was there anything new now. Knitting in the middle of the day wasn't a common occurrence for her, but she decided that would be an ideal way to spend the rest of the afternoon—perhaps sitting on the porch.

The rhythms of crisscrossing needles and looping yarn worked their magic. Add to that the perfect September day, not warm but not cool, and her thoughts were soon adrift. One thought led to another and another in an almost dreamlike state of free association.

The red sweater for her father was coming together nicely. She was only on the second sleeve, but she had until December to finish. The red yarn had been a good choice for Christmas—a bright red, not like the muted red that Flo had achieved with her salvaged yarn and the bloodroot dye. She pictured Flo at the knitting bee, contentedly laboring over a red sock.

Suddenly her mind was no longer adrift. A thought was taking shape, and her busy fingers ceased their motion. The red sock was to be a gift, of course! It was to join another red sock as a gift for the man Flo met for trysts in the Sufficiency House garden shed, the man she loved not wisely but too well.

She had described to Bettina her theory that Flo was killed because she was an accomplice in Dr. Critter's murder and then had a falling out with the killer. And Bettina, while serving herself the last few meatballs at the reception, had described that theory to the very next person she talked to. Pamela realized she had been right about why Flo was killed but wrong about whose accomplice she had been. And now . . .

She raised her eyes from her work. An unfamiliar car had appeared at the curb near the Frasers' house, a shabby car, unlike the cars typically seen on Orchard Street.

Pamela set her knitting aside and bounded down the porch steps, reaching the Frasers' door in less than a minute. Panting in time with her rapidly thumping heart, she pressed the doorbell, again and again. There was no response, not even—ominously—an answering bark from Woofus.

She darted around the side of the house and crept onto the patio, sneaking up to the edge of the sliding glass doors. As she approached the doors, she noticed that the nearest one was open a few inches.

She was distracted from the door, however, by an eager snuffling sound behind her. She turned to see Woofus, who greeted her in his diffident way but ignored her question about the whereabouts of Bettina. As he romped off onto the lawn, she approached the doors more boldly.

Bettina had entered the kitchen, apparently just returned from taking Woofus for a walk. She draped a leash over one of the chairs surrounding the scrubbed pine table and stepped toward the refrigerator. She was met by a figure emerging from the kitchen's deeper recesses, a figure carrying a knife. The knife was Wilfred's prized chef's knife, but the figure was not Wilfred. It was Bob Lombard.

I knew it, Pamela whispered to herself. Bettina hadn't realized it, but she been talking to the person who murdered Critter and Flo when she implied that she had figured out the murders and boasted of her connections with Detective Clayborn. Why, why, why, Pamela asked herself, why hadn't she taken a moment to grab her phone before running across the street?

When Bettina caught sight of Bob, she reacted with a yelp. Pamela hadn't imagined her heart could thump any more rapidly, but it sped up, and sweat prickled her forehead. She pounded on the glass door—if she distracted Bob, Bettina could flee through the dining room and living room and out the front door. But instead, Bettina stood her ground.

"What are you doing here?" she demanded.

Recognizing his mistress's voice, and perhaps sensing her alarm, Woofus bounded onto the patio. As a high-pitched whine emerged from his throat, he pawed at the narrow gap between the door and the doorframe. Taking the hint, Pamela slid the door back and Woofus sprang into the kitchen. Pamela followed.

The whine was replaced by a full-throated bark, which startled Bob, and the knife clattered to the floor. Then Woofus reared up, placed his front paws on Bob's shoulders, and nipped at his face.

"Off! No! Down!" Bob shouted frantically, retreating until his back was against the sink and then collapsing to the floor.

Meanwhile, Bettina had fetched her smart phone and was summoning the police. Satisfied that they were on their way, she sank trembling into the nearest chair as Woofus stood guard over Bob, warning him with a snarl or nip if he moved. Pamela joined her friend at the scrubbed pine table.

After a few minutes, Pamela felt her heartbeat slow, and Bettina had recovered enough to look over at Bob and ask, again, "What are you doing here?"

When there was no answer from the region of the sink, Pamela responded for him.

"He's our killer," she said. "He thought if you told Detective Clayborn that Flo was killed because she was the killer's accomplice, that tip would lead him to the truth about the murders."

"He killed Critter?" Bettina frowned and wrinkled her nose. "Why?"

"Resentment and jealousy," Pamela explained. "He and Dr. Critter are brothers. Bitsy told us Dr. Critter got Bob his job and somebody at Dermott's picnic mentioned that Bob's brother got Bob his job, so . . ."

"Half-brothers," came a mournful voice from the floor

near the sink. "The same mother. She married too young, and the wrong guy, then left him and abandoned me to be raised by my loser father. She remarried and had another son, and then I couldn't even have my own name. The new guy was named Robert and he wanted a namesake." He punctuated the sentence with a sound like a cross between a sob and a snort.

"Robert Greer-Gordon Critter! He's teaching at Wendelstaff and I'm working in maintenance. Sure he got me the job, and he even put me in his will, but he never let me forget how superior he was to me, how sorry for me he felt. Once his father and our mother were gone, he was loaded, believe me. But now he's gone and I'd be rich, except . . ."

"It *was* a clever plot," Pamela said.

"Did Flo put the poison in the coffee dispenser?" Bettina half-rose and peered toward where Bob was sitting.

It was Pamela who answered. "It wasn't that kind of poison. Among his other duties at Wendelstaff, Bob did some exterminating." *They won't know what hit them,* said a voice in her head, quoting from the pest control flyer that had appeared in her mailbox that afternoon.

"*Robert* was always bumming cigarettes off me." Bob's tone mocked the self-importance that Critter's eschewing a nickname implied. "So I dusted ricin powder on a whole pack and pulled out the pack every time he asked for one that Saturday. I figured the poison would kick in about midafternoon. All Flo had to do was make sure he drank some coffee to put the cops off the trail."

"You *used* her!" Bettina stood all the way up so she could address Bob directly.

"She wanted to help. We were going to take the inheritance and go off together. But then she started feeling guilty, and blaming me for pulling her into it. I couldn't have her going to the cops, could I?"

He leaned forward to emphasize his point and Woofus barked sharply. At that moment, a siren, faint at first, distinguished itself from the suburban sounds of traffic, children playing, and lawnmowers. It soared to a dramatic wail and subsided with a resentful moan.

"They're here," Pamela exclaimed. She sped toward the doorway that led to the dining room and the living room beyond and flung the front door open to admit Officer Anders and Officer Sanchez. "Back here," she said, "in the kitchen. An . . . intruder . . . broke in and threatened Bettina—my neighbor—with a knife. She's okay though."

They hurried ahead of her, Officer Sanchez a bit behind Officer Anders. As they approached the door leading to the kitchen, Officer Sanchez looked back at Pamela and said, "How did you two manage to . . ."

"Restrain him?" Pamela asked. A sharp bark greeted them as they stepped through the doorway, and Woofus advanced across the floor, leaving Bob slumped against the cabinet that housed the sink.

"Oh, I see." Officer Sanchez said, and both officers halted.

"There's the knife." Pamela pointed to Wilfred's prized chef's knife, which lay where it had landed when Bob dropped it.

Bettina was still sitting at the pine table. She held out a hand to Woofus and whispered, "Good doggie, good doggie. It's okay." Woofus crept forward and laid his shaggy head on her thigh. She stroked him and crooned, "*Hero* doggie." Then she swiveled to look at the officers and said, "Woofus won't hurt you."

"Is this the man who threatened you?" Officer Sanchez asked, gesturing at Bob.

Bettina nodded.

"With this knife." She gestured at the knife.

Bettina nodded again.

Officer Anders detached a pair of handcuffs from his belt and advanced toward the sink. Officer Sanchez, looking quite official despite her sweet heart-shaped face, focused her attention on Pamela. "How did you happen to be here?" she inquired, after producing a small notepad and a pen.

"Bettina and I are neighbors," Pamela said. "We pop back and forth across the street all the time. She didn't answer when I rang the bell, so I walked around the back and saw that the sliding door was open a little bit." Pamela nodded toward the door and went on. "And then Woofus came running into the backyard and Bettina walked into the kitchen and yelped when she saw the . . . intruder . . . and Woofus started pawing at the door so I pushed it all the way open and he dashed in and started barking."

"Lucky you happened by just when you did," Officer Sanchez commented when she had finished writing.

"Yes," Pamela said. "Yes, it was."

After the police had gone on their way, taking Bob Lombard with them, Pamela and Bettina sat at the kitchen table talking.

"Lucky you happened by just when you did," Bettina said, echoing Officer Sanchez.

"Not so lucky." Pamela laughed, if a bit shakily. She hadn't quite recovered from the shock of discovering she'd been correct to fear for her friend's safety. "I realized that you'd been talking to the killer when you described my theory about what Flo's murder had to do with Dr. Critter's—and that it was only a matter of time before he decided he had to silence you. I was knitting on the porch when I noticed a strange car near your house."

"How did you know Bob was the killer?"

"He was the man in the garden shed," Pamela explained. "Those red socks Flo was knitting at the bee were for him. He was wearing them the day he came crawling out from under the desk in the office of Fine and Professional Arts."

"Why didn't you tell the police Bob was the killer when they were here?" Bettina asked. "You solved that crime." She brought her fist down on the table to emphasize the point.

"Clayborn will figure it out once he looks into why Bob thought he had to silence you," Pamela said. "Let him have the credit. He doesn't like it when he thinks the taxpayers of Arborville are doing the work the police are paid to do."

CHAPTER 26

Pamela surveyed her handiwork, knowing that Bettina would be pleased. Arranged in two rows on a large platter were eight plum turnovers, glossy golden-brown semicircles with trickles of plummy syrup leaking from the steam vents pricked in their tops. The platter sat on her kitchen table, accompanied by a stack of small plates, six cups and saucers, forks and spoons, lacy napkins, and her cut-glass cream and sugar set. Stepping to the counter, she measured out coffee beans.

The morning had brought welcome news in the form of an article in the *Register*. Bob Lombard had been charged with killing Robert Greer-Gordon Critter and Flower Ransom. Police had interviewed Flo's neighbors and had learned of a "shabby car" frequently parked outside Sufficiency House, including—briefly—the afternoon of the day Flo was killed. When police arrested Bob for his attempt on Bettina's life, his car was identified as the same "shabby car" and Detective Clayborn was able to wrap up his case, despite that fact that Bob had been unwilling to explain the cause of his animus toward Bettina.

Pamela had granted an interview to Marcy Brewer of the *Register* and fielded relieved phone calls from Penny and Brian, as well as a relieved email from her boss. The email brought with it three articles to evaluate and a message saying a book for Pamela to review was en route via FedEx. But tonight it was her turn to host the Knit and Nibblers, and she had been grateful for the cleaning and baking chores that distracted her from the dramatic events of the previous day.

The doorbell's chime called her away from the coffee preparations. It was only a quarter to seven and, as she suspected, the early bird proved to be Bettina, wearing wide-legged trousers in olive-green linen and a silky flower-print blouse. She was escorted by Wilfred, who had hurried back from his fishing trip as soon as he learned what had happened.

"Safely delivered," he said with a bow. He focused on Pamela, his ruddy face serious. "I can't bear to think what would have happened if you hadn't crossed the street just at that moment."

"Very lucky timing." Pamela smiled.

"The three of us know it was more than that." Wilfred returned the smile and then bent toward Bettina. "I shall return at nine to escort you home, dear wife," he said and retreated toward the porch steps.

Bettina sailed across the threshold, grasped Pamela by the arms, and stood back to inspect her. "None the worse for wear," she pronounced. The pucker in her brow relaxed and she directed her gaze toward the kitchen doorway. "What is that heavenly smell?"

"Plum turnovers," Pamela said. "Do you want to see them?"

"I do," Bettina responded. "But first, you have to see this." She reached into her purse for her phone, brought up an image on its screen, and held it out to Pamela.

Something looked familiar, but for a moment Pamela couldn't think why. Lavender yarn shot through with silver lurex had been fashioned into a fetching sweater, a very small sweater—with four sleeves. It was worn by a winsome jet-black cat.

"Cat Walk and Putting on the Dog?" Pamela inquired.

Bettina nodded. "To benefit the Haversack animal shelter. And our own Roland DeCamp has raised two hundred dollars for them so far, with forty votes for his knit creation, modeled by Cuddles."

Pamela and Bettina were not the only Knit and Nibblers to have discovered what Roland was knitting from his lavender and silver yarn. Feet echoed on the porch steps, and a crescendo of voices announced the arrival of more Knit and Nibblers. Without waiting for the bell, Bettina pulled the door back to reveal Roland front and center, looking pleased in spite of himself. Holly and Karen were on his left and Nell on his right.

"No, really," Holly was saying, "it is the cutest thing I have ever seen. You are so talented—and so kindhearted to do that for the shelter. I already gave you five votes and Desmond gave you five too, and I'm telling everyone I meet about the shelter fashion show."

"Well, I just . . . it was . . ." Roland tightened his grip on his impressive briefcase as if to reassure himself that being kindhearted was compatible with being a high-powered corporate lawyer.

"Welcome! Come in, come in!" Bettina stepped aside

and waved the group into the entry. Ever the gentleman, Roland was last over the threshold.

"Please sit down." Pamela added her greeting. Holly and Karen settled next to each other on the sofa and Nell took the big armchair near the hearth. All three of them continued to heap praise on Roland, with Bettina and Pamela chiming in as well, as Roland perched on the hassock at the other side of the hearth, Bettina next to Holly on the sofa, and Pamela on the rummage-sale chair with the carved wooden back and needlepoint seat.

Soon needles were clicking busily on the pale green donkey, the burnt-orange tunic, the argyle sock, the creamy white turtleneck, and the red sweater—and Roland was casting on from a skein of yarn in a sedate shade of tan.

If Pamela had thought Roland's heartwarming contribution to the shelter fashion show would distract the group from her role in the arrest of the man who murdered Dr. Critter and Flo Ransom, she was soon proved wrong.

Holly looked up from the argyle sock to say, "Roland isn't the only celebrity in our midst tonight."

Perhaps eager to shrug off the burden of his fame, Roland spoke up. "That was quite a story in the *Register* this morning, and Pamela is to be congratulated for anticipating the danger Bettina was in."

"I'm certainly grateful to Pamela," Bettina said, "and to Woofus too."

With a hesitant glance across the room at Nell, who everyone knew disapproved of amateur sleuthing, Holly said, "Was it just a lucky chance that you came to visit right when he was there, Pamela?"

"Why, yes. Very lucky." Pamela glanced at Nell too and thought she saw the flicker of a smile. "Of course, after being so involved with the conference, I was concerned when the police seemed not to be making much progress. They did solve the murders though, when they were able to link Bob Lombard with Flo because of his car, and then got the report from the neighbor that the car was parked outside Sufficiency House the afternoon Flo was killed."

Holly shook her head. "And they had him right in their hands already because they'd responded to 911 when he was trying to attack Bettina." The streak in her raven hair was maroon tonight and she was wearing large silvery hoop earrings. She went on. "The timing was amazing though. If you'd showed up even a few minutes later, Woofus would have been watching outside that door while . . . while . . ." She shuddered, set her knitting down, and reached over to grab Bettina's hand.

"How did you know, Pamela?" Karen piped up in her little voice. "Was it a kind of sixth sense?"

Bettina had been watching and listening, looking alternately amused and annoyed. Finally she spoke, loudly. "Oh, for heaven's sake, Pamela! Credit where credit is due—to you, I mean. I brought it on myself because I just had to have those last few meatballs, and you saved my life and I'll never, never, never forget it!"

The moment Bettina started speaking, Nell looked up from her knitting, apparently alarmed at her tone. But alarm gave way to puzzlement. "Last few meatballs?" she said. "You brought it on yourself because you had to have those last few meatballs?"

Pamela started to rise. "She means . . . she thinks it was something she said. Bob Lombard was helping at the reception Wendelstaff had for Flo . . . and Bettina grabbed the last few meatballs before he cleared the chafing dish away. And . . ."

From the expression on Nell's face, this explanation was making things no clearer. The pale eyes regarding Pamela from their nests of wrinkles had narrowed.

"And . . ." Pamela searched the room for a more welcoming visage. Bettina still looked annoyed, Holly and Karen looked interested, and Roland . . . was checking his watch.

She whirled around and dashed toward the kitchen, hearing from a distance Roland's announcement that eight p.m. had arrived. After a few moments, Bettina joined her there.

"I will never, never, never forget it," she repeated, but she busied herself filling the cut-glass pitcher with heavy cream and then delicately transferring six plum tarts to six wedding-china plates.

"There's something you're not telling us, Pamela," came a cheerful voice from the doorway. Holly stepped into the kitchen, and speaking over the whir and clatter of the coffee grinder, she said, "It's not really about the last few meatballs, is it?"

"Actually"—the grinding wound down and Pamela turned from the counter—"it has more to do with red socks, and a tryst in a garden shed, and someone who loved not wisely but too well."

"What?" Holly greeted the statement with a dimple-inducing smile despite her puzzlement.

"Bettina and I will explain the whole thing," Pamela said. "Wait around after Nell leaves. But for now, as Nell would say, let's tend to our knitting."

"And nibbling," Bettina added. She stepped forward and handed Holly two plates bearing plum tarts. The kettle began to hoot, Pamela returned to her task, and soon the aroma of brewing coffee suffused the little kitchen.

KNIT

Cozy Knitted Hat

Death of a Knit Wit takes place in mid-September, but many of the knitters are already working on projects to be worn or given as gifts in winter. Once summer draws to a close, it's not too soon to think about being cozy in the months ahead. Here are directions for a cozy knitted hat.

Use yarn identified on the label as "Medium" and/or #4, and use size 6 needles (though size 5 or 7 is fine if that's what you have). With this yarn and these needles you will average about four stitches to the inch. The hat requires about 160 yards of yarn, and it will fit an average-sized head, male or female.

If you're not already a knitter, watching a video is a great way to master the basics of knitting. Just search the internet for "How to knit" and you'll have your choice of tutorials that show the process clearly. The hat looks best when worked in the stockinette stitch, the stitch you see, for example, in a typical sweater. To create the stock-inette stitch, you knit one row, then purl going back the other direction, then knit, then purl, knit, purl, back and forth. Again, it's easier to understand "purl" by viewing a video, but essentially when you purl you're creating the backside of "knit." To knit, you insert the right-hand needle front to back through the loop of yarn on the left-hand needle. To purl, you insert the needle back to front.

Cast on 72 stitches, using either the simple slip-knot process or the "long tail" process. Casting on is often included in internet "How to knit" tutorials, or you can search specifically for "Casting on." After you've cast on, start creating the ribbing that will form the hat's cuff. Ribbing is the basic knit 2, purl 2 concept. For your first row, knit 2 stitches, then purl 2, then knit 2 more, purl 2 more, and continue like that to the end of the row. On the way back, knit 2, purl 2 and so on again. If you've cast on a multiple of 4 (which 72 is), you'll see that now you're doing a knit where you did a purl, and vice versa. This is what creates the effect of ribs. After you do a few rows you will see the ribs starting to form and this concept will become clearer.

One important note: After you knit the first two stitches, you must shift the yarn you're working with to the front of your work by passing it between the needles. After the two purls, you must shift it to the back, and so on back and forth. If you don't do this, extra loops of yarn will accumulate on your needles and you will have a mess. Do the knitting and purling until you have about 3 inches of ribbing. You have now created the cuff of your hat.

You will use the stockinette stitch for the rest of your hat. Work 5½ more inches using the stockinette stitch, then begin the decreasing that will form the hat's rounded top. Starting on a "knit" row, knit two stitches together so that when you finish the row there are only 36 stitches on your needle. (Instead of inserting your right-hand needle through one of the loops on the left-hand needle, insert it through two.) Then purl a row without decreasing. Knit a row decreasing again so that you end up with 18 stitches on your needle. Purl a row without decreasing. Knit another row decreasing so that you end up with 9 stitches on your needle. Purl a row without decreasing. Knit a row knitting 3 stitches together instead of 2, then cast off the 3 stitches that remain. Casting off is often included in internet "How to knit" tutorials or you can search specifically for "Casting off." If you like, leave a tail of several inches when you clip your yarn and use that to sew up the seam that will complete your hat.

Thread a yarn needle—a large needle with a large eye and a blunt tip—with more of your yarn or with the tail you left when you cast off. With right sides together, stitch up the two long edges of your piece of knitting to form your hat. To make a neat seam, use a whip stitch and catch only the outer loops along each side. When you finish the seam, make a knot and work the needle in and out of the seam for an inch or so to hide the tail. Cut off what's left. Hide the tail from when you cast on too. Turn your hat right-side out.

Variations

It's fun to knit the hat with stripes. Here are directions for making a two-tone hat, but you can use many colors if you wish. You will need about 106 yards of color #1 and 54 yards of color #2. Cast on with color #1, create your 3 inches of ribbing, and then use the stockinette stitch for 4 more rows, ending with a purl row. Clip your yarn, leaving a tail of 3 inches or so. Take color #2 and tie it on to the tail of color #1 as close to the knitted edge as possible, leaving a tail of about 3 inches of the new color beyond the knot. (You'll have parallel tails of the two colors.)

Still using the stockinette stitch, work 4 rows with color #2, then switch back to color #1. Keep switching back and forth, tying on the new color each time, until you have 4 stripes of each color. You will end with color #2. Go back to color #1 and follow the instructions above for decreasing and for sewing up the seam, making sure that the tails end up hidden inside the hat when you turn the hat right-side out. You can hide them by threading the yarn needle with them, working the needle in and out of the seam for half an inch or so, and clipping what's left. Or you can just clip them a little shorter and leave them loose and hidden inside the hat.

You can also make the hat's cuff wider or narrower. Some knitted-hat wearers prefer a hat that sits higher on the head with a cuff that doesn't turn back. For this look, make the cuff only 2 or 2½ inches deep. Others prefer a deeper cuff and a hat that pulls down well over the ears. You can adjust the pattern by making the ribbing even wider than 3 inches and working more than 5½ inches before beginning to decrease.

For a picture of two finished cozy hats, one with stripes and one with a narrower cuff, visit the Knit & Nibble Mysteries page at PeggyEhrhart.com. Click on the cover for *Death of a Knit Wit* and scroll down on the page that opens.

NIBBLE

Plum Turnovers

Good peaches are often gone by mid-September, at least in New Jersey, but good plums can still be found. Use red or black plums for this recipe but not prune plums. Plum flesh varies in color from golden to deep pink. The recipe makes 8 turnovers. Each is a generous serving, or one can be shared.

Ingredients
4 or 5 large, ripe plums
1 cup flour
$\frac{1}{2}$ tsp salt
$\frac{1}{3}$ cup of butter (a little over 5 tbsp), allowed to warm up and cut into small bits
2 tbsp cream cheese (1 oz), allowed to warm up
2 to 3 tbsp ice water
8 tsp sugar
1 egg, for the egg wash (optional)

Prepare the plums.

First, peel the plums. In order to do this easily you will blanch them. Bring a pot of water to boil and prepare an ice bath by putting a tray's worth of ice cubes into a large bowl and filling the bowl three-quarters of the way with water. With a small knife, cut an X in the bottom of each plum—a serrated knife works best. There's a photo of this step on my website. Lower the plums into the boiling water. Let the water return to a boil and leave the plums in for 60 seconds. Remove them with a slotted spoon and lower them into the ice bath. Leave them for a minute or so. You will see the skin already start to peel away at the edges of the Xs you cut.

Use a sharp paring knife to peel each plum, starting at the center of the X where the skin is already coming away. The skin will come off easily. Now cut the flesh away from the pits in whatever size of chunks you can manage. Try to get as much flesh as possible but the pits might not be clean. Some varieties of plum are clingier than others. You should and up with 3 to 3½ cups of plum. Cut the chunks into small pieces no larger than a kidney bean.

Prepare the dough.

This recipe makes a very rich and buttery dough, but you can use your own recipe for pie crust if you wish, enough for a one-crust pie.

Sift flour and salt into a medium-sized bowl. Using two knives, cut in the butter and cream cheese until the mixture resembles pebbly sand. Toss with a fork while you sprinkle on 2 tbsp of ice water. Add more ice water until the dough comes together in large clumps. If dry spots remain, use a little more ice water.

With floured hands, push the dough into a compact disk. Wrap it in plastic wrap and refrigerate it for ½ hour. You can refrigerate it longer if you want to make it ahead, but in that case it will need to soften up a bit before you can work with it.

Assemble the turnovers.

Butter a large baking sheet.

Unwrap the disk of dough, cut it into 8 sections (like slices of pie), and press each into a ball. Liberally flour a cutting board, pastry cloth, or other surface. (I use a KitchenAid® Silicone Bakeware Baking Mat.) Put a dough ball on the rolling surface, sprinkle it with flour, and flatten it slightly with your hands. Flour your rolling pin and roll the dough ball into an oval about 5" x 7". As you work, turn the dough over frequently and sprinkle more flour on it and on your rolling surface.

Note: When I make turnovers or hand pies, I roll out separate balls like this instead of rolling out a large piece of dough and cutting round shapes from it. Small balls of dough are easier to work with and you don't waste any dough. In addition, I have found that an oval shape is easier than a circle to fill, fold, and seal.

Scoop $\frac{1}{3}$ to $\frac{1}{2}$ cup of plum pieces onto the dough oval. Put them nearer to one end rather than in the middle, but leave an inch or so between them and the edge. There's a photo of this step on my website. Sprinkle a tsp of sugar over the plum pieces. Moisten your index finger with water and dab water around the edge of the dough oval at the end with the plums on it. Carefully fold the other end of the dough oval over the plums, lining up the edges and pressing them together. Push at the edges to form a ridge. Use the tines of a fork to seal the edge, then use the fork to poke several holes in the top of the turnover. There's a photo of this step on my website.

Use a pancake turner to carefully transfer the turnover to the baking pan.

Repeat the process to make 7 more turnovers.

Beat the egg with a splash of water to make an egg wash and brush it over the tops of your turnovers. You can skip this step, but the egg wash makes them glossy.

Bake the turnovers for 35 minutes at 350°F. Some juice will escape and the egg wash will bake onto the baking pan around the edges of the turnovers. Loosen them with a pancake turner a few minutes after you remove the baking sheet from the oven.

They are especially delicious while still warm, and they can be served with vanilla ice cream.

For a picture of Plum Turnovers, as well as some in-progress photos, visit the Knit & Nibble Mysteries page at PeggyEhrhart.com. Click on the cover for *Death of a Knit Wit* and scroll down on the page that opens.